A BETTY NEELS Christmas

During this season of giving,
Bertha and Emily are about to receive
the greatest gift of their lives...love.

And they will discover that Christmas wishes *do*
come true, and "handsome princes" do *indeed* exist.

Romance readers around the world will be sad to note the passing of **Betty Neels** in June 2001. Her career spanned thirty years and she continued to write into her ninetieth year. To her millions of fans, Betty epitomized the romance writer, and yet she began writing almost by accident. She had retired from nursing, but her inquiring mind still sought stimulation. Her new career was born when she heard a lady in her local library bemoaning the lack of good romance novels. Betty's first book, *Sister Peters in Amsterdam,* was published in 1969, and she eventually completed 134 books. Her novels offer a reassuring warmth that was very much a part of her own personality. She was a wonderful writer, and she will be greatly missed. Her spirit will live on in all her stories, including those yet to be published.

A BETTY NEELS

Christmas

HARLEQUIN®

TORONTO • NEW YORK • LONDON
AMSTERDAM • PARIS • SYDNEY • HAMBURG
STOCKHOLM • ATHENS • TOKYO • MILAN • MADRID
PRAGUE • WARSAW • BUDAPEST • AUCKLAND

ISBN 0-373-83534-5

A BETTY NEELS CHRISTMAS

Copyright © 2002 by Harlequin Books S.A.

The publisher acknowledges the copyright holder of the individual works as follows:

A CHRISTMAS PROPOSAL
Copyright © 1996 by Betty Neels

WINTER WEDDING
Copyright © 1979 by Betty Neels

CONTENTS

A CHRISTMAS PROPOSAL

CHAPTER ONE

THE girl standing in a corner of the crowded room hardly merited a second glance; she was small, with light brown hair strained back into an unfashionable bun, a face whose snub nose and wide mouth did nothing to redeem its insignificance, and she was wearing an elaborate shrimp-pink dress. But after his first glance the man standing across the room from her looked again. Presently he strolled over to stand beside her. His 'Hello' was pleasant and she turned her head to look at him.

She answered him politely, studying him from large brown eyes fringed by curling lashes. Looking at her eyes, he reflected that one soon forgot the nose and mouth and dragged-back hair. He smiled down at her. 'Do you know anyone here? I came with friends—I'm staying with them and was asked to come along with them. A birthday party, isn't it?'

'Yes.' She looked past him to the crowded room, the groups of laughing, gossiping people waving to each other with drinks in their hands, the few couples dancing in the centre. 'Would you like me to introduce you to someone?'

He said in his friendly way, 'You know everyone here? Is it your birthday?'

'Yes.' She gave him a quick surprised look and bent her head to examine the beaded bodice of her dress.

'Then shouldn't you be the belle of the ball?'

'Oh, it's not my party. It's my stepsister's—that pretty girl over by the buffet. Would you like to meet Clare?'

'The competition appears too keen at the moment,' he said easily. 'Shouldn't you be sharing the party, since it's your birthday too?'

'Well, no.' She had a pretty voice and she spoke matter-of-factly. 'I'm sure you'd like to meet some of the guests. I don't know your name…'

'Forgive me. Hay-Smythe—Oliver.'

'Bertha Soames.' She put out a small hand and he shook it gently.

'I really don't want to meet anyone. I think that perhaps I'm a little on the old side for them.'

She scrutinised him gravely—a very tall, strongly built man, with fair hair thickly sprinkled with grey. His eyes were grey too, and he had the kind of good looks which matched his assured air.

'I don't think you're in the least elderly,' she told him.

He thanked her gravely and added, 'Do you not dance?'

'Oh, I love to dance.' She smiled widely at him, but as quickly the smile faded. 'I—that is, my stepmother asked me to see that everyone was enjoying themselves. That's why I'm standing here—if I see anyone on their own I make sure that they've got a drink and meet someone. I really think that you should…'

'Definitely not, Miss Soames.' He glanced down at her and thought how out of place she looked in the noisy room. And why, if it was her birthday, was she not wearing a pretty dress and not that ill-fitting, over-elaborate garment? 'Are you hungry?'

'Me? Hungry?' She nodded her head. 'Yes, I missed lunch.' Her eyes strayed to the buffet, where a number of people were helping themselves lavishly to the dainties upon it. 'Why don't you…?'

Dr Hay-Smythe, hard-working in his profession and already respected by older colleagues, a man who would never pass a stray kitten or a lost dog and who went out of his way to make life easy for anyone in trouble, said now, 'I'm hungry too. Supposing we were to slip away and have a meal somewhere? I don't imagine we should be missed, and we could be back long before this finishes.'

She stared at him. 'You mean go somewhere outside? But there isn't a café anywhere near here—besides…'

'Even Belgravia must have its pubs. Anyway, I've my car outside—we can look around.'

Her eyes shone. 'I'd like that. Must I tell my step-mother?'

'Certainly not. This door behind you—where does it lead? A passage to the hall? Let us go now.'

'I'll have to get my coat,' said Bertha when they were in the hall. 'I won't be long, but it's at the top of the house.'

'Haven't you a mac somewhere down here?'

'Yes, but it's very old…'

His smile reassured her. 'No one will notice in the pub.' He reflected that at least it would conceal that dreadful dress.

So, suitably shrouded, she went out of the house with him, through the important front door, down the imposing steps and onto the pavement.

'Just along here,' said the doctor, gesturing to where a dark grey Rolls-Royce was parked. He unlocked the door, popped her inside and got in beside her. As he drove off he asked casually, 'You live here with your parents?'

'Yes. Father is a lawyer—he does a lot of work for international companies. My stepmother prefers to live here in London.'

'You have a job?'

'No.' She turned her head to look out of the window, and he didn't pursue the subject but talked idly about this and that as he left the quiet streets with their stately houses and presently, in a narrow street bustling with people, stopped the car by an empty meter. 'Shall we try that pub on the corner?' he suggested, and helped her out.

Heads turned as they went in; they made an odd couple—he in black tie and she in a shabby raincoat—but the landlord waved them to a table in one corner of the saloon bar and then came over to speak to the doctor.

'Ain't seen yer for a while, Doc. Everything OK?'

'Splendid, thank you, Joe. How is your wife?'

'Fighting fit, thanks to you. What'll it be?' He glanced at Bertha. 'And the little lady here? A nice drop of wine for her?'

'We're hungry, Joe...'

'The wife's just this minute dished up bangers and mash. How about that, with a drop of old and mild?'

Dr Hay-Smythe raised an eyebrow at Bertha, and when she nodded Joe hurried away, to return presently with the beer and the wine and, five minutes later, a laden tray.

The homely fare was well cooked, hot and generous. The pair of them ate and drank in a friendly silence until the doctor said quietly, 'Will you tell me something about yourself?'

'There's nothing to tell. Besides, we're strangers; we're not likely to meet again.' She added soberly, 'I think I must be a little mad to be doing this.'

'Well, now, I can't agree with that. Madness, if at all, lies with people who go to parties and eat too much and drink too much and don't enjoy themselves. Whereas you and I have eaten food we enjoy and are content with each other's company.' He waited while Joe brought the coffee he had ordered. 'Being strangers, we can safely talk knowing that whatever we say will certainly be forgotten.'

'I've never met anyone like you before,' said Bertha.

'I'm perfectly normal; there must be thousands exactly like me.' He smiled a little. 'I think that perhaps you haven't met many people. Do you go out much? The theatre? Concerts? Sports club? Dancing?'

Bertha shook her head. 'Well, no. I do go shopping, and I take my stepmother's dog out and help when people come for tea or dinner. That kind of thing.'

'And your sister?' He saw her quick look. 'Stepsister Clare—has she a job?'

'No—she's very popular, you see, and she goes out a great deal and has lots of friends. She's pretty—you must have seen that...'

'Very pretty,' he agreed gravely. 'Why are you unhappy, Bertha? You don't mind my calling you Bertha? After all, as you said, we are most unlikely to meet again. I'm a very good listener. Think of me as an elder brother or, if you prefer, someone who is going to the other side of the world and never returning.'

She asked, 'How do you know that I'm unhappy?'

'If I tell you that I'm a doctor, does that answer your question?'

She smiled her relief. 'A doctor! Oh, then I could talk to you, couldn't I?'

His smile reassured her.

'You see, Father married again—oh, a long time ago, when I was seven years old. My mother died when I was five, and I suppose he was lonely, so he married my stepmother.

'Clare was two years younger than I. She was a lovely little girl and everyone adored her. I did too. But my stepmother—you see, I've always been plain and dull. I'm sure she tried her best to love me, and it must be my fault, because I tried to love her, but somehow I couldn't.

'She always treated me the same as Clare—we both had pretty dresses and we had a nice nanny and went to the same school—but even Father could see that I wasn't growing up to be a pretty girl like Clare, and my stepmother persuaded him that it would be better for me to stay at home and learn to be a good house-wife…'

'Was Clare not a partner in this, too?'

'Well, no. She has always had lots of friends—I mean, she hadn't time to be at home very much. She's really kind to me.' She laid a hand on a glimpse of pink frill which had escaped from the raincoat. 'She gave me this dress.'

'You have no money of your own?'

'No. Mother left me some, but I—I don't need it, do I?'

The doctor didn't comment on that. All he said was, 'There is a simple solution. You must find a job.'

'I'd like that, but I'm not trained for anything.' She added anxiously, 'I shouldn't have said all that to you. Please forget it. I have no right to complain.'

'Hardly complaining. Do you not feel better for talking about it?'

'Yes, oh, yes. I do.' She caught sight of the clock and gave a little gasp. 'Heavens, we've been here for ages…'

'Plenty of time,' said the doctor easily. 'I dare say the party will go on until midnight.' He paid the bill and stowed her in the Rolls once more, then drove her back and went with her into the house. Bertha shed the raincoat in the hall, smoothed the awful dress and went with him into the vast drawing room. The first person to see them was her stepmother.

'Bertha, where have you been? Go at once to the kitchen and tell Cook to send up some more vol-au-vents. You're here to make yourself useful—'

Mrs Soames, suddenly aware of the doctor standing close by, became all at once a different woman. 'Run along, dear.' She spoke in a quite different voice now, and added, 'Don't be long—I'm sure your friends must be missing you.'

Bertha said nothing, and slipped away without a glance at the doctor.

'Such a dear girl,' enthused Mrs Soames, her massive front heaving with pseudo maternal feelings, 'and such a companion and help to me. It is a pity that she is so shy and awkward. I have done my best—' she managed to sound plaintive '—but Bertha is an intelligent girl and knows that she is lacking in looks and charm. I can only hope that some good man will come along and marry her.'

She lifted a wistful face to her companion, who murmured the encouraging murmur at which doctors are so good. 'But I mustn't bother you with my little worries, must I? Come and talk to Clare—she loves a new face. Do you live in London? We must see more of you.'

So when Bertha returned he was at the other end of the room, and Clare was laughing up at him, a hand on his arm. Well, what did I expect? reflected Bertha, and went in search of Crook the butler, a lifelong friend and ally; she had had a good supper, and now, fired by a rebellious spirit induced by Dr Hay-Smythe's company, she was going to have a glass of champagne.

She tossed it off under Crook's fatherly eye, then took a second glass from his tray and drank that too. Probably she would have a headache later, and certainly she would have a red nose, but since there was no one to mind she really didn't care. She wished suddenly that her father were at home. He so seldom was…

People began to leave, exchanging invitations and greetings, several of them saying a casual goodbye to Bertha, who was busy finding coats and wraps and mislaid handbags. Dr Hay-Smythe was amongst the first to leave with his party, and he came across the hall to wish her goodbye.

'That was a splendid supper,' he observed, smiling down at her. 'Perhaps we might do it again some time.'

Before she could answer, Clare had joined them. 'Darling Oliver, don't you dare run off just as I've discovered how nice you are. I shall find your number in the phone book and ring you—you may take me out to dinner.'

'I'm going away for some weeks,' he said blandly. 'Perhaps it would be better if I phoned you when I get back.'

Clare pouted. 'You wretched man. All right, if that's the best you can do.'

She turned her head to look at Bertha. 'Mother's looking for you…'

Bertha went, but not before putting out a small, capable hand and having it shaken gently. Her, 'Goodbye Doctor,' was uttered very quietly.

It was after Bertha had gone to her bed in the modest room on the top floor of the house that Mrs Soames went along to her daughter's bedroom.

'A successful evening, darling,' she began. 'What do you think of that new man—Oliver Hay-Smythe? I was talking to Lady Everett about him. It seems he's quite well-known—has an excellent practice in Harley Street. Good family and plenty of money— old money...' She patted Clare's shoulder. 'Just the thing for my little girl.'

'He's going away for a while,' said Clare. 'He said he'd give me a ring when he gets back.' She looked at her mother and smiled. Then she frowned. 'How on earth did Bertha get to know him? They seemed quite friendly. Probably he's sorry for her—she did look a dowd, didn't she?'

Clare nibbled at a manicured hand. 'She looked happy—as though they were sharing a secret or something. Did you know that he has a great deal to do with backward children? He wouldn't be an easy man... If he shows an interest in Bertha, I shall encourage him.' She met her mother's eyes in the mirror. 'I may be wrong, but I don't think he's much of a party man—the Paynes, who brought him, told me that he's not married and there are no girlfriends— too keen on his work. If he wants to see more of Bertha, I'll be all sympathy!'

The two of them smiled at each other.

*   *   *

Dr Hay-Smythe parted from his friends at their house and took himself off to his flat over his consulting rooms. Cully, his man, had gone to his bed, but there was coffee warm on the Aga in the kitchen and a covered plate of sandwiches. He poured himself a mug of coffee and sat down at the kitchen table, and the Labrador who had been snoozing by the Aga got up sleepily and came to sit beside him, ready to share his sandwiches. He shared his master's thoughts too, chewing on cold roast beef and watching his face.

'I met a girl this evening, Freddie—a plain girl with beautiful eyes and wearing a truly awful frock. An uninteresting creature at first glance, but somehow I feel that isn't a true picture. She has a delightful voice—very quiet. She needs to get away from that ghastly stepmother too. I must think of something…'

Bertha, happily unaware of these plans for her future, slept all night, happier in her dreams than in her waking hours.

It was two days later that the doctor saw a way to help Bertha. Not only did he have a private practice, a consultancy at two of the major hospitals and a growing reputation in his profession, he was also a partner in a clinic in the East End of London, dealing with geriatrics and anyone else who could not or would not go to Outpatients at any of the hospitals.

He had spent the evening there and his last patient had been an old lady, fiercely independent and living on her own in a tiny flat near the clinic. There wasn't a great deal he could do for her; a hard working life and old age were taking their toll, but she stumped around with a stick, refusing to go into an old people's home, declaring that she could look after herself.

'I'm as good as you, Doctor,' she declared after he had examined her. 'But I miss me books—can't read like I used to and I likes a good book. The social lady brought me a talking book, but it ain't the same as a real voice, if yer sees what I mean.' She added, 'A nice, quiet voice...'

He remembered Bertha then. 'Mrs Duke, would you like someone to come and read to you? Twice or three times a week, for an hour or so?'

'Not if it's one of them la-de-da ladies. I likes a nice bit of romance, not prosy stuff out of the parish mag.'

'The young lady I have in mind isn't at all like that. I'm sure she will read anything you like. Would you like to give it a try? If it doesn't work out, we'll think of something else.'

'OK, I'll 'ave a go. When'll she come?'

'I shall be here again in two days' time in the afternoon. I'll bring her and leave her with you while I am here and collect her when I've finished. Would that suit you?'

'Sounds all right.' Mrs Duke heaved herself out of her chair and he got up to open the door for her. 'Be seeing yer.'

The doctor went home and laid his plans; Mrs Soames wasn't going to be easy, a little strategy would be needed...

Presently he went in search of Cully. Cully had been with him for some years, was middle-aged, devoted and a splendid cook. He put down the silver he was polishing and listened to the doctor.

'You would like me to telephone now, sir?'

'Please.'

'And if the lady finds the time you wish to visit her unacceptable?'

'She won't, Cully.'

Cully went to the phone on the wall and the doctor wandered to the old-fashioned dresser and chose an apple. Presently Cully put back the receiver.

'Five o'clock tomorrow afternoon, sir. Mrs Soames will be delighted.'

The doctor took a bite. 'Splendid, Cully. If at any time she should ring me here, or her daughter, be circumspect, if you please.'

Cully allowed himself to smile. 'Very good, sir.'

The doctor was too busy during the next day to give much thought to his forthcoming visit; he would have liked more time to think up reasons for his request, but he presented himself at five o'clock at Mrs Soames' house and was shown into the drawing room by a grumpy maid.

Mrs Soames, encased in a vivid blue dress a little too tight for her ample curves, rose to meet him. 'Oliver, how delightful to see you—I'm sure you must be a very busy man. I hear you have a large practice.' She gave rather a shrill laugh. 'A pity that

I enjoy such splendid health or I might visit your rooms.'

He murmured appropriately and she patted the sofa beside her. 'Now, do tell me why you wanted to see me—' She broke off as Clare came into the room. Her surprise was very nearly real. 'Darling, you're back. See who has come to see us.'

Clare gave him a ravishing smile. 'And about time, too. I thought you were going away.'

'So did I.' He had stood up when she'd joined them, and he now took a chair away from the sofa. 'A series of lectures, but they have been postponed for a couple of weeks.'

Clare wrinkled her nose enchantingly. 'Good; now you can take me out to dinner.'

'A pleasure. I'll look in my appointments book and give you a ring, if I may. I was wondering if you have any time to spare during your days? I'm looking for someone who would be willing to read aloud for an hour or two several times a week to an old lady.' He smiled at Clare. 'You, Clare?'

'Me? Read a boring book to a boring old woman? Besides, I never have a moment to myself. What kind of books?'

'Oh, romances...'

'Yuk. How absolutely grim. And you thought of me, Oliver?' She gave a tinkling laugh. 'I don't even read to myself—only *Vogue* and *Tatler*.'

The doctor looked suitably disappointed. 'Ah, well, I dare say I shall be able to find someone else.'

Clare hesitated. 'Who is this old woman? Someone

I know? I believe Lady Power has to have something done to her eyes, and there's Mrs Dillis—you know, she was here the other evening—dripping with diamonds and quite able to afford half a dozen companions or minders or whatever they're called.'

'Mrs Duke lives in a tiny flat on her own and she exists on her pension.'

'How ghastly.' Clare looked up and caught her mother's eye. 'Why shouldn't Bertha make herself useful? She's always reading anyway, and she never does anything or goes anywhere. Of course—that's the very thing.'

Clare got up and rang the bell, and when the grumpy maid came she told her to fetch Miss Bertha.

Bertha came into the room quietly and stopped short when she saw Dr Hay-Smythe.

'Come here, Bertha,' said Mrs Soames. 'You know Dr Hay-Smythe, I dare say? He was at Clare's party. He has a request to make and I'm sure you will agree to it—something to keep you occupied from time to time. Perhaps you will explain, Oliver.'

He had stood up when Bertha had come into the room, and when she sat down he came to sit near her. 'Yes, we have met,' he said pleasantly. 'I came to ask Clare to read to an old lady—a patient of mine—whose eyesight is failing, but she suggested that you might like to visit her. I believe you enjoy reading?'

'Yes, yes, I do.'

'That's settled, then,' said Mrs Soames. 'She's at your disposal, Oliver.'

'Would you like to go to this lady's flat—say, three

times a week in the afternoons—and read to her for an hour or so?'

'Yes, thank you, Doctor.' Bertha sounded politely willing, but her eyes, when she looked at him, shone.

'Splendid. Let me see. Could you find your way to my rooms in Harley Street tomorrow afternoon? Then my secretary will give you her address. It is quite a long bus ride, but it won't be too busy in the afternoon. Come about two o'clock, will you? And thank you so much.'

'You'll have a drink, won't you?' asked Mrs Soames. 'I must make a phone call, but Clare will look after you. Bertha, will you go and see Cook and get her list for shopping tomorrow?'

The doctor, having achieved his purpose, sat for another half-hour, drinking tonic water while Clare drank vodka.

'Don't you drink?' She laughed at him. 'Really, Oliver, I should have thought you a whisky man.'

He smiled his charming smile. 'I'm driving. It would never do to reel into hospital, would it?'

'I suppose not. But why work in a hospital when you've got a big practice and can pick and choose?'

He said lightly, 'I enjoy the work.' He glanced at his watch. 'I am most reluctant to go, but I have an appointment. Thank you for the drink. I'll take you out to dinner and give you champagne at the first opportunity.'

She walked with him to the door, laid a pretty little hand on his arm and looked up at him. 'You don't mind? That I don't want to go to that old woman? I can't bear poverty and old, dirty people and smelly children. I think I must be very sensitive.'

He smiled a little. 'Yes, I am sure you are, and I don't mind in the least. I am sure your stepsister will manage very well—after all, all I asked for was someone to read aloud, and she seems to have time on her hands.'

'I'm really very sorry for her—her life is so dull,' declared Clare, and contrived to look as though she meant that.

Dr Hay-Smythe patted her hand, removed it from his sleeve, shook it and said goodbye with beautiful manners, leaving Clare to dance away and find her mother and gloat over her conquest.

As for the doctor, he went home well pleased with himself. He found Clare not at all to his taste but he had achieved his purpose.

It was raining as Bertha left the house the following afternoon to catch a bus, which meant that she had to wear the shabby mackintosh again. She consoled herself with the thought that it concealed the dress she was wearing—one which Clare had bought on the spur of the moment and disliked as soon as she'd got home with it.

It was unsuitable for a late autumn day, and a wet one, being of a thin linen—the colour of which was quite brilliant. But until her stepmother decided that Bertha might have something more seasonal there was nothing much else in her wardrobe suitable for the occasion, and anyway, nobody would see her. The old lady she was to visit had poor eyesight…

She got off the bus and walked the short distance to Dr Hay-Smythe's rooms, rang the bell and was admitted. His rooms were elegant and restful, and the cosy-looking lady behind the desk in the waiting room had a pleasant smile. 'Miss Soames?' She had got up and was opening a door beside the desk. 'The doctor's expecting you.'

Bertha hadn't been expecting him! She hung back to say, 'There's no need to disturb him. I was only to get the address from you.'

The receptionist merely smiled and held the door wide open, allowing Bertha to glimpse the doctor at his desk. He looked up then, stood up and came to meet her at the door.

'Hello, Bertha. Would you mind waiting until I finish this? A few minutes only. Take this chair. You found your way easily?' He pushed forward a small, comfortable chair, sat her down and went back to his own chair. 'Do undo your raincoat; it's warm in here.'

He was friendly and easy and she lost her shyness and settled comfortably, undoing her raincoat to reveal the dress. The doctor blinked at its startling colour as he picked up his pen. Another of Clare's castoffs, he supposed, which cruelly highlighted Bertha's nondescript features. Really, he reflected angrily, something should be done, but surely that was for her father to do? He finished his writing and left his chair.

'I'm going to the clinic to see one or two patients. I'll take you to Mrs Duke and pick you up when I've finished. Will you wait for me there?' He noticed the small parcel she was holding. 'Books? How thoughtful of you.'

'Well, Cook likes romances and she let me have some old paperbacks. They may please Mrs Duke.'

They went out together and the receptionist got up from her desk.

'Mrs Taylor, I'm taking Miss Soames with me. If I'm not back by five o'clock, lock up, will you? I've two appointments for this evening, haven't I? Leave the notes on my desk, will you?'

'Yes, Doctor. Sally will be here at six o'clock...'

'Sally is my nurse,' observed the doctor. 'My right hand. Mrs Taylor is my left hand.'

'Go on with you, Doctor,' said Mrs Taylor, and chuckled in a motherly way.

Bertha, brought up to make conversation when the occasion warranted it, worked her way painstakingly through a number of suitable subjects in the Rolls-Royce, and the doctor, secretly amused, replied in his kindly way, so that by the time he drew up in a shabby street lined with small terraced houses she felt quite at ease.

He got out, opened her door and led the way across the narrow pavement to knock on a door woefully in need of a paintbrush. It was opened after a few moments by an old lady with a wrinkled face, fierce black eyes and an untidy head of hair. She nodded at the doctor and peered at Bertha.

'Brought that girl, 'ave yer? Come on in, then. I could do with a bit of company.' She led the way down the narrow hall to a door at the end. 'I've got me own flat,' she told Bertha. 'What's yer name?'

'Bertha, Mrs Duke.'

The doctor, watching her, saw with relief that she had neither wrinkled her small nose at the strong smell of cabbage and cats, nor had she let her face register anything other than friendly interest.

He didn't stay for more than a few minutes, and when he had gone Bertha, bidden to sit herself down, did so and offered the books she had brought.

Mrs Duke peered at their titles. 'Just me cup of tea,' she pronounced. 'I'll 'ave *Love's Undying Purpose* for a start.' She settled back in a sagging armchair and an elderly cat climbed onto her lap.

Bertha turned to the first page and began to read.

CHAPTER TWO

BERTHA was still reading when the doctor returned two hours later. There had been a brief pause while Mrs Duke had made tea, richly brown and laced with tinned milk and a great deal of sugar, but Bertha hadn't been allowed to linger over it. She had obediently picked up the book again and, with a smaller cat on her own knees, had continued the colourful saga of misunderstood heroine and swashbuckling hero.

Mrs Duke had listened avidly to every word, occasionally ordering her to 'read that bit again', and now she got up reluctantly to let the doctor in.

'Enjoyed yourselves?' he wanted to know.

'Not 'arf. Reads a treat, she does. 'Artway through the book already.' Mrs Duke subsided into her chair again, puffing a bit. 'Bertha's a bit of all right. When's she coming again?'

He looked at Bertha, sitting quietly with the cat still on her knee.

'When would you like to come again?' he asked her.

'Whenever Mrs Duke would like me to.'

'Tomorrow? We could finish this story…'

'Yes, of course. If I come about the same time?'

'Suits me. 'Ere, give me Perkins—like cats, do you?'

'Yes, they're good company, aren't they?' Bertha got up. 'We'll finish the story tomorrow,' she promised.

In the car the doctor said, 'I'll bring you over at the same time and collect you later. I want to take a look at Mrs Duke; she's puffing a bit.'

'Yes—she would make tea and she got quite breathless. Is she ill?'

'Her heart's worn out and so are her lungs. She's turned eighty and had a very hard life. She refuses to go into hospital. You have made her happy reading to her—thank you, Bertha.' She smiled and he glanced at her. 'You didn't find the smells and the cats too much for you?'

'No, of course not. Would she be offended if I took a cake or biscuits? I'm sure Cook will let me have something.'

'Would you? I think she would be delighted; she's proud, but she's taken to you, hasn't she?'

He reflected with some surprise that he had rather taken to Bertha himself...

'Could we settle on which days you would like to visit Mrs Duke? I'll bring you tomorrow, as I've already said, but supposing we say three times a week? Would Monday, Wednesday and Friday suit you? Better still, not Friday but Saturday—I dare say that will help her over the weekend. I'll give you a lift on Wednesdays and Saturdays and on Mondays, if you

will come to my rooms as usual, there will be someone to take you to Mrs Duke.'

'I'll go any day you wish me to, but I must ask my
stepmother... And I can get a bus—there's no
need...'

'I go anyway. You might just as well have a lift.
And on Mondays there is always someone going to
the clinic—I'm one of several who work there.'

'Well, that would be nice, if you are sure it's no
trouble?'

'None whatsoever. Is your stepmother likely to object to your going?'

'I don't think so.' Bertha paused. 'But she might
not like me going with you...' She spoke matter-of-
factly.

'Yes. Perhaps you are right. There is no need to
mention that, is there?'

'You mean it will be a kind of secret between us?'

'Why not?' He spoke lightly and added, 'I'm taking your stepsister out to dinner tomorrow evening.
She is a very popular girl, isn't she?'

Which somehow spoilt Bertha's day.

Two weeks went by and autumn showed signs of
turning into winter. Mrs Soames had decided that
Bertha, since she went out so seldom, needed no new
dresses; Clare had several from last year still in perfect condition. A little alteration here and there and
they would be quite all right for Bertha, she declared,
making a mental note that she would have to buy

something new for the girl when her father returned in a month's time.

So Bertha, decked out more often than not in a hastily altered outfit of Clare's—lime-green and too wide on the shoulders—went on her thrice-weekly visits to Mrs Duke: the highlights of her week. She liked Wednesdays and Saturdays best, of course, because then she was taken there by the doctor, but the young man who drove her there on Mondays was nice too. He was a doctor, recently qualified, who helped out at the clinic from time to time. They got on well together, for Bertha was a good listener, and he always had a great deal to say about the girl he hoped to marry.

It had surprised Bertha that her stepmother hadn't objected to her reading sessions with Mrs Duke, but that lady, intent on finding a suitable husband for Clare, would have done a good deal to nurture a closer friendship with Dr Hay-Smythe. That he had taken Clare out to dinner and accepted an invitation to dine with herself, Clare and a few friends she took as a good sign.

Clare had looked her best at the dinner party, in a deceptively simple white dress. Bertha had been there, of course, for there had been no good reason for her not to be, wearing the frightful pink frock again—quite unsuitable, but really, when the girl went out so seldom there was no point in buying her a lot of clothes.

Dr Hay-Smythe had been a delightful guest, Mrs Soames had noted, paying court to her darling Clare and treating Bertha with a friendly courtesy but at the same time showing no interest in the girl. Very satisfactory, Mrs Soames had reflected, heaving such a deep sigh that her corsets creaked.

It was at the end of the third week on the Saturday that Mrs Duke died. Bertha had just finished the third chapter of a novel that the old lady had particularly asked her to read when Mrs Duke gave a small sigh and stopped breathing.

Bertha closed her book, set the cat on her lap gently on the ground and went to take the old lady's hand. There was no pulse; she had known there wouldn't be.

She laid Mrs Duke's hands tidily in her lap and went into the tiny hall to where the doctor had left a portable phone, saying casually that she might need it and giving her a number to call. She hadn't thought much about it at the time, but now she blessed him for being thoughtful. She dialled the number—the clinic—and heard his quiet voice answer.

'Mrs Duke.' She tried to keep her voice steady. 'Please would you come quickly? She has just died…'

'Five minutes. Are you all right, Bertha?'

'Me? Yes, thank you. Only, please come…' Her voice wobbled despite her efforts.

It seemed less than five minutes until he opened the door and gave her a comforting pat on the shoulder as he went past her into the living room to examine Mrs Duke. He bent his great height over her for a few minutes and then straightened up.

'Exactly as she would have wished,' he said. 'In her own home and listening to one of her favourite stories.'

He looked at Bertha's pale face. 'Sit down while I get this sorted out.'

She sat with the two cats crouching on her lap—they were aware that something wasn't quite right—while he rang the clinic, and presently a pleasant elderly woman came and the doctor picked up Mrs Duke and carried her into her poky bedroom.

'I'll take you home,' he told Bertha. 'It's been a shock. I'm sorry you had to be here.'

'I'm not. I'm glad. If Mrs Duke didn't know anything about it... The cats—we can't just leave them.' She stroked their furry heads. 'I'd have them, only I don't think my stepmother...'

'I'll take them. There's room for them at my flat and Freddie will enjoy their company—my dog.'

'Mrs Duke would be glad of that; she loved them.' Bertha put the pair gently down and got to her feet. 'I could go by bus. I expect there's a lot for you to do.'

'Time enough for that. Come along.' He glanced at his watch. 'You need a cup of tea.'

'Please don't bother.' Two tears trickled slowly down her cheeks. 'It doesn't seem right to be talking about tea...'

'If Mrs Duke were here it would be the first thing that she would demand. Be happy for her, Bertha, for this is exactly what she wished for.'

Bertha sniffed, blew her nose and mopped up her

tears. 'Yes, of course. Sorry. I'll come now. You're sure about the cats?'

'Yes. Wait while I have a word with Mrs Tyler.' He went into the bedroom and presently came out of it again, and whisked Bertha into the car.

He stopped the car in a side-street close to Oxford Street and ushered her into a small café where he sat her down at a table, ordered a pot of tea and took a seat opposite her.

'There is no need to say anything to your step-mother for the moment. It so happens that a nursery school I know of needs someone to read to the children. Would you consider doing that? The times may be different, but I'm sure I can explain that to Mrs Soames. Will you leave it to me? You will want to come to the funeral, won't you? Will you phone my rooms—tomorrow evening? Can you do that?'

'Well, I take my stepmother's dog for a walk every evening—I could go to the phone box; it's not far...'

'Splendid.' His smile was kind. 'Now, drink your tea and I'll take you home.' He added casually, 'I don't think there is any need to say anything to your stepmother about your change of job or Mrs Duke's death, do you?' He gave her a sidelong glance. 'I can explain that it will suit everyone concerned if the times are changed.'

'If you wouldn't mind. I don't think my stepmother would notice. I mean...'

'I know what you mean, Bertha.' His quiet voice reassured her.

*　　*　　*

The funeral was to be on Wednesday, she was told when she telephoned the following evening on her walk, and if she went as usual to the doctor's rooms she would be driven to Mrs Duke's flat. 'And as regards Monday,' went on the doctor, 'come at the usual time and I'll take you along to the nursery school so that you can meet everyone and arrange your hours.'

As she went back into the house she met Clare in the hall, dressed to go out for the evening. She twirled round, showing off the short silky frock.

'Do you like it, Bertha? It shows off my legs very well, doesn't it? It's a dinner party at the Ritz.' She smiled her charming smile. 'I might as well have as much fun as possible before I settle down and become a fashionable doctor's wife.'

She danced off and Bertha took the dog to the kitchen. Was that why the doctor was being so kind to her, finding her work to fill her empty days? To please Clare, with whom he was in love? Well, who wouldn't be? reflected Bertha. Clare was so very pretty and such fun to be with.

She was surprised that her stepmother had had no objection to her changing the hours of her reading, but the doctor, driving her to the funeral, observed that there had been no trouble about it. 'Indeed, Mrs Soames seemed pleased that you have an outside interest.'

It was a remark which surprised Bertha, since her

stepmother had evinced no interest in her comings and goings. It was a thought which she kept to herself.

A surprisingly large number of people were in the church. It seemed that Mrs Duke while alive had had few friends, but now even mere acquaintances crowded into the church and returned to her flat, filling it to overflowing while her nephew, a young man who had come from Sheffield with his wife, offered tea and meat-paste sandwiches.

Bertha, in the habit of making herself useful, filled the teacups and cut more bread and listened to the cheerful talk. Mrs Duke was being given a splendid send-off, and there had been a nice lot of flowers at the funeral.

'Aunty left her bits and pieces to me,' said her nephew, coming into the kitchen to make another pot of tea, 'as well as a bit in the Post Office. She 'as two cats too—I'll 'ave ter 'ave 'em destroyed. We've got a dog at home.'

'No need. Dr Hay-Smythe has taken them to his home.'

'Up ter 'im. 'E did a good job looking after Aunty.'

The doctor came in search of her presently. 'I think we might leave—I'll get someone to take over from you. Did you get a cup of tea?'

She shook her head. 'It doesn't matter.'

He smiled. 'It's a powerful brew. Wait there while I get someone…'

Mrs Tyler came back with him. 'Off you go, dearie. Everyone'll be here for another few hours and you've done more than your fair share. It was good of you and the doctor to come.'

'I liked Mrs Duke,' said Bertha.

'So did I. She'd have enjoyed this turn-out.'

'Are you expected home?' asked the doctor as he drove away.

'My stepmother and Clare are at a picture gallery and then going to have drinks with some friends. I expect you're busy—if you'd drop me off at a bus stop...'

'And then what will you do?' he wanted to know.

'Why, catch a bus, of course,' said Bertha in her practical way. 'And have a cup of tea when I get home.'

'Someone will have it ready for you?'

'Well, no. Crook's got the afternoon off and so has Daisy—she's the housemaid—and Cook will have her feet up—her bunions, you know.'

'In that case we'll have tea at my place.'

'It's very kind of you to ask me, but really you don't have to be polite. I've taken up a lot of your time, and you must have an awful lot to do.'

He spoke testily. 'Bertha, stop being so apologetic. If you don't wish to have tea with me say so. If not, come back with me and discuss the funeral over tea and toast.'

She said indignantly, 'I'm not being apologetic.' Her voice rose slightly. 'I don't care to be—to be...'

'Pitied? The last thing you can expect from me, my girl.'

He stopped outside his rooms and got out to open

her door. She looked up at him as she got out and
found herself smiling.

Cully had the door open before they had reached
it. He was introduced to Bertha and offered her a
dignified bow before opening the sitting-room door.

'We would like tea, Cully,' said the doctor. 'Earl
Grey and hot buttered toast—and if you can find a
few cakes?'

'Certainly, sir. Shall I take the young lady's coat?'

He shuddered inwardly at the sight of the garish
dress, but his face was inscrutable; he had until now
had a poor opinion of any young ladies his master
had brought home from time to time for the occasional drink or lunch, but this one was different, never
mind the horrible garment she was wearing. He glided
away to arrange cakes on a plate. Made by himself,
of course. He didn't trust cakes bought in a shop.

Bertha, happily unaware of Cully's thoughts, went
into the sitting room with the doctor to be greeted by
Freddie before he went to his master's side.

'How very convenient,' said Bertha, 'having your
home over your consulting rooms. I didn't know you
lived here.'

She gently rubbed Freddie's head and looked
around her. The room was very much to her taste—
a pleasing mixture of comfortable chairs and sofas
and antique wall cabinets, lamp-tables, a magnificent
Georgian rent table under the window and a giltwood
mirror over the fireplace. That was Georgian too, she
was sure.

She gave a little sigh of pleasure. 'This is a beautiful room,' she told him gravely.

'I'm glad you like it. Do sit down.' He offered her a small bergère, with upholstery matching the mulberry brocade curtains, and took an armchair opposite her. When her eyes darted to the long-case clock as it chimed the hour of four, he said soothingly, 'Don't worry. I'll see that you get back home before anyone else.'

Cully came in then with a laden tray. He set everything out on a low table between them and slid away, but not before he had taken a good look at Bertha—nicely contrived from under lowered lids. His first impressions had been good ones, he decided.

Bertha made a good tea; she was hungry and Cully's dainty sandwiches and little cakes were delicious. Sitting there in the quiet, restful room with the doctor, whom she trusted and thought of as a friend, she was content and happy, and if their conversation dealt entirely with the visits she was to make to the nursery school she had no quarrel with that. She had been reminded so often by her stepmother and Clare that she was a dull companion and quite lacking in charm that she would have been surprised if the doctor had been anything else but briskly businesslike.

She was to go each morning from eleven o'clock until half past twelve, if that suited her, he told her, and she agreed at once. It might be a bit awkward sometimes, if she was needed to take the dog out or to go to the shops on some errand for her stepmother, but she would worry about that if and when it happened; there was no need to tell him.

'There are any number of books there; the children are various ages—two years to around four or five. You do understand that you need only read to them? There are plenty of helpers to do the necessary chores.'

'I think I shall like it very much.' Bertha smiled. 'Every day, too...'

He took her home presently, waiting until she had gone inside and then poked her head round the front door to tell him that no one was home.

Beyond telling Bertha how fortunate she was that Dr Hay-Smythe had found her something to do, her stepmother asked no questions. It was inconvenient that Bertha had to go each morning, of course, but since he was almost a friend of the family—indeed, almost more than that—she complied. 'Clare is quite sure that he's in love with her, so of course we would wish to do anything to oblige him in any way.'

So on Monday morning Bertha set off to go to the doctor's rooms. She was to go there first, he'd told her. The nursery school wasn't far from them and she would be shown the way and introduced to the matron who ran the place. She wasn't to feel nervous about going, for Matron already knew that she would be coming.

Mrs Taylor was at the rooms and greeted her with a friendly smile. 'Just a minute while I get Dr Hay-Smythe—he's in the garden with that dog of his.' She picked up the phone as she spoke, and a few minutes later he came in.

'I'll walk round with you, Bertha.' He glanced at his watch. 'I've time enough.'

She went with him down into the street and skipped along beside him to keep up.

'You can take a bus to the corner,' he told her. 'Go straight there after today.'

He turned down a narrow street and then turned again into a cul-de-sac lined with narrow, rather shabby houses. Halfway down he mounted the steps to a front door, rang the bell and then walked in.

The hall was rather bare, but the walls were a cheerful yellow and there was matting on the floor and a bowl of flowers on a table against the wall. The woman who came to meet them was small and stout with a jolly face and small bright eyes. She greeted the doctor like an old friend and looked at Bertha.

'So you're to be our reader,' she said, and shook hands. 'We are so glad to have you—we need all the help we can get. Come and see some of the children.'

She opened the door into a large, airy room full of children and several younger women. 'Of course, you won't be reading to them all,' she explained, 'but I've picked out those who will understand you, more or less. They love the sound of a voice, you know...'

They were in the centre of the room now with children all around them. 'We have children with special needs—three who are blind, several who had brain damage at birth and quite a few physically disabled...'

The doctor was watching Bertha's face. It showed surprise, compassion and a serene acceptance. Perhaps it had been unkind of him not to have told her, but he had wanted to see how she would react and she had reacted just as he had felt sure she would— with kindness, concern and not a trace of repugnance.

She looked at him and smiled. 'I'm going to like coming here,' she told him. 'Thank you for getting me the job.' She turned to the matron. 'I do hope I'll do…'

'Of course you will, my dear. Come along and take your jacket off and we'll get you settled.'

Bertha put out a hand to the doctor. 'I dare say I shan't see you again—well, perhaps when you come to see Clare, but you know what I mean. I can't thank you enough for your kindness.'

The doctor shook her hand in his large, firm one. 'Probably we shall see each other here occasionally. I come quite often to see the children.'

He went away then, and Bertha was led away by the matron, introduced to the other helpers and presently began to read to the circle of children assembled round her chair. It was an out-of-date book—an old fairy tale collection—and she started with the first story.

It wasn't going to be straightforward reading; she was interrupted frequently by eager little voices wanting her to read certain parts again, and some of them needed to have parts of the story explained to them, but after a time she got the hang of it and by half past twelve she and the children understood each other very well. She would do better tomorrow, she promised herself, going home to a solitary lunch, since her stepmother and Clare were out.

Within a few days Bertha had found her feet. It was a challenging job but she found it rewarding; the children were surprisingly happy, though sometimes difficult and frequently frustrated. They were lovable, though, and Bertha, lacking love in her own home, had plenty of that to offer.

At the end of two weeks she realised that she was happy, despite the dull life she led at home. Her stepmother still expected her to run errands, walk the dog and fetch and carry for her, so that she had little time to call her own. She was glad of that, really, as it gave her less time to think about Dr Hay-Smythe, for she had quickly discovered that she missed him.

She supposed that if Clare were to marry him— and, from what her stepsister said occasionally, Bertha thought that it was very likely—she would see him from time to time. He had been to the house once or twice, and Clare would recount their evenings together at great length, making no attempt to hide the fact that she had made up her mind to marry him.

When Bertha had asked her if she loved him, Clare had laughed. 'Of course not, but he's exactly what I want. Plenty of money, a handsome husband, and a chance to get away from home. Oh, I like him well enough...'

Bertha worried a lot about that; it spoilt her happiness. Dr Hay-Smythe wasn't the right husband for

Clare. On the other hand, being in love with someone wasn't something one could arrange to suit oneself, and if he loved Clare perhaps it wouldn't matter.

It was towards the middle of the third week of her visits to the nursery school that Clare unexpectedly asked her to go shopping with her in the afternoon. 'I've some things I simply must buy and Mother wants the car, and I hate taxis on my own. You'll have to come.'

They set out after lunch, and since it had been raining, and was threatening to do so again, Crook hailed a taxi. Clare was in good spirits and disposed to be friendly.

'It's time you had something decent to wear,' she said surprisingly. 'There's that jersey two-piece of mine—I never liked it; it's a ghastly colour—you can have that.'

'I don't think I want it if it's a ghastly colour, Clare. Thank you all the same.'

'Oh, the colour is ghastly on *me*. I dare say you'll look all right in it.' She glanced at Bertha. 'You'd better take it. Mother won't buy you anything until Father gets home, and he's been delayed so you'll have to wait for it.'

Bertha supposed that the jersey two-piece wouldn't be any worse than the lime-green outfits and there was no one to see her in it anyway. She wondered silently if there would ever be a chance for her to earn some money. She was a voluntary worker, but if she worked longer hours perhaps she could ask to be paid? She wouldn't want much.

The idea cheered her up, so that she was able to stand about patiently while Clare tried on dresses and then finally bought a pair of Italian shoes—white kid with high heels and very intricate straps. Bertha, watching them being fitted, was green with envy; she had pretty feet and ankles, and Clare's were by no means perfect. The shoes were on the wrong feet, she reflected in a rare fit of ill-humour.

The afternoon had cleared. Clare gave Bertha the shoes to carry and said airily that they would walk home. 'We can always pick up a taxi if we get tired,' she declared. 'We'll cut through here.'

The street was a quiet one, empty of traffic and people. At least, it was until they were halfway down it. The elderly lady on the opposite pavement was walking slowly, carrying a plastic bag and an umbrella, with her handbag dangling from one arm, so she had no hands free to defend herself when, apparently from nowhere, two youths leapt at her from a narrow alleyway. They pushed her to the ground and one of them hit her as she tried to keep a hand on her bag.

Clare stopped suddenly. 'Quick, we must run for it. They'll be after us if they see us. Hurry, can't you?'

Bertha took no notice. She pushed away Clare's hands clinging to her arm, ran across the street and swiped at one of the youths with the plastic bag containing Clare's new shoes. It caught him on the shins and he staggered and fell. She swung the bag again, intent on hitting the other youth. The bag split this time and the shoes flew into the gutter.

Confronted by a virago intent on hurting them, the pair scrambled to their feet and fled, dropping the lady's handbag as they went. Short of breath and shaking with fright, Bertha knelt down by the old lady.

'My purse—my pension...' The elderly face was white with fear and worry. It was bruised, too.

'It's all right,' said Bertha. 'They dropped your handbag. I'll get it for you. But, first of all, are you hurt?'

Before the old lady could answer, Clare hissed into Bertha's ear, 'My shoes—my lovely new shoes. You've ruined them. I'll never forgive you!'

'Oh, bother your shoes,' said Bertha. 'Go and bang on someone's door and get an ambulance.'

Just for once, Clare, speechless at Bertha's brisk orders, did as she was told.

She was back presently, and there were people with her. Bertha, doing her best to make the old lady as comfortable as possible, listened with half an ear to her stepsister's voice.

'Two huge men,' said Clare, in what Bertha always thought of as her little-girl voice. 'They ran at this poor lady and knocked her down. I simply rushed across the street and hit them with a shopping bag— one of them fell over and they ran away then.' She gave a little laugh. 'I've never been so scared in my life...'

'Very plucky, if I might say so,' said a voice.

Another voice asked, 'You're not hurt, young lady? It was a brave thing to do.'

'Well, one doesn't think of oneself,' murmured Clare. 'And luckily my sister came to help me once the men had gone.'

The old lady stared up at Bertha's placid face. 'That's a pack of lies,' she whispered. 'It was you; I saw you…' She closed her eyes tiredly. 'I shall tell someone…'

'It doesn't matter,' said Bertha. 'All that matters is that you're safe. Here is your handbag, and the purse is still inside.'

She got to her feet as the ambulance drew up and the few people who had gathered to see what was amiss gave her sidelong glances with no sign of friendliness; she could read their thoughts—leaving her pretty sister to cope with those violent men… Luckily there were still brave girls left in this modern day and age of violence…

Bertha told herself that it didn't matter; they were strangers and never likely to see her again. She wondered what Clare would do next—beg a lift from someone, most likely.

There was no need for that, however.

By good fortune—or was it bad fortune?—Dr Hay-Smythe, on his way from somewhere or other, had seen the little group as he drove past. He stopped, reversed neatly and got out of his car. Clare, with a wistful little cry, exactly right for the occasion, ran to meet him.

CHAPTER THREE

'OLIVER!' cried Clare, in what could only be described as a brave little voice. 'Thank heaven you're here.' She waved an arm towards the ambulancemen loading the old lady onto a stretcher. 'This poor old woman—there were two enormous men attacking her. She's been hurt—she might have been killed—but I ran as fast as I could and threw my bag at them and they ran away.'

The onlookers, gathering close, murmured admiringly. 'Proper brave young lady,' said one.

'Oh, no,' Clare said softly. 'Anyone would have done the same.' She had laid a hand on the doctor's arm and now looked up into his face.

He wasn't looking at her. He was watching the stretcher being lifted into the ambulance. The old lady was saying something to Bertha, who had whipped a bit of paper and pencil from her bag and was writing something down.

He removed Clare's hand quite gently. 'I should just take a look,' he observed.

He spoke to the ambulance driver and then bent over the old lady, giving Bertha a quick smile as he did so. 'Can I help in any way? I'm told there's nothing broken, but you had better have a check-up at the hospital.'

The shrewd old eyes studied his face. 'You're a doctor? Don't you listen to that girl's tale. Not a word of truth in it. Seen it with my own eyes—tried to run away, she did. It was this child who tackled those thugs—twice her size too.' She gave a weak snort of indignation. 'Mad as fire because her shoes had been spoilt. Huh!'

'Thank you for telling me. Do we have your name? Is there anyone who should be told?'

'This young lady's seen to that for me, bless her. Gets things done while others talk.'

'Indeed she does.' He took her hand. 'You'll be all right now.'

He went back to the driver and presently, when the ambulance had been driven away, he joined Bertha. 'Let me have her name and address, will you? I'll check on her later today. Now I'll drive you both home.'

Clare had joined them. 'What was all that about? You don't need to bother any more; she'll be looked after at the hospital. I feel awfully odd—it was a shock…'

'I'll drive you both back home. I dare say you may like to go straight to bed, Clare.'

Clare jumped into the car. 'No, no—I'm not such a weakling as all that, Oliver. I dare say Bertha would like to lie down for a bit, though—she was so frightened.' She turned her head to look at Bertha on the back seat, who looked out of the window and didn't answer.

The doctor didn't say anything either, so Clare went on uncertainly, 'Well, of course, it was enough to scare the wits out of anyone, wasn't it?'

No one answered that either. Presently she said pettishly, 'I had a pair of new shoes—wildly expensive—they've been ruined.' Quite forgetting her role of brave girl, she turned on Bertha. 'You'll have to pay for them, Bertha. Throwing them around like that—' She stopped, aware that she had let the cat out of the bag. 'What was the good of flinging the bag at those men when they had already run away?'

'I'm sure you can buy more shoes,' said the doctor blandly. 'And what is a pair of shoes compared with saving an old lady from harm?'

He glanced in his mirror, caught Bertha's eye and smiled at her, and lowered an eyelid in an unmistakable wink.

It gave her a warm glow. Never mind that there would be some hard words when she got home; she had long since learned to ignore them. He had believed the old lady and she had the wit to see that he wouldn't mention it—it would make it so much worse for her and would probably mean the end of her job at the nursery school. If any special attention from him were to come to Clare's or her stepmother's notice, they would find a way to make sure that she never saw him again...

The doctor stopped the car before their door, and Clare said coaxingly, 'Take me out to dinner this evening, Oliver? I do need cheering up after all I've just gone through. Somewhere quiet where we can talk?'

He had got out to open her door and now turned to do the same for Bertha. 'Impossible, I'm afraid. I've a meeting at seven o'clock which will last for hours—perhaps at the weekend...'

He closed the car door. 'I suggest that you both have an early night. If there is any news of the old lady I'll let you have it. I shall be seeing her later this evening. Bertha, if you will give me her address, I'll see that her family are told.'

She handed it over with a murmured thank-you, bade him goodbye and started up the steps to the door, leaving Clare to make a more protracted leave-taking—something which he nipped in the bud with apparent reluctance.

Clare's charm turned to cold fury as they entered the house. 'You'll pay for this,' she stormed. 'Those shoes cost the earth. Now I've nothing to wear with that new dress...'

Bertha said matter-of-factly, 'Well, I can't pay for them, can I? I haven't any money. And you've dozens of shoes.' She looked at Clare's furious face. 'Are they really more important than helping someone in a fix?' She wanted to know. 'And what a lot of fibs you've told everyone. I must say you looked the part.'

She stopped then, surprised at herself, but not nearly as surprised as Clare. 'How dare you?' Clare snapped. 'How dare you talk to me like that?'

'Well, it's the truth, isn't it?' asked Bertha placidly. 'But, don't worry, I shan't give you away.'

'No one would believe you...'

'Probably not.' Bertha went up to her room, leaving Clare fuming.

The full weight of her stepmother's displeasure fell upon her when she went downstairs presently. She was most ungrateful, careless and unnaturally mean towards her stepsister, who had behaved with the courage only to be expected of her. Bertha should be bitterly ashamed of herself. 'I had intended to take you to a charity coffee morning at Lady Forde's, but I shall certainly not do so now,' she finished.

Bertha, allowing the harsh voice to wash over her head, heaved a sigh of relief; the last time she had been taken there she had ended up making herself useful, helping Lady Forde's meek companion hand round the coffee and cakes. She looked down at her lap and didn't say a word. What would be the use?

She would have been immensely cheered if she had known of the doctor's efforts on her behalf. There had to be a way, he reflected, sitting in his sitting room with Freddie at his feet, in which he could give Bertha a treat. It seemed to him that she had no fun at all—indeed, was leading an unhappy life.

'She deserves better,' he told Freddie, who yawned. 'Properly dressed and turned out, she might stand a chance of attracting some young man. She has beautiful eyes, and I don't know another girl who would have held her tongue as she did this afternoon.'

It was much later, after Cully had gone to his bed and the house was quiet, that he knew what he would do. Well satisfied, he settled Freddie in his basket in the kitchen and went to bed himself.

The doctor waited another two days before calling at Mrs Soames's house. He had satisfied himself that Bertha was still going to the nursery. Matron had been enthusiastic about her and assured him that there had been no question of her leaving, so he was able to dispel the nagging thought that her stepmother might have shown her anger by forbidding her to go.

He chose a time when he was reasonably sure that they would all be at home and gave as his excuse his concern as to whether the two girls had got over their unfortunate experience. All three ladies were in the drawing room—something which pleased him, for if Bertha wasn't there, there was always the chance that she would hear nothing of his plans.

Mrs Soames rose to meet him. 'My dear Oliver, most kind of you to call—as you see, we are sitting quietly at home. Dear Clare is somewhat shocked still.'

'I'm sorry to hear it,' said the doctor, shaking Clare's hand and giving Bertha a smiling nod. 'Perhaps I can offer a remedy—both for her and for Bertha, who must also be just as upset.'

Mrs Soames looked surprised. 'Bertha? I hardly think so. She isn't in the least sensitive.'

The doctor looked grave and learned. He said weightily, 'Nevertheless, I think that both young ladies would benefit from my plan.'

His bedside manner, reflected Bertha, and very impressive and effective too, for her stepmother nodded and said, 'Of course. I bow to your wisdom, Oliver.'

'Most fortunately I am free tomorrow. I should be delighted if I might drive them into the country for the day, away from London. To slow down one's lifestyle once in a while is necessary, especially when one has had a shock such as Clare had.' He looked at Bertha. 'And I am sure that Bertha must have been upset. I haven't had the opportunity to ask her—'

'There's no need,' Clare interrupted him hastily. 'I'm sure she needs a break just as I do. We'd love to come with you, Oliver. Where shall we go?'

'How about a surprise? Is ten o'clock too early for you?'

'No, no. Not a minute too early.' Clare was at her most charming, and then, as he got up to go, she said suddenly, 'But of course Bertha won't be able to go with us—she reads to old ladies or something every morning.'

'Tomorrow is Saturday,' the doctor reminded her gently. 'I doubt if she does that at the weekends.' He glanced at Bertha. 'Is that not so, Bertha?'

Bertha murmured an agreement and saw the flash of annoyance on Clare's face. All of a sudden she was doubtful as to whether a day spent in the company of Clare and the doctor would be as pleasant as it sounded.

After he had gone, Clare said with satisfaction, 'You haven't anything to wear, Bertha. I hope Oliver won't feel embarrassed. It's a great pity that you have to come with us. You could have refused.'

'I shall enjoy a day out,' said Bertha calmly, 'and I shall wear the jersey two-piece you handed down to me. I'll have to take it in…'

Clare jumped up. 'You ungrateful girl. That outfit cost a lot of money.'

'It's a ghastly colour,' said Bertha equably, and went away to try it on. It was indeed a garment which Clare should never have bought—acid-yellow, and it needed taking in a good deal.

'Who cares?' said Bertha defiantly to the kitchen cat, who had followed her upstairs, and began to sew—a tricky business since her eyes were full of tears. To be with the doctor again would be, she had to admit, the height of happiness, but she very much doubted if he would feel the same. He was far too well-mannered to comment upon the two-piece—probably he would be speechless when he saw it—but it would be nice to spend a day with him wearing an outfit which was the right colour and which fitted.

'I suppose I am too thin,' she observed to the cat, pinning darts and cobbling them up. The sleeves were a bit too long—she would have to keep pushing them up—and the neck was too low. Clare liked low necks so that she could display her plump bosom, but Bertha, who had a pretty bosom of her own, stitched it up to a decent level and hoped that no one would notice.

Dr Hay-Smythe noticed it at once, even though half-blinded by the acid-yellow. An appalling outfit, he reflected, obviously hastily altered, for it didn't fit

anywhere it should and the colour did nothing for
Bertha's ordinary features and light brown hair. He
found that he was full of rage at her treatment, although he allowed nothing of that to show. He wished
her good morning and talked pleasantly to Mrs
Soames while they waited for Clare.

She came at last, with little cries of regret at keeping him waiting. 'I wanted to look as nice as possible
for you, Oliver,' she said with a little laugh. And indeed she did look nice—in blue and white wool, simply cut and just right for a day in the country. She
had a navy shoulder-bag and matching shoes with
high heels. The contrast between the two girls was
cruel.

The doctor said breezily, 'Ah, here you are at last.
I was beginning to think that you had changed your
mind!' He smiled a little. 'Found someone younger
and more exciting with whom to spend the day.'

This delighted Clare. 'There isn't anyone more exciting than you, Oliver,' she cooed, and Bertha looked
away, feeling sick and wishing that the day was over
before it had begun.

Of course Clare got into the seat beside Oliver,
leaving him to usher Bertha into the back of the car
where Freddie, delighted to have company, greeted
her with pleasure.

Clare, turning round to stare, observed tartly, 'Oh,
you've brought a dog.' And then said, with a little
laugh, 'He'll be company for Bertha.'

'Freddie goes wherever I go when it's possible. He

sits beside me on long journeys and is a delightful companion.'

'Well, now you have me,' declared Clare. 'I'm a delightful companion too!'

A remark which the doctor apparently didn't hear.

He drove steadily towards the western suburbs, apparently content to listen to Clare's chatter, and when he was finally clear of the city he turned off the main road and slowed the car as they reached the countryside. They were in Hertfordshire now, bypassing the towns, taking minor roads through the woods and fields and going through villages, peaceful under the morning sun. At one of these he stopped at an inn.

'Coffee?' he asked, and got out to open Clare's door and then usher Bertha and Freddie out of the car.

The inn was old and thatched and cosy inside. The doctor asked for coffee, then suggested, 'You two girls go ahead. I'll take Freddie for a quick run while the coffee's fetched.'

The ladies' was spotlessly clean, but lacked the comforts of its London counterparts. Clare, doing her face in front of the only mirror, said crossly, 'He might have stopped at a decent hotel—this is pretty primitive. I hope we shall lunch somewhere more civilised.'

'I like it,' said Bertha. 'I like being away from London. I'd like to live in the country.'

Clare didn't bother to reply, merely remarking as they went to join the doctor that the yellow jersey looked quite frightful. 'When I see you in it,' said Clare, 'I can see just how ghastly it is!'

It was an opinion shared by the doctor as he watched them cross the bar to join him at a table by the window, but nothing could dim the pleasure in Bertha's face, and, watching it, he hardly noticed the outfit.

'The coffee was good. I'm surprised,' said Clare. 'I mean, in a place like this you don't expect it, do you?'

'Why not?' The doctor was at his most genial. 'The food in some of these country pubs is as good or better than that served in some of the London restaurants. No dainty morsels in a pretty pattern on your plate, but just steak and kidney pudding and local vegetables, or sausages and mash with apple pie for a pudding.'

Clare looked taken aback. If he intended giving her sausages and mash for lunch she would demand to be taken home. 'Where are we lunching?' she asked.

'Ah, wait and see!'

Bertha had drunk her coffee almost in silence, with Freddie crouching under the table beside her, nudging her gently for a bit of biscuit from time to time. She hoped that they would lunch in a country pub—sausages and mash would be nice, bringing to mind the meal she and the doctor had eaten together. Meeting him had changed her life...

They drove on presently into Buckinghamshire, still keeping to the country roads. It was obvious that the doctor knew where he was going. Bertha stopped herself from asking him; it might spoil whatever surprise he had in store for them.

It was almost noon when they came upon a small village—a compact gathering of Tudor cottages with a church overlooking them from the brow of a low hill.

Bertha peered and said, 'Oh, this is delightful. Where are we?'

'This is Wing—'

'Isn't there a hotel?' asked Clare. 'We're not going to stop here, are we?' She had spoken sharply. 'It's a bit primitive, isn't it?' She saw his lifted eyebrows. 'Well, no, not primitive, perhaps, but you know what I mean, Oliver. Or is there one of those country-house restaurants tucked away out of sight?'

He only smiled and turned the car through an open wrought-iron gate. The drive was short, and at its end was a house—not a grand house, one might call it a gentleman's residence—sitting squarely amidst trees and shrubs with a wide lawn before it edged by flowerbeds. Bertha, examining it from the car, thought that it must be Georgian, with its Palladian door with a pediment above, its many paned windows and tall chimneystacks.

It wasn't just a lovely old house, it was a home; there were long windows, tubs of japonica on either side of the door, the bare branches of Virginia creeper rioting over its walls and, watching them from a wrought-iron sill above a hooded bay window, a majestic cat with a thick orange coat. Bertha saw all this as Clare got out, the latter happy now at the sight of a house worthy of her attention and intent on making up for her pettishness.

'I suppose we are to lunch here?' she asked as the doctor opened Bertha's door and she and Freddie tumbled out.

His 'yes' was noncommittal.

'It isn't a hotel, is it?' asked Bertha. 'It's someone's home. It's quite beautiful.'

'I'm glad you like it, Bertha. It is my home. My mother will be delighted to have you both as her guests for lunch.'

'Yours?' queried Clare eagerly. 'As well as your flat in town? I suppose your mother will live here until you want it for yourself—when you marry?' She gave him one of her most charming smiles, which he ignored.

'Your mother doesn't mind?' asked Bertha. 'If we are unexpected...'

'You're not. I phoned her yesterday. She is glad to welcome you—she is sometimes a little lonely since my father died.'

'Oh, I'm sorry.' Bertha's plain face was full of sympathy.

'Thank you. Shall we go indoors?'

The house door opened under his hand and he ushered them into the wide hall with its oak floor and marble-topped console table flanked by cane and walnut chairs. There was a leather-covered armchair in one corner too, the repository of a variety of coats, jackets, walking sticks, dog leads and old straw hats, giving the rather austere grandeur of the hall a pleasantly lived-in look. The doctor led the way past the oak staircase with its wrought-iron balustrade at the back of the hall and opened a small door.

'Mother will be in the garden,' he observed. 'We can go through the kitchen.'

The kitchen was large with a vast dresser loaded with china against one wall, an Aga stove and a scrubbed table ringed by Windsor chairs at its centre. Two women looked up as they went in.

'Master Oliver, good morning to you, sir—and the two young ladies.'

The speaker was short and stout and wrapped around by a very white apron. The doctor crossed the room and kissed her cheek.

'Meg, how nice to see you again.' He looked across at the second woman, who was a little younger and had a severe expression. 'And Dora—you're both well? Good. Clare, Bertha—this is Meg, our cook, and Dora, who runs the house.'

Clare nodded and said, 'hello,' but Bertha smiled and shook hands.

'What a heavenly kitchen.' Her lovely eyes were sparkling with pleasure. 'It's a kind of haven…' She blushed because she had said something silly, but Meg and Dora were smiling.

'That it is, miss—specially now in the winter of an evening. Many a time Mr Oliver's popped in here to beg a slice of dripping toast.'

He smiled. 'Meg, you are making my mouth water. We had better go and find my mother. We'll see you before we go.'

Clare had stood apart, tapping a foot impatiently, but as they went through the door into the garden beyond she slipped an arm through the doctor's.

'I love your home,' she told him, 'and your lovely old-fashioned servants.'

'They are our friends as well, Clare. They have been with us for as long as I can remember.'

The garden behind the house was large and rambling, with narrow paths between the flowerbeds and flowering shrubs. Freddie rushed ahead, and they heard his barking echoed by a shrill yapping.

'My mother will be in the greenhouses.' The doctor had disengaged his arm from Clare's in order to lead the way, and presently they went through a ramshackle door in a high brick wall and saw the greenhouses to one side of the kitchen garden.

Bertha, lingering here and there to look at neatly tended borders and shrubs, saw that Clare's high heels were making heavy weather of the earth paths. Her clothes were exquisite, but here, in this country garden, they didn't look right. Bertha glanced down at her own person and had to admit that her own outfit didn't look right either. She hoped that the doctor's mother wasn't a follower of fashion like her stepmother.

She had no need to worry; the lady who came to meet them as the doctor opened the greenhouse door was wearing a fine wool skirt stained with earth and with bits of greenery caught up in it, and her blouse, pure silk and beautifully made, was almost covered by a misshapen cardigan of beige cashmere as stained as the skirt. She was wearing wellies and thick gardening gloves and looked, thought Bertha, exactly as the doctor's mother should look.

She wasn't quite sure what she meant by this, it was something that she couldn't put into words, but she knew instinctively that this elderly lady with her plain face and sweet expression was all that she would have wanted if her own mother had lived.

'My dear.' Mrs Hay-Smythe lifted up her face for her son's kiss. 'How lovely to see you—and these are the girls who had such an unpleasant experience the other day?'

She held out a hand, the glove pulled off. 'I'm delighted to meet you. You must tell me all about it, presently—I live such a quiet life here that I'm all agog to hear the details.'

'Oh, it was nothing, Mrs Hay-Smythe,' said Clare. 'I'm sure there are many more people braver than I. It is so kind of Oliver to bring us; I had no idea that he had such a beautiful home.'

Mrs Hay-Smythe looked a little taken aback, but she smiled and said, 'Well, yes, we're very happy to live here.'

She turned to Bertha. 'And you are Bertha?' Her smile widened and her blue eyes smiled too, never once so much as glancing at the yellow jersey. 'Forgive me that I am so untidy, but there is always work to do in the greenhouse. We'll go indoors and have a drink. Oliver will look after you while I tidy myself.'

They wandered back to the house—Clare ahead

with the doctor, his mother coming slowly with Bertha, stopping to describe the bushes and flowers that would bloom in the spring as they went, Freddie and her small border terrier beside them.

'You are fond of gardening?' she wanted to know.

'Well, we live in a townhouse, you know. There's a gardener, and he comes once a week to see to the garden—but he doesn't grow things, just comes and digs up whatever's there and then plants the next lot. That's not really gardening. I'd love to have a packet of seeds and grow flowers, but I—I don't have much time.'

Mrs Hay-Smythe, who knew all about Bertha, nodded sympathetically. 'I expect one day you'll get the opportunity—when you marry, you know.'

'I don't really expect to marry,' said Bertha matter-of-factly. 'I don't meet many people and I'm plain.' She sounded quite cheerful and her hostess smiled.

'Well, as to that, I'm plain, my dear, and I was a middle daughter of six living in a remote vicarage. And that, I may tell you, was quite a handicap.'

They both laughed and Clare, standing waiting for them with the doctor, frowned. Just like Bertha to worm her way into their hostess's good books, she thought. Well, she would soon see about that.

As they went into the house she edged her way towards Mrs Hay-Smythe. 'This is such a lovely house. I do hope there will be time for you to take me round before we go back.' She remembered that that would leave Bertha with Oliver, which would never do. 'Bertha too, of course…'

Mrs Hay-Smythe had manners as beautiful as her son's. 'I shall be delighted. But now I must go and change. Oliver, give the girls a drink, will you? I'll be ten minutes or so. We mustn't keep Meg waiting.'

It seemed to Bertha that the doctor was perfectly content to listen to Clare's chatter as she drank her gin and lime, and his well-mannered attempts to draw her into the conversation merely increased her shyness. So silly, she reflected, sipping her sherry, because when I'm with him and there's no one else there I'm perfectly normal.

Mrs Hay-Smythe came back presently, wearing a black and white dress, which, while being elegant, suited her age. A pity, thought Bertha, still wrapped in thought, that her stepmother didn't dress in a similar manner, instead of forcing herself into clothes more suitable to a woman of half her age. She was getting very mean and unkind, she reflected.

Lunch eaten in a lovely panelled room with an oval table and a massive sideboard of mahogany, matching shield-back chairs and a number of portraits in heavy gilt frames on its walls, was simple but beautifully cooked: miniature onion tarts decorated with olives and strips of anchovy, grilled trout with a pepper sauce and a green salad, followed by orange cream soufflés.

Bertha ate with unselfconscious pleasure and a good appetite and listened resignedly to Clare tell her hostess as she picked daintily at her food that she adored French cooking.

'We have a chef who cooks the most delicious

food.' She gave one of her little laughs. 'I'm so fussy, I'm afraid. But I adore lobster, don't you? And those little tartlets with caviare…'

Mrs Hay-Smythe smiled and offered Bertha a second helping. Bertha, pink with embarrassment, accepted. So did the doctor and his mother, so that Clare was left to sit and look at her plate while the three of them ate unhurriedly.

They had coffee in the conservatory and soon the doctor said, 'We have a family pet at the bottom of the garden. Nellie the donkey. She enjoys visitors and Freddie is devoted to her. Shall we stroll down to see her?'

He smiled at Bertha's eager face and Freddie was already on his feet when Clare said quickly, 'Oh, but we are to see the house. I'm longing to go all over it.'

'In that case,' said Mrs Hay-Smythe in a decisive voice, 'you go on ahead to Nellie, Oliver, and take Bertha with you, and I'll take Clare to see a little of the house.' When Clare would have protested that perhaps, after all, she would rather see the donkey, Mrs Hay-Smythe said crisply, 'No, no, I mustn't disappoint you. We can join the others very shortly.'

She whisked Clare indoors and the doctor stood up. 'Come along, Bertha. We'll go to the kitchen and get a carrot…'

Meg and Dora were loading the dishwasher, and the gentle clatter of crockery made a pleasant background for the loud tick-tock of the kitchen clock and the faint strains of the radio. There was a tabby cat before the Aga, and the cat with the orange coat was sitting on the window-sill.

'Carrots?' said Meg. 'For that donkey of yours, Master Oliver? Pampered, that's what she is.' She smiled broadly at Bertha. 'Not but what she's an old pet, when all's said and done.'

Dora had gone to fetch the carrots and the doctor was sitting on the kitchen table eating a slice of the cake that was presumably for tea.

'I enjoyed my lunch,' said Bertha awkwardly. 'You must be a marvellous cook, Meg.'

'Lor' bless you, miss, anyone can cook who puts their mind to it.' But Meg looked pleased all the same.

The donkey was in a small orchard at the bottom of the large garden. She was an elderly beast who was pleased to see them; she ate the carrots and then trotted around a bit in a dignified way with a delighted Freddie.

The doctor, leaning on the gate to the orchard, looked sideways at Bertha. She was happy, her face full of contentment. She was happily oblivious of her startling outfit too—which was even more startling in the gentle surroundings.

Conscious that he was looking at her, she turned her head and their eyes met.

Good gracious, thought Bertha, I feel as if I've known him all my life, that I've been waiting for him…

Clare's voice broke the fragile thread which had been spun between them. 'There you are. Is this the donkey? Oliver, you do have a lovely house—your really ought to marry and share it with someone.'

CHAPTER FOUR

THEY didn't stay long in the orchard—Clare's high-heeled shoes sank into the ground at every step and her complaints weren't easily ignored. They sat in the conservatory again, and Clare told them amusing tales about her friends and detailed the plays she had recently seen and the parties she had attended.

'I scarcely have a moment to myself,' she declared on a sigh. 'You can't imagine how delightful a restful day here is.'

'You would like to live in the country?' asked Mrs Hay-Smythe.

'In a house like this? Oh, yes. One could run up to town whenever one felt like it—shopping and the theatre—and I dare say there are other people living around here...'

'Oh, yes.' Mrs Hay-Smythe spoke pleasantly. 'Oliver, will you ask Meg to bring tea out here?'

After tea they took their leave and got into the car, and were waved away by Mrs Hay-Smythe. Bertha waved back, taking a last look at the house she wasn't likely to see again but would never forget.

As for Mrs Hay-Smythe, she went to the kitchen, where she found Meg and Dora having their own tea. She sat down at the table with them and accepted a cup of strong tea with plenty of milk. Not her favourite brand, but she felt that she needed something with a bite to it.

'Well?' she asked.

'Since you want to know, ma'am,' said Meg, 'and speaking for the two of us, we just hope that the master isn't taken with that young lady what didn't eat her lunch. High and mighty, we thought—didn't we, Dora?'

'Let me put your minds at rest. This visit was made in order to give the other Miss Soames a day out, but to do so it was necessary to invite her stepsister as well.'

'Well, there,' said Dora. 'Like Cinderella. Such a nice quiet young lady too. Thanked you for her lunch, didn't she, Meg?'

'That she did, and not smarmy either. Fitted into the house very nicely too.'

'Yes, she did,' said Mrs Hay-Smythe thoughtfully. Bertha would make a delightful daughter-in-law, but Oliver had given no sign—he had helped her out of kindness but shown no wish to be in her company or even talk to her other than in a casual friendly way. 'A pity,' said Mrs Hay-Smythe, and with Flossie, her little dog, at her heels she went back to the greenhouse, where she put on a vast apron and her gardening gloves and began work again.

The doctor drove back the way they had come, listening to Clare's voice and hardly hearing what she was saying. Only when she said insistently, 'You will take me out to dinner this evening, won't you, Oliver?

Somewhere lively where we can dance afterwards? It's been a lovely day, but after all that rural quiet we could do with some town life…'

'When we get back,' he said, 'I am going straight to the hospital where I shall be for several hours, and I have an appointment for eight o'clock tomorrow morning. I am a working man, Clare.'

She pouted. 'Oh, Oliver, can't you forget the hospital just for once? I was so sure you'd take me out.'

'Quite impossible. Besides, I'm not a party man, Clare.'

She touched his sleeve. 'I could change that for you. At least promise you'll come to dinner one evening? I'll tell Mother to give you a ring.'

He glanced in the side-mirror and saw that Bertha was sitting with her arm round Freddie's neck, looking out of the window. Her face was turned away, but the back of her head looked sad.

He stayed only as long as good manners required when they reached the Soameses' house, and when he had gone Clare threw her handbag down and flung herself into a chair.

Her mother asked sharply, 'Well, you had Oliver all to yourself—is he interested?'

'Well, of course he is. If only we hadn't taken Bertha with us…'

'She didn't interfere, I hope.'

'She didn't get the chance—she hardly spoke to him. I didn't give her the opportunity. She was with his mother most of the time.'

'What is Mrs Hay-Smythe like?'

'Oh, boring—talking about the garden and the

Women's Institute and doing the flowers for the church. She was in the greenhouse when we got there. I thought she was one of the servants.'

'Not a lady?' asked her mother, horrified.

'Oh, yes, no doubt about that. Plenty of money too, I should imagine. The house is lovely—it would be a splendid country home for weekends if we could have a decent flat here.' She laughed. 'The best of both worlds.'

Bertha, in her room, changing out of the two-piece and getting into another of Clare's too-elaborate dresses, told the kitchen cat, who was enjoying a stolen hour or so on her bed, all about her day.

'I don't suppose Oliver will be able to withstand Clare for much longer—only I mustn't call him Oliver, must I? I'm not supposed to have more than a nodding acquaintance with him.' She sat down on the bed, the better to address her companion. 'I think that is what I must do in the future, just nod. I think about him too much and I miss him…'

She went to peer at her face in the mirror and nodded at its reflection. 'Plain as a pikestaff, my girl.'

Dinner was rather worse than usual, for there were no guests and that gave her stepmother and Clare the opportunity to criticise her behaviour during the day.

'Clare tells me that you spent too much time with Mrs Hay-Smythe…'

Bertha popped a morsel of fish into her mouth and chewed it. 'Well,' she said reasonably, 'what else was I to do? Clare wouldn't have liked it if I'd attached myself to Dr Hay-Smythe, and it would have looked very ill-mannered if I'd just gone off on my own.'

Mrs Soames glared, seeking for a quelling reply. 'Anyway, you should never have gone off with the doctor while Clare was in the house with his mother.'

'I enjoyed it. We talked about interesting things—the donkey and the orchard and the house.'

'He must have been bored,' said her stepmother crossly.

Bertha looked demure. 'Yes, I think that some of the time he was—very bored.'

Clare tossed her head. 'Not when he was with me,' she said smugly, but her mother shot Bertha a frowning look.

'I think you should understand, Bertha, that Dr Hay-Smythe is very likely about to propose marriage to your stepsister...'

'Has he said so?' asked Bertha composedly. She studied Mrs Soames, whose high colour had turned faintly purple.

'Certainly not, but one feels these things.' Mrs Soames pushed her plate aside. 'I am telling you this because I wish you to refuse any further invitations which the doctor may offer you—no doubt out of kindness.'

'Why?'

'There is an old saying—two is company, three is a crowd.'

'Oh, you don't want me to play gooseberry. I looked like one today in that frightful outfit Clare passed on to me.'

'You ungrateful—' began Clare, but was silenced by a majestic wave of her mother's hand.

'I cannot think what has come over you, Bertha.

Presumably this day's outing has gone to your head. The two-piece Clare so kindly gave you is charming.'

'Then why doesn't she wear it?' asked Bertha, feeling reckless. She wasn't sure what had come over her either, but she was rather enjoying it. 'I would like some new clothes of my own.'

Mrs Soames's bosom swelled alarmingly. 'That is enough, Bertha. I shall buy you something suitable when I have the leisure to arrange it. I think you had better have an early night, for you aren't yourself... The impertinence...'

'Is that what it is? It feels nice!' said Bertha.

She excused herself with perfect good manners and went up to her room. She lay in the bath for a long time, having a good cry but not sure why she was crying. At least, she had a vague idea at the back of her head as to why she felt lonely and miserable, but she didn't allow herself to pursue the matter. She got into bed and the cat curled up against her back, purring in a comforting manner, so that she was lulled into a dreamless sleep.

Her mother and Clare had been invited to lunch with friends who had a house near Henley. Bertha had been invited too, but she didn't know that. Mrs Soames had explained to their hosts that she had a severe cold in the head and would spend the day in bed.

Bertha was up early, escorting the cat back to her rightful place in the kitchen and making herself tea. She would have almost the whole day to herself;

Crook was to have an afternoon off and Cook's sister was coming to spend the day with her.

Mrs Soames found this quite satisfactory since Bertha could be served a cold lunch and get her own tea if Cook decided to walk down to the nearest bus stop with her sister. The daily maid never came on a Sunday.

All this suited Bertha; she drank her tea while the cat lapped milk, and decided what she would do with her day. A walk—a long walk. She would go to St James's Park and feed the ducks. She went back upstairs to dress and had almost finished breakfast when Clare joined her. Bertha said good morning and she got a sour look, which she supposed was only to be expected.

It was after eleven o'clock by the time Mrs Soames and Clare had driven away. Bertha, thankful that it was a dull, cold day, allowing her to wear the lime-green which she felt was slightly less awful than the two-piece, went to tell Crook that she might be late for lunch and ask him to leave it on a tray for her before he left the house and set out.

There wasn't a great deal of traffic in the streets, but there were plenty of people taking their Sunday walk as she neared the park. She walked briskly, her head full of daydreams, not noticing her surroundings until someone screamed.

A young woman was coming out of the park gates pushing a pram—and running across the street into the path of several cars was a small boy. Bertha ran. She ran fast, unhampered by high heels and handbag, and plucked the child from the nearest car's wheels just before those same wheels bowled her over.

The child's safe, she thought hazily, aware that every bone in her body ached and that she was lying in a puddle of water, but somehow she felt too tired to get up. She felt hands and then heard voices, any number of them, asking if she were hurt.

'No—thank you,' said Bertha politely. 'Just aching a bit. Is that child OK?'

There was a chorus of 'yes', and somebody said that there was an ambulance coming. 'No need,' said Bertha, not feeling at all herself. 'If I could get up…'

'No, no,' said a voice. 'There may be broken bones…'

So she stayed where she was, listening to the voices; there seemed to be a great many people all talking at once. She was feeling sick now…

There were no broken bones, the ambulanceman assured her, but they laid her on a stretcher, popped her into the ambulance and bore her away to hospital. They had put a dressing on her leg without saying why.

The police were there by then, wanting to know her name and where she lived.

'Bertha Soames. But there is no one at home.'

Well, Cook was, but what could she do? Better keep quiet. Bertha closed her eyes, one of which was rapidly turning purple.

Dr Hay-Smythe, called down to the accident and emergency department to examine a severe head injury, paused to speak to the casualty officer as he left.

The slight commotion as an ambulance drew up and a patient was wheeled in caused him to turn his head. He glanced at the patient and then looked again.

'Will you stop for a moment?' he asked, and bent over the stretcher. It was Bertha, all right, with a muddy face and a black eye and hair all over the place.

He straightened up. 'I know this young lady. I'll wait while you take a look.'

'Went after a kid running under a car. Kid's OK but the car wheel caught her. Nasty gash on her left leg.' The ambulanceman added, 'Brave young lady.'

Dr Hay-Smythe bent his great height again. 'Bertha?' His voice was quiet and reassuring. She opened the good eye.

'Oliver.' She smiled widely. 'You oughtn't to be working; it's Sunday.'

He smiled then and signalled to the men to wheel the stretcher away. It struck him that despite the dirt and the black eye nothing could dim the beauty of her one good eye, its warm brown alight with the pleasure of seeing him again.

There wasn't too much damage, the casualty officer told him presently—bruising, some painful grazes, a black eye and the fairly deep gash on one leg. 'It'll need a few stitches, and there's a good deal of grit and dirt in the wound. She'd better have a whiff of anaesthetic so that I can clean it up. Anti-tetanus jab too.'

He looked curiously at his companion; Dr Hay-Smythe was a well-known figure at the hospital, oc-

casionally giving anaesthetics and often visiting the
patients in his beds on the medical wards. He was
well liked and respected, and rumour had it that he
was much in demand socially; this small girl didn't
seem quite his type...

Dr Hay-Smythe looked at his watch. 'If you could
see to her within the next half-hour I'll give a hand.
It'll save calling the anaesthetist out.'

Bertha, getting stiffer with every passing minute and
aware of more and more sore places on her person,
had her eyes closed. She opened the sound one when
she heard his voice.

'You have a cut on your leg, Bertha,' he told her.
'I'm going to give you a whiff of something while
it's seen to, then you will be warded.'

'No, no, I must go back home. Cook might wonder
where I am.'

'Only Cook?' he gueried gently.

'Crook's got a half-day and my stepmother and
Clare have gone to Henley to lunch with friends.
There's no need to bother Cook; her sister's there.'

'Very well, but you are to stay here, Bertha. I'll
see that your stepmother knows when she returns.
Now, how long ago is it since you had your breakfast?'

'Why ever do you want to know? About eight
o'clock.'

'Purely a professional question. No, close your
eyes; I'm going to give you an injection in the back
of your hand.' He turned away and spoke to someone

she couldn't see and presently, eyes obediently shut, she felt a faint prick. 'Count up to ten,' he said, his voice reassuringly casual.

She got as far as five.

When she opened her eyes again she was in bed— a corner bed in a big ward—and the casualty officer and Dr Hay-Smythe were standing at the foot of it.

'Ah, back with us.' He turned away for a moment while two nurses heaved her up the bed, rearranged a cradle over her leg and disappeared again.

He studied her thoughtfully; anywhere else she would have minded being stared at like that, but here in hospital it was different; here he was a doctor and she was just another patient.

'Can I go home soon?' she asked.

It was the last place he wished her to go. She looked very small, engulfed in a hospital gown far too large for her, with her face clean now but pale and the damaged eye the only colour about her. Her hair, its mousy abundance disciplined into a plait, hung over one shoulder.

He said after a moment, 'No, you can't, Bertha. You're in one of my beds and you'll stay here until I discharge you.' He smiled suddenly. 'This is Dr Turner, the casualty officer who stitched you up.' And as another young man joined them he went on, 'And this is the medical officer who will look after you— Dr Greyson. I'll go and see your stepmother this afternoon and she will doubtless arrange to send in whatever you need.'

He offered a hand and she took it and summoned

up a smile. 'Thank you for all your trouble. I hope I haven't spoilt your day.'

She closed her eyes, suddenly overcome by sleep.

Dr Hay-Smythe waited until the late afternoon before calling at the Soameses' house—too late for tea and too early for drinks—since he had no wish to linger there. He was admitted by Cook, since Crook was still enjoying his half-day, and ushered into the drawing room, where Mrs Soames and Clare were sitting discussing the lunch party. They greeted him eagerly, bored with each other's company.

'Oliver!' Clare went to meet him. 'How lovely—I was just wondering what I would do with the rest of this dull day, and you're the answer.'

He greeted her mother before replying, 'I'm afraid not. I have to return to the hospital very shortly. I have come to tell you that Bertha has had an accident—'

'The silly girl,' interposed Mrs Soames.

'She saved the life of a small boy who had run into the street in front of a car.' His voice was carefully expressionless. 'She is in hospital with a badly cut leg and severe bruising, so she must stay there for a few days at least. Would you take her whatever is necessary when you go to see her?'

'You've seen her?' Clare's voice was sharp.

'Yes. I happened to be in the accident and emergency department when she was admitted. She is in very good hands. I'll write down the name of the ward for you—there is no reason why you shouldn't visit her this evening.'

'Quite impossible, Oliver. I've guests coming for

dinner.' Mrs Soames uttered the lie without hesitation. 'And I can't allow Clare to go. She is so sensitive to pain and distressing scenes; besides, who knows what foul germs there are in those public wards? She *is* in a public ward?'

'Yes. Perhaps you would ask one of your staff.' He paused, and then went on silkily, 'Better still, if you could give me whatever is needed, I will take it to Bertha.'

This suggestion met with the instant rejection he had expected. 'No, no!' cried Mrs Soames. 'Cook shall go with Bertha's things, and at the same time make sure that she has all she wants. The poor child!' she added with sickening mendacity. 'We must take good care of her when she comes home.'

She gave Clare a warning glance so that the girl quickly added her own sympathy. 'I hope she comes home soon.' Clare sounded wistfully concerned. 'I shall miss her.'

As indeed she would, reflected the doctor. There would be no one to whom she might pass on her unsuitable clothes. She was wearing a ridiculous outfit now, all frills and floating bits; he much preferred Bertha in her startling lime-green. Indeed, upon further reflection he much preferred Bertha, full-stop.

He took his leave presently and went back home to fetch Freddie and take him for a long walk in Hyde Park. And that evening, after he had dined, he got into his car once more and drove to the hospital. Visiting hours were long over and the wards were quiet, the patients drinking their milk or Ovaltine and being settled down for the night. Bertha was asleep when, accompanied by the ward sister, he went to look at her.

'Someone came with her nightclothes and so on?' he wanted to know.

'Oh, yes, Doctor. The family cook—a nice old soul. Gave her a large cake in a tin too, and said she would come again and that if she couldn't come someone called Crook would.'

'Ah, yes, the butler.'

'Has she no family?'

'A stepmother and a stepsister and a father who at present is somewhere in the States. He's a well-known QC.'

Sister looked at him. There was nothing to see on his handsome features, but she sensed damped-down rage. 'I'll take good care of her, Doctor,' she said.

He smiled at her then. 'Good—and will you be sure and let me know before she goes home?'

Bertha, after a refreshing sleep, felt quite herself in the morning. True, she was still stiff and sore, and it was tiresome only having the use of one eye, but she sat up and ate her breakfast and would have got out of bed armed with towel and toothbrush if she hadn't been restrained.

The leg must be rested, she was told. The cut had been deep and very dirty, and until it had been examined and re-dressed she would have to remain in her bed.

There was plenty to keep her interested, however. The elderly lady in the bed next to hers passed half an hour giving her details of her operation, most of

them inaccurate, but Bertha listened enthralled until
Sister came down the ward with a Cellophaned pack-
age.

'These have just come for you, Bertha. Aren't you
a lucky girl?'

It was a delicate china bowl filled with a charming
mixture of winter crocuses.

'There's a card,' prompted Sister.

Bertha took it from its miniature envelope. The
writing on it was hard to read. 'Flowers for Bertha',
it said, and then the initials 'O.H-S.'

Sister recognised the scrawl. 'Just the right size for
your locker top,' she said breezily, and watched the
colour flood into Bertha's pale face. Who'd have
thought it? the sister asked herself, sensing romance.

There were visitors later—the small boy whom she
had saved led into the ward by his mother and bearing
a bunch of flowers. The mother cried all over Bertha
and wrung her hand and, very much to Bertha's embarrassment, told everyone near enough to listen how
Bertha had saved her small son from being run over.

'Killed, he would have been—or crippled for life.
A proper heroine, she is.'

That evening Crook came, bearing more flowers
and a large box of chocolates from Cook and the daily
and the man who came to do the garden each week.

'Is everything all right at home, Crook?' asked
Bertha.

'Yes, Miss Bertha. I understand that there is a letter
from your father; he hopes to return within the next
few weeks. Mrs Soames and Miss Clare have been

down to Brighton with friends; they are dining out this evening.'

'I'm not sure how long I am to stay here, Crook…'

'As long as it takes you to get quite well, Miss Bertha. You're not coming home before.'

He got up to go presently, with the promise that someone would come to see her again.

'Thank you for coming, and please thank the others for the chocolates and flowers. It's so kind of them and I know how busy you all are, so I won't mind if none of you can spare the time to visit. You can see how comfortable I am, and everyone is so friendly.'

On his way out, Sister stopped him. 'You come from Mrs Soames's household? Is she coming to see Miss Soames? She must wish to know about her injuries and I'd like to advise her about her convalescence.'

'Mrs Soames is most unlikely to come, Sister. If you will trust me with any details as to the care of Miss Bertha when she returns home, I shall do my utmost to carry them out,' said Crook.

When Dr Hay-Smythe came onto the ward later that evening, as she was going off duty, Sister paused to talk to him and tell him and the medical officer, who had come to do an evening round, what Crook had told her. 'I'll keep her as long as possible, but I'm always pushed for beds. And although I know you have beds in this ward, doctor, it is a medical unit and Bertha's a surgical case.'

'A couple more days, Sister?' He glanced at the young doctor with him. 'Turn a blind eye, Ralph? At least until the stitches come out. If she goes home too soon she'll be on that leg all day and ruin the CO's painstaking surgery. How is she, by the way?'

'A model patient; she's next to Mrs Jenkins—a thrombosis after surgery—and she's delighted to have such a tolerant listener.' She glanced at the doctor. 'She was delighted with your flowers, doctor.'

'Good. May I see Miss Arkwright for a moment? She wasn't too good yesterday.'

Miss Arkwright was at the other end of the ward from Bertha, but she could see Dr Hay-Smythe clearly as he went to his patient's bedside. She was feeling sleepy, but she kept her eye open; he would be sure to come and say goodnight presently. Only he didn't. After a few minutes he went away again without so much as a glance in her direction.

Bertha discovered that it was just as easy to cry with one eye as two.

The next few days were pleasant enough—the nurses were friendly, those patients who were allowed up came to sit by her, bringing their newspapers and reading out the more lurid bits, since her eye, now all the colours of the rainbow and beginning to open again, was still painful. Cook came too, this time with a bag of oranges.

Everything was much as usual, she told Bertha comfortably, omitting to mention that Mrs Soames's temper had been worse than usual and that Clare was having sulking fits.

'That nice doctor what she's keen on—always asking 'im ter take 'er out, she is, and 'im with no time to spare. 'E's taking 'er out to dinner this evening, though.'

Bertha stayed awake for a long time that night, listening to the snores and mutterings around her, the occasional urgent cry for a bedpan, the equally urgent whispers for tea. She closed her eyes each time the night nurse or night sister did her round and she heard the night sister say quietly, 'She'll have to go home in a couple of days; she's only here as a favour to Dr Hay-Smythe.'

Bertha lay and thought about going home. She had no choice but to do so for she had no money. It would mean seeing Clare and Oliver together, and she wasn't sure if she could bear that.

I suppose, she reflected, with the clarity of mind which comes to everybody at three o'clock in the morning, that I've been in love with him since he came over to me and asked me if it was my birthday. I'll have to go away… Once Father's back home, perhaps he'll agree to my training for something so that I can be independent. I'll have my own flat and earn enough money to be able to dress well and to go to the hairdresser and have lots of friends… She fell into an uneasy doze.

She was allowed out of bed now, and later the next day Staff Nurse took out alternate stitches.

'I'll have the rest tomorrow,' she said briskly. 'Don't run around too much; it's not quite healed yet. I expect you'll be going home in a day or two now.'

Bertha told Crook that when he came that afternoon. 'Please don't tell anyone, will you? I wouldn't want to upset any plans…'

They both knew Mrs Soames wasn't likely to change any plans she had made just because Bertha was coming home.

Dr Hay-Smythe came to see her that evening. 'You're to go home the day after tomorrow. I'll take you directly after lunch. You feel quite well?'

'Yes, thank you, I'm fine. Some of the stitches are out and it's a very nice scar—a bit red...'

'You won't see it in a few months. Will you be able to rest at home?'

'Oh, of course,' said Bertha airily. 'I can sit in the drawing room. But I don't need to rest, do I? I'm perfectly well. I know my eye's still not quite right, but it looks more dramatic than it is.'

He sat down on the side of the bed. 'Bertha, my mother would like you to go and stay with her for a week or two, perhaps until Christmas. How would you like that?'

Her eyes shone. 'Oh, how kind of her. I'd have to ask my stepmother first...'

He found himself smiling at her eager face. The few days in hospital had done her good; she had a pretty colour and she looked happy. He took her hand in his, conscious of a deep contentment. He had cautioned himself to have patience, to give her time to get to know him, but he had fallen in love with her when he had first seen her and his love had grown over the weeks. She was the girl he had been waiting for, and somehow or other he had managed to keep close to her, despite the dreadful stepmother and the tiresome Clare. He wouldn't hurry her, but after a few days he would go home and tell her that he loved her in the peace and quiet of the country.

He said now, 'We have to talk, Bertha. But not here.'

The ward was very quite and dim. He bent and kissed her gently and went away. Mrs Jenkins, feigning sleep and listening to every word, whispered, 'Now go to sleep, ducks. Nothing like a kiss to give you sweet dreams.'

The next day Oliver realized that he would have to see Mrs Soames before taking Bertha home. There was bound to be unpleasantness and he wanted that dealt with before she arrived. Not that he intended to tell her that he was in love with Bertha and was going to marry her, only that his mother had invited her to stay for a short time.

Mrs Soames gushed over him and then listened to his plans, a smile pinned onto her face. He was surprised at her readiness to agree with him that a week or so's rest was necessary for Bertha, but, thinking about it later, he concluded that it might suit her and Clare to have Bertha out of the way—she would be of no use to them around the house until her leg was quite healed. All the same, he had a feeling of unease.

CHAPTER FIVE

OLIVER'S feeling of unease was justified. Mrs Soames, left to herself, paced up and down her drawing room, fuming. Bertha had gone behind her back and was doing her best to put a spoke in Clare's wheel. The wretched girl! Something would have to be done.

Mrs Soames, by now in a rage, spent some time thinking of the things she would like to do to Bertha before pulling herself together. Anger wasn't going to help. She must keep a cool head and think of ways and means. She heard Clare's voice in the hall and went to the door and called for her to come to the drawing room.

'Presently,' said Clare, who was halfway up the stairs. 'I've broken a fingernail and I must see to it at once…'

Something in her mother's voice brought her downstairs again.

'What's the matter?'

'Oliver has been here. Bertha is to come home to-morrow and his mother has invited her to stay with her for a couple of weeks.' Mrs Soames almost choked with fury as she spoke. 'The ungrateful girl—going behind our backs. She's cunning enough—

she'll have him all to herself if she goes to his home.'
She looked thoughtful. 'I wonder—Clare, get me the
telephone directory.'

His receptionist was still at his rooms, and, in answer to Mrs Soames's polite enquiry, said that she
was afraid that Dr Hay-Smythe wouldn't be seeing
new patients during the coming week. 'And he will
be going on holiday the following week. But I could
book you for an appointment in three weeks' time.'

Mrs Soames put down the phone without bothering
to answer.

'He's going on holiday in a week's time—he'll go
home, of course, and they'll have a whole week together. We have this week to think of something,
Clare.'

Clare poured them each a drink and sat down.
'She'll have to go away—miles away. Now, who do
we know...?'

'She'll have to go immediately—supposing he calls
to see her?'

'We can say she's spending the weekend with
friends.' Clare sat up suddenly. 'Aunt Agatha,' she
said triumphantly. 'That awful old crow—Father's elder sister, the one who doesn't like us. We haven't
seen her for years. She lives somewhere in the wilds
of Cornwall, doesn't she?'

'Perfect—but will she have Bertha to stay? Supposing she refuses?'

'She doesn't need to know. You can send Bertha
there—tell her that Aunt Agatha isn't well and has
asked if she would go and stay with her.'

'What are we to say? Bertha may want to see the letter…'

'No letter. A phone call.' Clare crowed with laughter. 'I'd love to see her face when Bertha gets there.' She paused to think. 'We'll have to wait until Oliver has brought her home and then pack her off smartly. Do you suppose that he's interested in her? It's ridiculous even to think it. Why, Bertha's plain and dull—it's not possible. Besides, he's taken me out several times…'

'He will again, darling,' said Mrs Soames. She smiled fondly at her daughter; she could rest assured that Clare would get her way.

Bertha was ready and waiting when the doctor came for her. Her leg was still bandaged and her cheek under the black eye was grazed, but all he saw was the radiance of her smile when she saw him. He held down with an iron will a strong desire to gather her into his arms and kiss her, and said merely, 'Quite ready? The leg is comfortable? I can see that the eye is better.'

'I'm fine,' declared Bertha—a prosaic statement, which concealed her true feelings. 'It's very kind of you to take me home.'

He only smiled, waiting while she said goodbye to Sister and the nurses; she had already visited each bed to shake hands with its occupant.

He carried on a gentle, rambling conversation as he drove her home and as he drew up before the door he said, 'I'm coming in with you, Bertha.' Mrs

Soames had seemed pleasant enough, but he still had an uneasy feeling about her.

Mrs Soames and Clare were both there, waiting for them. Clare spoke first.

'Bertha, are you quite better? Ought you to rest?' She gave a small, apologetic smile. 'I'm sorry I didn't come and see you—you know how I hate illness and dreary hospitals. But I'll make it up to you.'

Bertha, recognising this as a deliberate act to put her stepsister in a good light, murmured back and replied suitably to her stepmother's enquiries, which gave Clare the opportunity to take the doctor aside on the pretext of enquiring as to Bertha's fitness.

'Is she all right to walk about? Not too much, of course. We'll take good care of her.' She smiled up into his face. 'It is so kind of your mother to have her to stay. Will you be going to your home too?'

He looked down at her, his face bland. 'I shall do my best.' He got up from the sofa where they were sitting. 'I must go. I have several patients to see this afternoon.' He crossed the room to where Bertha was in uneasy conversation with her stepmother. 'I will come for you in three days' time, Bertha. Mrs Soames, I'm sure you'll take good care of her until then.' He shook hands then turned to Bertha. 'I hope to get away at half past twelve— will you be ready for me then?'

'Yes—yes, thank you.'

'Don't try and do too much for a few days.'

No one could fault the way in which he spoke to her—a detached kindness, just sufficiently friendly. Only his eyes gleamed under their lids.

Bertha's stepmother, once the doctor had gone, was so anxious to make sure that Bertha had everything she wanted, wasn't tired, wasn't hungry, or didn't wish to lie down on her bed that Bertha was at pains to discover what had brought about this change of heart.

She wasn't the only one. Crook, going back to the kitchen after he had served dinner, put down his tray and said darkly, 'Depend upon it, this won't last—there's madam begging Miss Bertha to have another morsel and is she comfortable in that chair and would she like to go to bed and someone would bring her a warm drink. Poppycock—I wonder what's behind it?'

Apparently nothing; by the end of the second day Bertha's surprise at this cosseting had given way to pleased relief, and Crook had to admit that Mrs Soames seemed to have had a change of heart. 'And not before time,' he observed.

Bertha went to bed early. She had packed her bag with the miserable best of her wardrobe, washed her hair and telephoned the nursery school to tell the matron that she would be coming back after Christmas if they still wanted her. Since her stepmother was showing such a sympathetic face, Bertha had told her that she was no longer reading to an old lady but to a group of children.

'Why didn't you tell me this?' Mrs Soames strove to keep the annoyance out of her voice.

'I didn't think that it was important or that you would be interested.'

Mrs Soames bit her tongue and summoned up a

smile. 'Well, it really doesn't matter, Bertha. I'm sure it is very worthwhile work. Oliver arranged it for you, I expect?'

Bertha said that yes, he had, and didn't see the angry look from her stepmother.

Clare, when told of this, burst into tears. 'You see, Mother, how she has been hoodwinking us all this time. Probably seeing him every day. Well, she'll be gone when he comes. Is it all arranged?'

It was still early morning when Bertha was roused by her stepmother. 'Bertha, I've just had a phone call from your aunt Agatha. She's not well and asks for you. I don't think she's desperately ill, just needs someone there other than the servants. She has always been fond of you, hasn't she? She begged me to ask you to go as soon as possible, and I couldn't refuse.'

'I'm going to Mrs Hay-Smythe today, though…'

'Yes, yes, I know. But perhaps you could go to your aunt just for a day or two.'

'Why must I go? Why should she ask for me?'

'She's elderly—and she's always been eccentric.' Mrs Soames, sensing that she was losing the battle, said with sudden inspiration, 'Suppose you go today? I'll phone her doctor and see if he can arrange for someone to stay with your aunt, then you can come straight back. A day's delay at the most. Your father would want you to go.'

'Oliver expects me to be ready—'

'Write him a note and I'll explain. Believe me, Bertha, if Clare could go in your place she would, but you know how your aunt dislikes her.'

Bertha threw back the bed clothes. 'Very well, but I'm coming back, whatever arrangements are made.'

'Well, of course you are. Get dressed quickly and I'll find out about trains.'

Mrs Soames went away to tell Clare that their plan was working so far. 'I told her that I was finding out about the next train.' She glanced at the clock. 'I've just time to dress and drive her to Paddington. She can have breakfast on the train.' She turned at the door. 'Bertha's writing a note for Oliver. Get rid of it before he comes—and not a word to the servants. I'll see them when I get back. I don't mean to tell them where she has gone.'

An hour later, sitting in the train, eating a breakfast she didn't want, Bertha tried to sort out the morning's happenings. It didn't occur to her that she had been tricked; she knew that her stepmother didn't like her, but that she would descend to such trickery never crossed her mind. She had written to Oliver—a careful little note, full of apologies, hoping that he wouldn't be inconvenienced and hoping to see his mother as soon as she could return.

Clare had read it before she'd torn it into little pieces.

The train journey was a lengthy one. Bertha, eating another meal she didn't want, thought about Oliver. He would have been to her home by now, of course, and been told about her sudden departure. She wished she could have written a longer letter, but there hadn't been time. She could think of nothing else, her head full of the whys and wherefores of something she couldn't understand. It was a relief when Truro was reached at last and she got out to change to a local train, which stopped at every station until it stopped, at last, at her destination.

The village was small and she remembered it well from visits when she was a child. Miss Soames lived a mile or two away from the narrow main street, and Bertha was relieved to see a taxi in the station yard. She had been given money for her expenses—just sufficient to get her to her aunt's house—and since her stepmother had pointed out that there was no point in getting a return ticket as she herself would drive down and fetch Bertha she had accepted the situation willingly enough. Her head full of Oliver, nothing else mattered.

Her aunt's house looked exactly the same as she remembered it—solid and rather bleak, with a splendid garden. Bertha toiled up the path with her suitcase and knocked at the door.

After a moment it was flung open and Miss Agatha Soames, majestic in a battered felt hat and old and expensive tweeds, stood surveying Bertha.

'Well, upon my word. Why are you here, gel?'

Bertha, not particularly put out by this welcome, for her aunt was notoriously tart, said composedly that her stepmother had sent her. 'She told me that you were ill and needed a companion and had asked for me urgently.'

Miss Soames breathed deeply. 'It seems to me from the look of you that it is you who needs a companion. Your stepmother is a vulgar, scheming woman who would be glad to see me dead. I am in the best of

health and need no one other than Betsy and Tom.
You may return home.' She bent a beady eye on
Bertha. 'Why have you a black eye? She actually sent
you here to me?'

'Yes, Aunt Agatha.' Awful doubts were crowding
into Bertha's tired head.

Miss Soames snorted. 'Then she's up to something.
Wants you out of the way in a hurry. Been upsetting
the applecart, have you? Poaching on that Clare's pre-
serves, are you?'

When Bertha's cheeks grew pink, she said, 'Took
a fancy to you instead of her, did he? Well, if he's
got any sense he will come after you.'

Bertha shook her head. 'No, I don't think so. He
doesn't know where I am—I didn't tell him.'

'They won't tell him either. But if he's worth his
salt he'll find you. Love him?'

'Yes, Aunt Agatha. But he doesn't think of me like
that, though he's a kind man.'

'We will see.' Miss Soames thrust the door wide
open and said belatedly, 'Well, come in. Now you're
here you'd better stay. Where's your father?'

'I'm not exactly sure, but he's coming home soon.'

Aunt Agatha said, 'Pah!' and raised her voice.
'Betsy, come here and listen to this.' Betsy came so
quickly that Bertha wondered if she had been standing
behind the door.

'No need to tell, I heard it all. Poor lamb. I'll get
the garden room ready and a morsel of food. The
child looks starved—and look at that eye! A week or
two here with good food and fresh air is what she
needs.'

*   *   *

During the next few days that was what Bertha got. Moreover, her aunt ordered Tom to bring the elderly Rover to the front door and she and Bertha were driven into Truro, where she sailed in and out of various shops buying clothes for her niece.

When Bertha protested, she said, 'I'll not have a niece of mine wearing cast-off clothes which are several sizes too big and quite unsuitable. I shall speak to your father. Don't interfere, miss.'

So Bertha thanked her aunt and got joyfully into skirts and blouses and dresses which fitted her slender person and were made of fine material in soft colours. If only Oliver could see her now. She had talked to her aunt about what she should do and that lady had said, 'Do nothing, gel. Let your stepmother wonder, if she can be bothered to do so. You are not to write to her nor are you to telephone. You will stay here until this doctor finds you.'

'He won't,' said Bertha. 'He'll never find me…'

'Have you never heard of the proverb "Love finds a way"? I have great faith in proverbs,' said Aunt Agatha.

Oliver had presented himself at half past twelve exactly to collect Bertha, and had been shown into the drawing room. Mrs Soames had come to meet him.

'Oliver, thank heaven you have come. I tried to get you on the phone, but there was no answer.'

She'd found his calm unnerving.

'Bertha!' she'd exclaimed. 'She must be ill—that accident. She got me out of bed early this morning and insisted on being driven to Euston Station. I begged her to stay, to phone you, to wait at least until you came. She was quite unlike herself—so cold and determined.'

'You did as she asked?' His voice had been very quiet.

'What else could I do? She wouldn't listen to reason.'

'She had money? Did she say where she was going?'

'I gave her what I had. She told me that she was going to an aunt—a relation of her mother's, I believe, who lives somewhere in Yorkshire. I begged her to tell why she wanted to leave us and I reminded her that she was to visit your mother—she said she would write to you.' Mrs Soames managed to squeeze out a tear. 'I really don't know what to do, Oliver. Clare is terribly upset.'

Oliver sounded quite cheerful. 'Why, I suggest that we wait until one or other of us gets a letter. She is quite capable of looking after herself, is she not?'

'Yes, of course. Will you come this evening so that we three can put our heads together? Dinner, perhaps?'

'Not possible, I'm afraid, Mrs Soames.' He spoke pleasantly, longing to wring the woman's neck. There was something not right about the story she had told him. He would get to the bottom of it if it took him weeks, months...

'The whole thing is fishy,' he told Freddie as he drove away. Someone somewhere would know where Bertha had gone; he would send Cully round later with some excuse or other and he could talk to

Crook—both he and Cook were obviously fond of Bertha, and in the meanwhile he would see if the nursery school knew anything.

'Gone?' asked Matron. 'Without a word to anyone? I find that hard to believe. Why, she telephoned not a day or two ago to say that she would be coming back after Christmas, when she had had a short holiday.'

Oliver thanked her. It hadn't been much help, but it was a start.

Cully's visit had no success, either. Crook was disturbed that Bertha had gone so unexpectedly, but he had no idea where she might be. Certainly there was an aunt of hers somewhere in the north of England, and the master had a sister living, but he had no idea where.

The doctor phoned his mother and sat down to think. Mrs Soames had been very glib, and he didn't believe a word of what she had said, but there was no way of getting her to tell the truth. To find this aunt in Yorkshire when he had no idea of her name or where she lived was going to be difficult. Her father's sister—unmarried, Crook had said—was a more likely possibility. He went to bed at last, knowing what he would do in the morning.

Mr Soames QC was well-known in his own profession. The doctor waited patiently until a suitable hour the next morning and then phoned his chambers.

'No,' he was told. 'Mr Soames is still in the States. Would you like to make an appointment at some future date?'

The doctor introduced himself. 'You are his chief

clerk? So I can speak freely to you? I am a friend of the Soames family and there is a personal matter I should like to attend to—preferably with Mr Soames. Failing that, has he a relation to whom I could write? This is a family matter, and Mrs Soames is not concerned with it.'

'Dr Hay-Smythe? You have a practice in Harley Street. I remember that you were called to give evidence some time ago.'

'That is so. You would prefer me to come and see you?'

'No. No, that won't be necessary. Mr Soames has a sister living in Cornwall. I could give you her address.' The clerk sounded doubtful.

'I will come to your chambers to collect it, and if you wish to let Mr Soames know of my request, please do so.'

It was impossible to go down to Cornwall for at least two days; he had patients to see, a ward round at the hospital, an outpatients clinic, and then, hours before he intended to leave, an urgent case. So, very nearly a week had passed by the time he got into his car with Freddie and began the long drive down to Cornwall.

It was already later than he had intended; he had no hope of reaching Miss Soames's house at a reasonable hour. He drove steadily westward, Freddie alert beside him, and stopped for the night at Liskeard in an old friendly pub where he was given a hearty supper before going to his room, which was low-ceilinged and comfortable. Since Freddie had behaved in a very well-bred manner he accompanied his master, spreading his length across the foot of the bed.

'This is definitely not allowed,' Oliver told him. 'But just this once, since it is a special occasion. I only hope that Bertha's aunt likes dogs.'

Freddie yawned.

They were on their way again after breakfast—bacon, mushrooms freshly picked, fried bread, a sausage or two and egg garnished with a tomato. A meal to put heart into a faint-hearted man—something which the doctor was not. In an hour or so he would see his Bertha again, beyond that he didn't intend to think for the moment. He whistled as he drove and Freddie, no lover of whistling, curled his lip.

It was shortly after ten o'clock when Betsy carried the coffee tray into Miss Soames's sitting room, which was small and pleasant, overlooking the wide stretch of garden at the back of the house. Bertha was out there, walking slowly, her hair in a plait over one shoulder, and wearing one of the pretty winter dresses which Miss Soames had bought for her.

Her aunt, peering over her spectacles at her, observed, 'The girl's not pretty, but there's something about her... Takes after our side of the family, of course.' She poured her coffee. 'Leave the child for the moment, Betsy. She's happy.'

Betsy went away, but she was back again within a minute.

'There's an 'andsome motor car coming up to the door...'

Miss Soames sipped her coffee. 'Ah, yes, I was

expecting that. Show the gentleman in here, Betsy, and say nothing to Bertha.'

The doctor came in quietly. 'Miss Soames? I apologise for calling upon you unexpectedly. I believe that Bertha is staying with you?' He held out a hand. 'Oliver Hay-Smythe.'

She took the hand. 'What kept you, young man?' she wanted to know tartly. 'Of course, I knew that you would come, although Bertha is sure that she will never see you again.'

He followed her gaze out of the window; Bertha looked very pretty, and his rather tired face broke into a smile.

'I told her that if a man was worth his salt he would find her even if he had to search the world for her.' She gave him a level gaze. 'Would you do that, Doctor?'

'Yes. I do not quite understand why she is here. I think that her stepmother wanted her out of the way. That doesn't matter for the moment, but it took me some time to discover where she was.'

'You have driven down from London? What have you done with your patients?'

He smiled. 'It took a good deal of organising, but I'd planned a holiday this week.'

'You'll stay here, of course.' She looked over his shoulder. 'What is it, Betsy?'

'There's a dog with his head out of the car window.'

'Freddie. Might I allow him out? He's well-mannered.'

'Get the beast, Betsy,' commanded Miss Soames,

and when Freddie, on his best behaviour, came into the room, she offered him a biscuit.

'Well, go along, young man. There's a door into the garden at the back of the hall.'

Freddie, keeping close to his heels, gave a pleased bark as he saw Bertha, and she turned round as he bounded towards her. She knelt and put her arms round his neck and watched Oliver crossing the lawn to her. The smile on her face was like a burst of sunshine as she got slowly to her feet. He saw with delight that she had a pretty colour in her cheeks and a faint plumpness which a week's good food had brought about. Moreover, the dress she was wearing revealed the curves which Clare's misfits had so successfully hidden.

He didn't say anything, but took her in his arms and held her close. Presently he spoke. 'I came as soon as I could, my darling. I had to find you first...'

'How?' asked Bertha. 'Who...?'

'Later, my love.' He bent his head and kissed her.

Bertha, doing her best to be sensible, said, 'But I want to know why my stepmother sent me here—she'll be so angry when she finds out.'

'Leave everything to me, dear heart. You need never see her or Clare again if you don't want to. We'll marry as soon as it can be arranged. Would you like Christmas Eve for a wedding?'

He kissed her again, and eventually, when she had stopped feeling light-headed, she said, 'You haven't asked me—you haven't said—'

'That I love you?' He smiled down at her. 'I love you, darling Bertha. I fell in love with you the moment I clapped eyes on you in that hideous pink dress. Will you marry me and love me a little?'

She reached up to put her arms round his neck. 'Of course I'll marry you, dear Oliver, and I'll love you very much for always. Will you kiss me again? Because I rather like it when you do.'

Aunt Agatha, unashamedly watching them from her chair, took out her handkerchief and blew her nose, and to Betsy, who was peering over her shoulder, she said, 'I must need new glasses, for my eyes keep watering!'

She sounded cross, but she was smiling.

WINTER WEDDING

CHAPTER ONE

IT WAS snowing outside, and the pallid faces of the night nurses coming off duty looked even more pallid in its glaring whiteness. Emily Seymour, one of the last to go, traipsed down the stairs from the top floor, where she had been in charge of the Ear, Nose and Throat wards, yawning widely, longing for her bed and knowing that it would be some time before she could get into it; it would be even longer today, she decided gloomily, glancing out of a landing window. The snow had settled and cycling through the streets would be a slow business. A pretty girl in staff nurse's uniform, bounding up the staircase towards her, paused to join her at the window.

'Lucky you, Emily,' she exclaimed cheerfully, 'going home to a nice warm bed. Had a busy night?' She glanced at her companion with sympathy. 'No, don't answer, I can see you did. What happened?'

'Terry had to have a trachy at two o'clock this morning. I got Mr Spencer up—or at least, I rang his flat when Night Sister told me to—and she couldn't be there because the Accident Department was going hell for leather—and he brought Professor Jurres-Romeijn with him.' She paused, staring out into the freshly whirling snow. 'I had everything ready, he did it in seconds flat.'

The pretty girl rolled a pair of fine eyes. 'Oh, him. He's the answer to every girl's dream; such a pity that no one knows anything about him and that he's not going to stay for ever. I must think up some good reason for going along to ENT this morning and see if I can soften him up a bit. I daresay...' she paused, listening. 'Oh, God, that sounds like Sister Gatesby trundling our way. 'Bye, love, be good.'

And when have I ever had the chance to be anything else? thought Emily, going on her way once more.

She met Sister Gatesby at the bottom of the second flight and that lady, stoutish and almost due to retire, seized on her at once. 'Just the girl!' she breathed happily. 'Just run back for me, Staff Nurse, and get the keys off the hook in Sister Reeves' office in ENT, will you? You can leave them at the Porter's Lodge as you go out; Theatre Sister wants them.'

She turned and wheezed her way down again, leaving Emily to trail all the way upstairs once more, muttering darkly under her breath. But she had finished her muttering by the time she had reached the top floor; for one thing she was a little short of wind and for another she had just remembered that her nights off were due in two days' time; she occupied the last few yards in making plans, then opened the swing doors and went through, into the landing which opened into the two wards, the kitchen, Sister's Office, the dressing room and the linen cupboard. The keys would be in Sister's Office, the first door on the left. She could hear the nurses in the ward, already well started on the day's routine; by the time Sister came on everything would be as it should be. She crossed the landing and then stopped with her hand on the door; Mr Spencer and Professor Jurres-Romeijn were in the dressing room, their backs towards her. She could see Mr Spencer's bald patch on the back of his head about which he was so sensitive because he was still quite a young man, and she could see the Professor's iron-grey cropped head, towering over his companion, for he was a vast man and very tall. He was speaking now, his voice, with its faint Dutch accent, very clear, although not loud.

'Good lord, Harry, am I to be fobbed off with that prim miss? Surely there's another nurse...?' He sounded annoyed.

Mr Spencer put up a hand to rub the bald patch. 'Sorry, sir—she's first class at her job...'

'I take your word for that—we are talking about the same girl, I suppose? A small, plump creature who merges into the background from whatever angle one looks at her.'

Mr Spencer chuckled. 'That's our Emily—a splendid worker and marvellous with children. You'll find that she grows on you, sir.'

'Heaven forbid! The only females who grow on me are beautiful blondes who don't go beetroot red every time I look at them.'

Emily forced herself to move then and in direct contradiction to the Professor's words, her face was chalk white, not red at all. She went silently into Sister's Office, took the keys and went back down the endless stairs, the Professor's words ringing in her ears. She had the nasty feeling that she was never going to forget them for as long as she lived, and through her tired brain the beginnings of a fine temper began to flare.

She was prim, was she, and plump and given to blushing, something which the Professor, loathesome type that he was, found both amusing and tiresome! She gained the Porter's Lodge, slammed down the keys in old Henry's astonished face and pranced out of the hospital entrance. Well, he had made it known all too clearly that he didn't want her for some job or other; she would make it just as clear to him that she wasn't going to oblige him. Let him find another nurse to wait on him hand and foot; someone with blonde curls and blue eyes… Emily, in the cupboard-like room by the bicycle shed where the nurses who lived out were expected to change, tore the cap off her own unspectacular brown hair, coiled so neatly, and began to race out of her uniform. Presently, buoyed up with her rage, she got her bike from the shed and oblivious of snow and slush, pedalled home.

Home was a small semi-detached villa on the very outskirts of the town. Emily, giving up a good post in London, had searched desperately for some months until she had found both a large hospital and a home close by. The hospital was one of the new ones, magnificently equipped, destined to take the overspill from London, ten miles away, and still a source of some astonishment to the inhabitants of the small town where it had been built. It took her ten minutes to cycle home, but today, because of the snow, she took a good deal longer and arrived at the wrought iron gate with 'Homelea' written on it, in a breathless state. Louisa, her younger sister, would be waiting with her breakfast, something she hated to do. She parked her bike in the little shed at the side of the house and went in through the back door.

Louisa was in the kitchen, her pretty face screwed up with peevishness.

'You're late,' she began. 'The twins are being little devils and they've both been sick.'

Emily made soothing murmurs; probably Louisa, who was only eighteen and impatient, had given them their morning feeds so fast that they had no choice but to bring the lot up again.

'I can't wait,' went on Louisa loudly, 'until I can get away from this hole...only another month, thank God!'

Emily unwound the scarf from her neck. 'Yes, dear.' She could have voiced her nightmare fears of what was going to happen when Louisa went; Mary, their elder sister, and the twins' mother, was still in the Middle East, unable to leave until her husband had been cleared of some trumped-up charge about something or other to do with his work. She, and her husband, should have been home months ago; the twins were to have been left with Emily for three months, no longer, an arrangement which seemed sensible at the time; they were too young to take with her, Mary had decided, and besides, she had had no idea if she would be able to get adequate help, even a good doctor. Louisa, waiting to go into a school for modelling, was staying with Emily, and a month or two in a London flat, with both sisters to look after them, was the answer.

Only it hadn't worked out like that. At the end of the three months, Mary had managed to get a message to Emily, begging her to look after the twins for another few months at least, and she, looking at them, rapidly growing from small babies to energetic large ones, quite overflowing the small flat close to the big London teaching hospital where she worked, decided that the only thing to do was to move to a small town where she might with luck find a house with a garden. Louisa hadn't liked the idea, of course, but as Emily had pointed out in her sensible way, the babies mattered; she had promised to look after them until Mary and George came home again and until they did there was nothing else to do about it.

'And after all, darling,' Emily had explained patiently, 'you'll be starting your course in a few months' time and probably they'll be back by then— I know Mary said several months, but she couldn't have meant that.'

She had been lucky, getting a post as staff nurse at the new hospital on the outskirts of London, with the prospect of a Sister's post in a few months' time. Of course it wasn't a patch on Paul's, where she had trained, but she couldn't complain; she had found a house at a reasonable rent, and furnished it rather sparsely with the things she had brought from the London flat, odds and ends of furniture she had brought from home after her parents died. But the house had a small garden and the air was fresh, and if one looked out of the kitchen window one could see fields and trees—not real country, of course, it was too near London for that, but at least the twins could be taken out in their pram along the quieter roads around them.

Emily took off her coat and looked round the little kitchen. It looked untidy and not as clean as she would have liked. Louisa, understandably, hated housework, it spoilt her hands with their long fingers and tapering nails—although she tried hard, Emily told herself loyally, coping with the shopping and the babies.

She dismissed as unimportant the fact that Louisa only did what she had to do, and that grudgingly. At Louisa's age—and with her pretty face and figure, it was understandable that she should want to avoid all the humdrum jobs; if she had been as pretty herself, she would doubtless have felt just the same. But she wasn't pretty—oh, pleasant enough; at least she didn't squint or have enormous ears, but her face was unspectacular and she was a little too plump; Louisa was always telling her so. Emily took it in good part. After all, Louisa hadn't had the happy childhood and girlhood that she had had and she had loved her three years' training, going home for days off and holidays while her parents were alive, and Mary in a good job at the local library until she had met George and married him. Louisa had been at school then, impatient to leave and make her mark in the world. She had known what she wanted to do; modelling—and as she had a small legacy due to her when she was eighteen and a half, no one could stop her enrolling at one of the London modelling schools; in a month she would be able to start. In the meantime, she cooled her heels with Emily and the twins and Emily used the money Mary had left for the twins' needs, to house and feed Louisa too. It was a difficult business, making ends meet, and she had had to give up several small luxuries in order to do it, and when Louisa went she didn't dare to think of the extra expense of getting baby-sitters to look after the twins while she was working. She would have to continue on night duty until Mary came to collect them and it was to be hoped that it would be soon, before Louisa went away.

Emily stifled a sigh and went upstairs to the babies' room. They were both sitting up in their cots, a bouncing eight-month-old and disarmingly beautiful. William was an hour or so older than Claire but it was almost impossible to tell the difference between them, for each reflected the other one's face. Emily, forgetting her tiredness, picked them up to cuddle them, and it wasn't until Louisa called from the kitchen that she popped them back with their toys and went downstairs.

At the table Louisa said with faint defiance: 'The hairdresser can only do me at half past nine—I'll have to go.'

Emily, her mouth full of toast, did her best to sound cheerful. 'Oh well, yes, of course, love——How long will you be?'

'I'll be back by eleven o'clock—I can take the twins out then. I'll bath them this evening…'

Emily poured more tea. 'I'll bath them,' and added without a vestige of truth, 'I'm not tired.' She smiled cheerfully in case Louisa felt guilty. 'I'll dress them ready to go out when you get back. It's a beastly day, but they'll be all right wrapped up.'

Louisa pouted. 'Oh, Emily, must they go out? Pushing the pram in all this snow…'

'I cycled back—it wasn't too bad. It's not for much longer, dear; think how you're going to enjoy yourself living in London and meeting all sorts of exciting people. Did you hear about the flat?'

Louisa's pretty face became animated. 'Yes, it's all settled; four of us, so it won't cost much. The course only lasts two months and I'm bound to get a job.'

Emily, eyeing her pretty sister, thought that she most certainly would. It would be nice, she thought a little wistfully, to be as pretty as Louisa, so that men looked at one twice instead of not at all. She frowned, remembering Professor Jurres-Romeijn's remarks, and Louisa said in a surprised way: 'Gosh, you look simply furious—what's wrong with me sharing a flat, for heaven's sake?'

Emily blinked. 'Not you, love, I was thinking about something quite different. Oughtn't you to be going? I'll wash up.'

She washed up and tidied the little house as well

as seeing to the twins, and as Louisa didn't get home until twelve o'clock, she wasn't in bed until an hour later than that and by then too tired to bother her head about the Professor's opinion of her. The snow was worse when she got up and she had to walk to the hospital after helping to feed the twins and get them to bed and then eating a meal herself, a kind of high tea so that she wouldn't be too hungry during the night. Food in the canteen was expensive and although she managed very well, she had to be careful. She told herself often enough that it was good for her to eat less, she'd get slim that way.

The wards were full and busy and it took her and her junior nurse quite two hours to settle their occupants. Men in one ward, women in the other and a small ward for children besides. Terry, who had slept soundly all day after his tracheotomy, was wide awake, sitting up against his pillows, declaring that he wouldn't be able to sleep like that, anyway. Emily soothed him in a reassuring voice and didn't tell him that she would have to disturb him frequently throughout the night when she changed and cleaned the tube. She made sure that the suction machine was in position with plenty of Toronto catheters and that there was a tracheotomy mask handy in case she should need one, together with dilators, a spare tube and scissors. Her junior nurse was very junior, unfortunately, and it wouldn't be fair to expect her to undertake any of the treatment; there should have been a special, thought Emily worriedly as she trotted off to see why the tonsillectomy was bawling. He wanted a drink; she gave him one, tucked him up and promised him ice cream in the morning and sped back to the Men's ward.

Most of the men had settled for the night, so she did a quick round and then went to the nurses' station between the wards—but not for long. She had pulled the first of the pile of charts to be filled in towards her when old Mrs Crewe, suffering from a small tumour in one ear, demanded attention. She was a nice old lady who had lived alone for years and was of an independent turn of mind; she made it clear now that she had had enough of bed, enough, moreover, of hospital, and wanted to go home.

Emily took time to talk her out of it. She still had a lot to do and she would have to see to Terry again very shortly, but she gave no sign of impatience and presently, with the old lady sufficiently satisfied to agree to stay until the morning at least, she got up off the bed where she had perched herself. 'A nice cup of tea?' she suggested. 'Just the thing to send you off to sleep.'

Mrs Crewe didn't answer her at once because she was peering towards the end of her bed, so Emily turned round to look too. Night Sister was standing there and with her, Professor Jurres-Romeijn.

Sister Gatesby nodded and smiled. 'Nurse shall make the tea,' was all she said. 'Staff Nurse, the Professor wants to talk to you—come into the office.'

The strip lighting in Sister's office was glaringly bright and not in the least kind to one's looks. Emily put up an absent hand to her cap and hoped that her nose wasn't shining too much. Not that it would matter; was she not small and plump and prim? She felt a surge of indignation at the sight of the Professor standing there; the bright light didn't detract from his good looks in the very least. His thick brows were drawn together in a frown and his arrogant nose and stern mouth didn't make any difference either.

He looked back at her. His eyes were very blue and rather cold and because it annoyed her that he should look so stunning without making any effort at all, she said tartly: 'I'm very busy; there's Terry to see to in five minutes.'

Sister Gatesby looked shocked. She was a tolerant woman and prided herself on being with it, but one thing she had never quite managed to swallow—the attitude of the nurses towards the doctors. The Professor's expression didn't alter. 'This will take three minutes, provided that you listen and don't interrupt.'

Emily drew a calming breath, stuffed back the retort which she longed to utter and went on staring at him.

'You worked for Mr Wright at your teaching hospital, I believe, Staff Nurse?' He hardly gave her time to nod her head. 'He has CA of pharynx, unfortunately no symptoms presented until I examined him last week and found an enlarged gland. He will be coming here as a patient and I shall be operating upon him. I shall be obliged if you will undertake to nurse him.'

Emily had liked Mr Wright. She had worked in ENT theatre with him and specialled several of his cases; it was tragic that he should be struck down by condition which he had so often diagnosed and treated himself. It would have given her the greatest satisfaction to have refused to work for the Professor, but her personal feelings didn't really matter.

'Well?' asked the Professor in a voice which brooked no delay.

'Certainly I'll nurse Mr Wright. Am I to work under you, Professor?'

'Yes. Mr Spencer will give you the details in the morning.' He sounded annoyed; perhaps she should have said no... His goodnight was brief and unsmiling as he turned on his heel and stalked away. Even from the back he looked super, mused Emily, watching him go. And elegant too—a trendy dresser, even if he wasn't all that young.

Sister Gatesby's voice broke into her thoughts. 'Well, that's settled, Staff Nurse. I'm not quite sure when you're to take up your new duties, but you'll get your nights off first. Such a nice man, the Professor, always so polite...'

The dear old thing must be joking, thought Emily—or perhaps he was, to those he liked or tolerated. Anyone else, and that meant her, she supposed, was treated as though they just didn't matter. She stifled a giggle, remembering that he had said that she merged into the background whichever way he looked at her.

'Why are you smiling?' asked Sister Gatesby quite sharply.

'Oh, nothing—nothing at all, Sister. Would you ex-

cuse me if I went along to see to Terry? He's doing
fine, but he needs an eye kept on him.'

Sister Gatesby tutted worriedly. 'There should have
been a special for him, but there just aren't the nurses.
I'll send someone up to relieve you for your meal
break, Nurse Weekes is far too inexperienced.' She
frowned, already busy with who she could send.
'Give me a bleep if you're not happy,' she counselled
Emily as she went.

The night went rapidly; too fast for Emily, strug-
gling to get finished by the time the day staff came
on duty. She had sent Nurse Weekes off duty and was
wrapping herself in her cloak when Mr Spencer came
through the swing doors exclaiming: 'Ah, just the girl
I want. Can you spare a few minutes?' He looked at
her tired face, and added kindly: 'You've had the hell
of a night, I suspect. Here, we'll borrow Sister's office
until she's ready to come into it. Just a minute.'

He went off down the ward to where the Day Sister
was in the middle of her morning round, and when
he came back he swept Emily into the little room, sat
her down in the chair beside the desk and went away
again.

'Coffee,' he told her, seconds later. 'Sister says we
may have some while we talk.'

Emily beamed at him. 'I hope it's not too complicated—I mean I'm half asleep…'

'All very easy. Professor Jurres-Romeijn came to
see me last night and we got it all sorted out. Mr
Wright's being admitted in two days' time, you're to
have two nights off—that's tonight and tomorrow

night, and report for duty at nine o'clock, perhaps earlier, on the following morning. You're to do day duty and probably you'll have to do a few extra hours, Emily. You're to go to theatre with your patient and assist the anaesthetist, got to ITU with him and stay there until he's fit to take to the ward and you'll hand over at the Professor's wish, and if he wants you back on duty you'll just have to do that, any time. He wants that clearly understood.'

The ward maid brought in their coffee and Emily poured it out. She said in a level voice: 'I'm surprised that Professor Jurres-Romeijn gets anyone to work for him, but I'll do exactly as he wishes because I like Mr Wright and I'd want him to recover—that's my only reason for agreeing to work for the Professor.'

Mr Spencer spooned far too much sugar into his mug. 'Yes, well…he's good at his job, you know, Emily.'

'I'm sure he is. But why's Mr Wright coming here?'

'Because he doesn't want everyone to know about it. It's bound to leak out, of course, but not at once, and Professor Jurres-Romeijn is going up to Edinburgh in a few weeks and Mr Wright wouldn't stand the journey. Besides that, you know as well as I do that speed is of the essence for him.'

Emily re-filled their mugs. 'Yes. Has he a good chance, do you think?'

Mr Spencer thought for a moment. 'Jurres-Romeijn is about the best there is; he's done a number of pharyngectomies and had a high percentage of successes.

Of course it's a severe operation, you know that, and
it means Mr Wright will have to learn oesophageal
speech or have an electric larynx fitted, but from what
I hear of him he sounds very able to cope with the
difficulties.' He smiled at Emily, visibly wilting but
listening carefully. 'Besides, he'll have you to nurse
him; you've got yourself a marvellous reputation
since you've been with us, Emily, and it was just as
good at Paul's, wasn't it?'

She smiled a little and just for a moment was
tempted to tell him that she had overheard his conversation with the Professor, but that wouldn't do any
good to anybody and she would regret it afterwards.
She finished her coffee and said: 'I'd better go to the
office, I suppose.'

And that was a speedy business; she was in and
out again within five minutes. Apparently the Professor had made his wishes known and had paved the
way for her. Not because he was taken with her, Emily reminded herself wryly as she wobbled home in
the slush which was all that was left of the snow. It
was warmer too, but then it was still only the middle
of November, time enough for snow during the next
month or two.

She told Louisa her news over breakfast and her
sister said at once: 'Oh, good, I wanted to go to London—to see about the flat, you know, and I was wondering how I could manage it before your next nights
off. I'll go tomorrow.'

Emily agreed, pointing out that once she started on
her case, she might not have much free time for a

little while. 'Oh, well, perhaps he'll die,' observed Louisa airily.

'Not if I can help it. He's got a splendid surgeon and there's no reason why he shouldn't be perfectly OK.'

Louisa shrugged her shoulders. 'Well, darling, let's hope he'll get over it. It sounds grisly to me; I don't know how you can stand it, and for a pittance, too. I'll earn as much in a week as you do in a month once I get a modelling job.' She smiled, well pleased at the thought. 'I'll wash up if you like while you see to the twins, then I'll take them out while you have a sleep.'

Emily sighed gratefully and then sighed again as Louisa went on: 'There's a film on this evening, that girl across the road asked me to go with her—you won't mind?'

Emily said that she didn't; Louisa was only eighteen and being eighteen didn't last long. She dealt with the twins' small wants, put them down for their morning nap and went to bed herself.

Her nights off went very quickly. She had more than enough to do when Louisa went to London, but she enjoyed her day; the twins, although hard work, were delightful. She pushed them for miles through the common behind the road where she lived and returned to give the house a good clean. And the next day was almost wholly taken up with shopping and listening to Louisa's ecstatic description of the flat and her future flatmates. Emily, tired out, slept like a log, got up early to see to the twins, advised her sister that she had no idea when she would be home, and cycled to the hospital.

Mr Wright was to have one of the private rooms attached to the Men's ENT ward. After a briefing from Sister she retired into it, readied it for its occupant, checked the equipment she would be using, arranged the flowers which her patient's friends had sent to welcome him, and went down to her dinner, where she shared a table with several of her friends.

'Lucky you,' observed one of them, 'working for that Professor Jurres-Romeijn. I could go for someone like him—I suppose he's married, they always are.' The speaker cocked a questioning eyebrow at Emily, who shook her head.

'I've no idea, but I should think so, I mean, he's not awfully young, is he?'

'Who cares?' The ENT staff nurse, Carol Drew, joined in. 'I'm going to have to go.'

Emily said mildly: 'Why not?' And why not indeed? Carol was pretty, as pretty as Louisa, all pink and white and golden with large blue eyes to melt a stone, and surely the Professor as well. She got up to fetch the puddings and when she got back someone asked: 'Why you, Emily?'

She spooned steamed pudding before she answered. 'Well, Mr Wright comes from Paul's and I worked for him there.'

'The Professor didn't actually choose you, then? I mean, Mr Wright wanted you, I suppose?'

'I suppose so.' Emily bolted the rest of her pudding and got up. 'I'd better get back, he was supposed to be here before one o'clock, but he hasn't turned up yet…'

'Don't blame him,' declared Carol. 'I wouldn't turn up either.' She got up too. 'I'll come back with you, Emily, you never know, the Professor might be there.' She whipped out a compact and peered into it. 'Do I look all right?'

'You always look all right. I daresay when he sees you he'll ask us to do a swap,' said Emily.

But she was wrong. The Professor was waiting in his patient's room, sitting on the side of the carefully made bed, rucking up the quilt in a careless fashion. He got up as Emily, with Carol hard on her heels, went in, and beyond a coldly polite 'Good morning,' showed no signs of being bowled over by Carol's looks, let alone suggesting that she might do instead of Emily. Indeed, he waited silently and rather pointedly until Carol had gone before addressing himself to Emily.

'You're quite ready, Nurse Seymour? Mr Wright will be here within the hour. You will be good enough to let me know when he arrives. I shall probably be in theatre. I should like him to undress and get to bed as soon as possible; there are a number of tests to be done and I shall wish to examine him.'

He strolled to the door. 'You enjoyed your nights off?' he asked her surprisingly.

'Me? Oh—yes, thank you.'

'Good. I hope Mr Spencer made it plain to you that your off duty is likely to be irregular and curtailed for the next few days. I hope to operate tomorrow—

in the morning; you will probably be on duty until late in the evening.'

'Yes, sir.'

'If I am not quite satisfied with Mr Wright's condition, you may have to stay on call.'

'Yes, sir.'

He glanced at her curiously. 'You can make arrangements for this?'

She just stopped herself from saying 'Yes, sir,' yet again, and changed it to: 'Certainly I can.'

He nodded unsmilingly, said, 'H'm,' and went away, leaving her to fly to Sister's office and telephone Louisa, who wasn't at all pleased at the idea of being left with the twins, even for one night.

'Well,' observed Emily, 'you'll be all right, love, and probably I'll be home, and it's not until tomorrow night, you know—I'll be back tonight. Only I thought I'd better give you plenty of warning.'

'I was going to that disco with Roy'—Roy was the rather vapid youth who lived next door. 'I suppose I'll have to stay home, now.'

'I'm afraid so.' Emily felt a little surge of impatience. Louisa was her sister and a dear girl, even if a bit spoilt, but she was making an awful fuss about nothing, especially as Emily was the one who was earning their bread and butter. She squashed the thought, cautioned Louisa about several small chores which would need to be done, and hung up.

Mr Wright arrived presently, the shadow of his former chubby self but remarkably cheerful. 'Best surgeon in Europe,' he told her in a frighteningly hoarse voice, 'and best nurse, too—can't help but get better, can I?'

He had brought his wife with him, a pretty little woman with grey hair, exquisitely cut, and elegant clothes. She was as determinedly cheerful as he was and nice to Emily. 'I'll go away for a bit, shall I?' she suggested. 'If you'll tell me when I can come back?'

'Ten minutes,' said Emily promptly. 'Mr Wright has to undress and get into bed while I get Professor Jurres-Romeijn. I expect he'll want to talk to you— there's a waiting room...'

'I'll find it, Staff Nurse—no, I shall call you Emily, if I may. Ten minutes, then.'

Mr Wright was in bed and Emily was drawing the covers over him when the Professor walked in. He greeted his patient affably, said briefly: 'Don't go,' to Emily, and sat down on the bed. 'You've brought Maud with you?' he wanted to know. 'I'll have a look at you now; and then I'll have a chat with her, shall I?'

The look, a very thorough one, took half an hour and Emily was kept on her toes, handing this and that and the other, filling in forms and unscrewing specimen bottles. She was surprised when the Professor thanked her for her service, albeit laconically, and asked her to go and tell Mrs Wright that he would be along to see her in a few minutes, a request which she took to mean that he wanted her out of the way for a bit while he and his patient talked. She found Mrs Wright in the waiting room, leafing through an old copy of *Woman* and not attempting to read it, gave her message and then sat down and made conversation until the Professor came through the door.

She was about to slip away when he said: 'I shall want to talk to you presently, Nurse Seymour,' before turning his attention to Mrs Wright.

It was fifteen minutes or more before he returned to Mr Wright's room where Emily was making a neat list of the flower givers so that Mrs Wright could send thank-you letters. She wrote the last name without undue haste and looked up at the Professor, towering over her. He looked cross, but then he often did; perhaps he had a gastric ulcer...

'You're looking at me as though I were the patient,' he said blandly.

She said hastily that she really hadn't been looking at him, 'Only into the background,' she added, just as blandly, and saw his eyebrows go up. 'And that will give you something to think about,' she told him silently.

The Professor turned away to speak to his patient for a moment, then invited her to follow him out of the room. 'Sister's office,' he suggested, and opened its door for her.

'This is going to be rather touch and go,' he began without preamble. 'Mr Wright isn't over-optimistic and quite realises that his chances are on the small side. All the more reason for us to make a success of it.' He smiled suddenly at her, so that she caught her breath. He looked quite different; it was like someone opening a door... 'I shall ask a great deal of you, Emily; you'll have your work cut out. Will you stay until this evening—until the night nurse comes on duty? and I'll want you here by seven o'clock tomorrow morning—you'll be here all day and I'll want you on call for the night. Probably the next couple of days as well.'

She eyed him calmly. 'Very well, sir. May I know what you're going to do?'

'Yes, of course. I'll have to do a laryngectomy as well as remove the tumour of the pharynx and do a block resection of the glands as well...' He elaborated at some length and she listened carefully, stopping him now and again so that he might make something she hadn't understood clear. Presently he got up from the table where he had been sitting. 'That's the lot, I think,' and just for a moment she thought that he was going to say something else, but he didn't, only opened the door for her, remarking that he would be along to see his patient later on in the day, bringing the anaesthetist with him.

The rest of her day was spent in preparing Mr Wright for the morning, explaining just where everything would be when he came round from the anaesthetic; that she would be with him all the time, and that on no account was he to get fussed about anything. 'There'll be a pad and pencil under your hand,' she reminded him, 'as well as a bell within reach and me.'

He laughed at her, a funny cracked sound. 'Never mind the pad and bell,' he whispered, 'you'll do on your own, Emily. I've great faith in you, my dear.,

I've never seen you put out by anything yet and I've never seen you look defeated, either.'

'Who's talking about defeat?' asked Emily strongly.

The Professor came about nine o'clock, spent five minutes with his patient, and then leaving the anaesthetist with him, went off to brief the night nurse, an elderly staff nurse, recently widowed and returned to nursing, a solid, sensible woman who liked Emily and could be relied upon to do all she could for her patient. He was away for half an hour; it was ten o'clock by the time Emily got on to her bike for the ride home, and midnight before she got to bed. Louisa had been tearful at the prospect of looking after the house and the twins, and resentful too. You'd think, decided Emily, getting ready for bed, that I was going on holiday or something! She got into bed, curled up into a tight ball round her hot water bottle, and went to sleep at once.

CHAPTER TWO

IT WAS DARK, cold and wet when Emily left the house at half past five the next morning. The twins and Louisa were still sleeping and she hadn't bothered with breakfast, only a quick, strong cup of tea. She tied her overnight bag on to her bike and pedalled briskly through the almost deserted streets. Bar the odd milkman and a police car idling along, giving her a nice sense of security, there were few people about. The rather ugly modern town looked bleak and un-friendly and before many minutes the rain was drip-ping steadily down the back of her neck. She hadn't had time to do much to her face and her hair was going to be sopping by the time she arrived. She changed in the cold little room, scraped her fine brown hair back into some sort of a bun, pinned her cap on top of it and went through to the hospital. The early morning rush was on; almost no noise, only the steady hurried tread of the nurses trying to get done before the day staff arrived. Emily gained ENT with-out seeing anyone at all, checked with the night staff nurse, telephoned Night Super that she was on duty and went along to Mr Wright's room.

He'd had a bad night, that was obvious, but his

cheerfulness was unabated, so Emily was cheerful too, telling him silly little tales of her training at Paul's and not mentioning the day's dire work while she readied him.

She was relieved for breakfast after an hour, a meal she swallowed in no time at all, and when she got back she found Mrs Wright had just arrived.

'I'm not supposed to be here,' the little lady hadn't slept either—'and I'm going again at once, dear.' She smiled at Emily. 'I know you'll do your very best.'

'I will, Mrs Wright, and don't worry, Mr Wright is going to be all right. Professor Jurres-Romeijn is tops, you know, he's done this op before a good many times and he's successful...'

'A generous statement, Nurse Seymour.' The Professor's voice held mockery and she swung round to see him standing in the doorway, immaculate as usual even at that early hour and the only one of them who looked as though he had had a good sleep. She didn't speak; she couldn't think of anything to say and there was no point in it. She stared at his faintly sneering mouth, and disliked him very much.

He didn't speak to her again but addressed himself to his patient and Mrs Wright, only as he went away he reminded her that Mr Wright would be going to theatre in exactly half an hour and as from now was to receive no more visitors, nor talk, or rather, try to talk. He paused at the door to allow Mrs Wright to say goodbye to her husband, then swept her away with him, not looking at Emily at all.

Mr Wright broke the Professor's rules the moment

the door was closed. He said in his strained voice: 'I wonder if Renier knows what a treasure he's got working for him? I must remember to point it out to him—in writing, of course.' He grinned at her and closed his eyes.

'Now you be a good boy,' begged Emily in a motherly voice, 'or I'll turn into an old battleaxe!'

The operation lasted a very long time. The Professor worked quickly but meticulously too, muttering to himself from time to time, requesting some instrument or other in an almost placid voice, asking details from the anaesthetist from time to time regarding his patient's blood pressure and condition. Emily, standing at the anaesthetist's elbow, had to admire his skill, and he must be getting a frightful backache, she thought inconsequently, bending like that. They were all three very close together with Mr Spencer on the other side of the Professor and an assistant across the table ready to hold things and tie off and cut gut when required. Theatre Sister was scrubbed, of course, and so was the senior staff nurse, and there were other nurses there too. A splendid turn-out, thought Emily, counting heads without taking her mind off her work.

The atmosphere was nicely relaxed; she had worked for surgeons who had everyone biting their nails with nerves because they were so ill-tempered. She could remember one occasion when a surgeon had flung an instrument on to the ground and then had to wait while it was picked up, scrubbed, sterilised and handed back to him; a bad-tempered man he had been, and give the Professor his due, with the exception of herself, he appeared to have everyone there eating out of his hand.

The morning wore on until finally the Professor straightened his great back and stood back from the table. His thanks were pleasantly uttered before he turned on his heel and went along to the changing room. Not that he'd be there long, Emily decided, he'd be in and out of ITU for the next hour or so, getting in her way...

She knew her job well and set about connecting tubes to sealed bottles, setting up a drip again, checking the cardiac arrest trolley, the tracheotomy trolley, the oxygen, the ventilator... She had a student nurse to help her, to fetch and carry, but she was responsible for her patient to the Professor and any mistakes, whether she made them or not, would be her fault.

Just as she had thought, the Professor was in and out of the room for the rest of the day and a good deal of the night as well, and when he had come to examine his patient in the early evening he had requested her politely to remain on duty for a few more hours. Doctor Wright was conscious but fretful and worried because he couldn't speak. Emily, reassuring him gently, found it pathetic that he had assured so many of his own patients in like case and still needed that reassurance himself, and her opinion of the Professor was considerably heightened by the kindly understanding he showed towards his patient. 'We'll keep him doped,' he told her. 'I've written him up again for another jab at ten o'clock and I'll be in just after to see how he is. He'll need more blood—is there plenty available?'

Emily said, 'Yes, sir.'

'And I'll take a blood gas estimation.'

She produced the tray without a word, waited while he withdrew the blood, signed to her assistant to take it to the Path. Lab. at once, and applied a swab to the puncture, standing patiently for five minutes while the Professor leaned over the foot of the bed, watching the patient and, from time to time, her.

'I should be obliged if you could be on duty as early as possible in the morning,' he observed quietly.

Emily had her eyes on her watch. 'Would half past seven suit, sir?'

'Very well. I'm afraid you're in for a rough time for the next few days.'

'Not half as rough as Mr Wright,' she told him matter-of-factly.

But the next few days were rough. Mr Wright was a good patient but naturally enough irritable, for Emily was constantly busy with something or other, turning him, with the other nurse, from side to side, sucking him out, charting her observations, feeding him through his intranasal naso-gastric tube, tending his tracheotomy. He vented his spleen on to his writing pad, scrawling the invective he would have liked to utter so that on occasion she was forced to admit that she had no idea of what he meant. 'You see,' she told him apologetically, 'there's no man about the house to swear, so I'm a bit out of touch.'

'Then it's high time there was,' Doctor Wright

scribbled furiously. 'Does Professor Jurres-Romeijn know? about the twins—and your sister?'

Her 'No!' was so fierce that he had added hastily: 'All right, keep your brown hair on; I shan't tell.' He put his pencil down and then picked it up again. 'You don't like him.'

Emily's hazel eyes flashed. 'Never mind that, Doctor Wright. He's a splendid surgeon.'

'He's a man as well,' wrote her patient slowly, 'a bit crusty sometimes, but I'd like him on my side in a fight. Nice with children too.'

'I have no doubt of it,' said Emily tartly, 'and now lie still while I see to your feed…'

She was a first class nurse—besides, she had made up her mind that Doctor Wright was going to recover. True, life wouldn't be quite the same for him ever again, but he had a loving wife and children and in time he might do a little consulting work; there was nothing wrong with his needle-sharp brain and he had been a top man at his job. Emily told him this, over and over again; each time she saw the worried lines deepen on his face, she trotted out her arguments with such sincerity that after a time he began to believe her, and when his wife, primed by Emily, joined in on Emily's side it was obvious that he had made up his mind to have a future after all. Perhaps not such a lengthy one as most people, but still a future. When the Professor called that evening, he stayed twice as long as usual, listening to Mrs Wright, and reading his friend's scribbled conversation. And he added his certainty as to the patient's ability to work again in a calm unhurried manner which carried conviction.

Emily was tired by the end of a week. She had been sleeping at the hospital, working long hours—busy ones too, and over and above that she wasn't happy about leaving Louisa alone for so long a time. She had managed to get home on several afternoons, just for an hour, but Louisa had sulked and the babies didn't seem happy. If only the longed-for letter from Mary would come! thought Emily, racing back to duty again. She would miss the twins, but the life they were leading now wasn't good enough. They should have someone's undivided attention. Luckily she would have a good deal of off duty and days off to come to her by the time Doctor Wright left, she would make it up to them then, and Louisa too. No wonder she had sulked, tied to the house and the shopping and washing and only the twins for company. Emily, carefully schooling her pleasant features into a look of relaxed ease, presented herself at her patient's door, declaring cheerfully that in such weather it was better to be in than out.

She had just completed all the many chores attached to her care of Doctor Wright, ensconced his wife beside him and declared her intention of going to supper herself when the Professor joined them. His 'Don't go, Nurse Seymour' left her standing, rather crossly, by the door while he sat himself down on the end of the bed for what she could see was to be a leisurely chat. If he wasn't quick about it, her supper time would be over and done with and she without her meal—and she had agreed to stay on duty until ten o'clock that evening so that Mrs Crewe, the night nurse, could go to the cinema. The canteen would be closed by then; if she wanted to of course she could wait until the night nurses' evening meal at midnight, but she knew she'd never stay awake.

The Professor rose presently and turned round and looked at her. 'Ah, yes, Staff Nurse—I should like a word with you.'

She followed him out of the room and stood in the middle of the landing. It was quiet there. Sister, back from her own supper, was writing the report in her office and the two nurses left on duty were in the ward. She was totally surprised when the Professor said: 'I have to thank you for your part in Doctor Wright's recovery. You have worked very well, I am grateful to you as I am sure he and his wife are.' He smiled and she thought suddenly that in other circumstances she might have liked him.

'I must admit,' he went on smoothly, 'that when you were suggested to me I wasn't quite sure...'

Emily broke in: 'No, I know—I heard you; you didn't like to be fobbed off with a prim miss.' She paused and quoted: 'A small plump creature who merges into the background from whatever angle one looks at her.'

The Professor was looking at her in astonishment. 'Good God—yes, I said that; I'd forgotten. Do you want me to apologise?' He neither looked nor sounded in the least put out.

Emily eyed him thoughtfully. 'No,' she said at

length. 'Words don't mean a thing—you could say you were sorry and not mean it.'

He shrugged. 'Just as you like, although I might point out that I'm not in the habit of apologising unless I mean it.' He added outrageously: 'You are small, you know, and a bit plump, too.'

Emily made a cross sound, but before she could say anything he went on in a quite different voice: 'I shall change the drugs this evening—you are on duty until ten o'clock, I understand? Observe Doctor Wright carefully, will you, and ask the night nurse to do the same. We must start talking about speech therapy, too.' He nodded his head carelessly. 'I'll see you later.'

He left her standing there. There were just five minutes left of her supper break; she'd barely reach the canteen in that time, let alone get a chance to eat anything. In a bad humour, she went back to her patient.

'You were quick over your supper,' remarked Mrs Wright. 'Wasn't it nice?'

'Professor Jurres-Romeijn was talking to me—I didn't get down to the canteen.' And when Mrs Wright protested: 'I'll go later.'

It was a little after ten o'clock when the Professor came again. He didn't speak to her although he gave her a close look as he came into the room. He altered the drugs, checked that his patient was in good shape for the night, said something quietly to him and went away, leaving Emily to give the report to Mrs Crewe, wish her patient goodnight and gather up her cloak and bag. She was very hungry, but it was really too late to go out to one of the small cafés which ringed the hospital. Besides, it was dark and cold and the streets weren't quiet; the pubs would be shutting. She would have to go to bed hungry...

The Professor was standing on the landing, staring in front of him, doing nothing, but at her quiet step he turned round. 'I had no idea that I made you miss your supper,' he observed without preamble. 'You should have told me.'

'Why?' asked Emily baldly.

He ignored that. 'Allow me to take you out for a meal.'

'No, thank you.' It was annoying that as she spoke her insides gave a terrific rumble.

The Professor's mouth twitched. 'You're hungry.'

Emily's mouth watered at the thought of food—any food. 'Not in the least,' she told him haughtily. She wished him goodnight just as haughtily and left him standing there.

Half an hour later, coming from the bathroom on the top floor of the Nurses' Home, where she had a temporary room on the night nurses' corridor, she was met by the night cook. 'There you are, Staff,' said that lady comfortably. 'I've put the tray in your room, Night Sister said you was ter 'ave it pronto; special orders from Professor Jurres-Romeijn.'

Emily, her hair hanging damply down her back, her face red and shiny from too hot a bath, goggled at her. 'Me? A tray?' she asked.

'That's right, love. And be a dear and bring it down to the canteen at breakfast, will you?'

'Yes—yes, of course—thanks a lot, Maggie.' She sped down the passage and into her room where there indeed was a tray laden with a teapot, milk, sugar and a mug, soup in a covered bowl and a wedge of meat pie flanked by peas and chips. Emily put the tray on the bed and got in beside it and wolfed the lot. It was over her third cup of tea that she took time to think about the Professor. It had been generous of him to see that she had some supper, or perhaps it was gratitude because he hadn't had to take her out? All her friends would think her out of her mind to have refused him anyway. But he must have taken the trouble to telephone Night Sister and speak to her about it, and considering he didn't like her, that had been good-natured of him, to say the least. She would have to thank him in the morning.

But when she did just that after his visit to Doctor Wright, all he said was: 'But my dear girl, you're wasting your gratitude; I can't afford to have you going off sick. I want you here for another four days.'

A remark which effectively nipped in the bud any warmer feelings she might have begun to cherish towards him.

The four days seemed unending. She went home every afternoon, just for an hour or so, and because it was obvious that Louisa was becoming more and more impatient and irritable, she spent the hours there catching up on the chores which her sister declared she had neither the time nor the inclination to do. And the twins looked peaky too. She suspected that Louisa wasn't taking them out enough, but hesitated to say so, and she would be home for four days. Louisa could be free to do what she liked while she set her little house in order and took long walks with the babies. It would make a nice change too.

Doctor Wright was leaving the hospital the day before she herself was due for her days off; he was going home with Mrs Crewe in attendance and it wasn't until he was writing his last note to Emily that she discovered that he had asked for her to go with him. When she had given him a questioning look he had taken the pad and scrawled: 'Jurres-Romeijn wouldn't allow it; said you were in need of a rest—made him promise that if anything went wrong you'd come and nurse me.'

'Yes, of course,' said Emily instantly, thrusting the question of what to do with the twins on one side. 'I'll come like a shot, but you're going to be fine. Do press on with the oesophageal speech, won't you?'

'You're as bad as Renier, badgering me back to living again.' But he smiled at her as he wrote, and his goodbye had been warm with gratitude. So had Mrs Wright's, accompanied by a large box wrapped in gay paper and tied with ribbon. Before Emily set about clearing the room of its complicated equipment and readying it for whoever was to occupy it next, she opened it. Elizabeth Arden, and lashings of it; lotions and powder and perfume, soap and several jars of face creams and a large bottle of bath essence. Emily drew in an excited breath; surely her mediocre looks would improve with such a galaxy of beauty aids? She wrapped everything up again and when she had finally finished her work bore it carefully home.

Louisa, looking it over that evening, agreed that it was a lovely present. 'Though personally I don't go for her,' she observed. 'I mean, everyone, just everyone, uses Fifth Avenue.'

But Emily refused to be put out. 'I shall use the lot,' she declared. 'It's bound to do something for me.'

Her young sister looked at her with affection tinged with irritation. Emily was a dear and she had always been able to twist her round her little finger, but she was a bit wet; it would take more than Elizabeth Arden to change her ordinary features into anything glamorous. 'It's worth a try,' she agreed. 'I say, now you're back for a day or two, I can go up to London, can't I? I simply must have some undies...'

There was really no need to go up to town. The shops were adequate enough for Louisa's modest wants; Emily recognised it as an excuse and agreed without demur. Louisa had earned some fun. It didn't occur to her that she had earned some fun too, but she was happy enough in the ugly little house, cleaning and washing and taking the twins out for the long walks she had promised. The weather had cheered up a little too, so she took them down the road and then pushed the pram along the bridle path, rutted and muddy, but the woods and fields on either side, although not quite country, were pleasant. She marched along briskly, thinking about Doctor Wright and the

Professor. She had heard from various friends at the hospital that he wouldn't be there much longer and she felt a strange regret, which considering she didn't like him, seemed strange.

Louisa, happy now that she had no need to be tied to the house all day, was disposed to be generous on Emily's last day. 'I'll take the twins,' she offered, 'so you can go to the shops if you want to.'

There were one or two things Emily wanted, she accepted at once and then at the last minute had to alter her plans because William, cutting a tooth, became fretful and feverish. 'He'll have to stay indoors,' she said, hiding disappointment. 'If you don't mind staying with him, I'll take Claire out this afternoon.'

'What about your shopping?'

'I'll do that on the way home tomorrow.'

It was a cold day and grey as was to be expected in November, but there was no wind and Emily, pushing Claire briskly in her pram, was quickly glowing. She had taken the bridle path again, away from the streets of small prim houses because although she never said so, she hated them. One day if she was lucky, she would have a small cottage in the country with a garden. There was plenty of time, she was only twenty-three and if she got a Sister's post soon she would start to save money. It didn't need to be full of mod cons, she could improve it over the years, and sometimes one could buy up a small place fairly cheaply if it hadn't been modernised.

There was no point in dwelling on the fact that she would probably not marry. She only met the young

doctors she worked with in hospital and none of them
had shown any interest in her to date. It would be
nice if she did, of course…her mind wandered off
into a vague dream so that she didn't at first hear the
horse's hooves ahead of her, and when she did she
merely turned the pram towards the hedge so that
there was room for the beast to pass. She was leaning
over the pram handle, encouraging Claire to take a
look at the animal, when it trotted round the bend
which had been hiding it. It was a very large horse,
which was a good thing, for its rider was large too—
the Professor, sitting at his ease and looking, as always, elegant. Emily, taken by surprise, gaped. The
Professor's handsome features, however, remained
calm. He reined in his horse, got down and said civilly: 'Good afternoon, Nurse Seymour.'

She muttered a greeting, rather red in the face, and
bent to inspect Claire. 'I didn't know that you were
married.' He turned to smile at Emily, and the red
deepened.

'I'm not,' said Emily.

His expression didn't alter, only his heavy lids
drooped over his eyes so that she had no idea what
he was thinking. 'She is very like you,' he observed.
'What is her name?'

'Claire.'

'Charming. You live close by?'

She jerked her head sideways. 'Yes, in one of those
houses over there—the last in a row, so it's not too
bad.' She added earnestly: 'I was lucky to get it.' She

went on, to make it clear: 'It's not so easy to get a house, you know—not if you're not married.'

'Er—probably not. I'm lost in admiration that you can work full time and run a house and a baby as well.'

'Well, Louisa—she's my sister, is staying with me until she can go to school for modelling—she's waiting for a place.'

His eyes flickered over her sensible coat, wellingtons and woolly cap pulled well down. 'She must be a pretty girl.'

'Oh, she is,' said Emily enthusiastically, 'and she's only just eighteen.'

He smiled faintly. 'And you, Emily? how old are you?'

'Twenty-three, almost twenty-four.'

'And Claire?'

'Eight months.'

'You moved here because of her, of course,' he suggested smoothly.

Emily had her mouth open to explain and then thought better of it. He couldn't possibly be interested. She frowned a little and said 'Yes' and nothing more. And then, because he just stood there, saying nothing, she said: 'I must be getting on; it's cold for Claire if I stand still.'

'Of course.' He got on his horse, raised his crop in salute and rode on, leaving her to continue her walk while she discussed the meeting with Claire, who chuckled and crowed and didn't answer back, which was nice. She was almost home again when the thought crossed her mind that the Professor might have thought Claire to be her baby. She stopped in the middle of the pavement, so that people hurrying past had to push against her.

'But that's absurd,' said Emily, out loud. 'I'm not married.'

The elderly woman squeezing past her, running over her wellingtons with one of those beastly little carriers on wheels, paused to say: 'Then you ought to be, my girl!'

Emily delivered a telling kick at the carrier; better than nothing, for she could think of nothing to answer back.

She went back on duty the next morning, on day duty now, but still on ENT. The wards were as busy as ever and Mr Spencer cheered her up by the warmth of his welcome. Of the Professor there was no sign; she went back home that evening wondering what had happened to him. She hadn't liked to ask and she had gone late to her dinner, so that she hadn't had a chance to talk to any of her friends.

He was there on the following morning, though, doing a round with Mr Spencer and his house surgeon, Sister and the speech therapist, a young woman whom Emily envied, for she was tall and slim and always said the right thing so that even the Professor listened to her when she had something to say, and smiled too. He didn't smile at Emily, only wished her a chilly good morning and requested a patient's notes. On her way home later, pedalling briskly through the crowded streets, she saw him again, driving a beautiful Jaguar XJ Spider. It was a silver-grey, Italian designed and probably worth a very great deal of money. He lifted a nonchalant hand in greeting as he slid past her which she had to ignore; there was so much traffic about that if she had lifted a hand from the handlebar she would certainly have fallen off.

Louisa wanted to go to the cinema, so Emily stayed home, contentedly enough because she had had a hard day. The little sitting room, rather bare of furniture, yet looked cosy enough in the firelight; she sat by it and sewed for the twins by the light of the lamp at her elbow.

There was a good programme on Radio Three and she allowed her thoughts to idle along with Brahms and Grieg and Delius. They returned over and over again to the Professor—too much so, she told herself severely; it was pointless to get even the faintest bit interested in him when he could hardly bear the sight of her. Besides, with a car like that, he obviously came from an entirely different background from her own. She folded her needlework carefully, left everything ready for Louisa to make herself a hot drink when she came in, and went to bed.

CHAPTER THREE

EMILY SAW saw almost nothing of Professor Jurres-Romeijn during the next few days; beyond stopping one morning to tell her that Doctor Wright was progressing just as he should, he had nothing to say to her other than a good morning or a good evening when he came to the ward. For some reason she felt vaguely discontented and miserable, perhaps because William had caught Claire's cold. She was worried about Mary too; she had had a guarded letter saying that they hoped to come home before very long, but it really held no news. She confided her worries to Louisa, who treated the matter more lightly. 'Well, they must be safe enough,' she pointed out, 'otherwise Mary wouldn't write, would she? I expect there's some sort of delay—you know what it is—some form not filled in properly...'

Emily told herself that she was fussing unnecessarily and resolved not to worry about it. Instead she worried about money. They lived on a tight budget, getting tighter every day, and sooner or later she would have to face up to what she was going to do when Louisa left home. She had suggested tentatively that Louisa might postpone the modelling school for a month or two, to be met with such a shower of reproaches that she hadn't said any more about it. She had a few savings, she would have to use them, every penny, to pay for a babyminder—if she could find one she could trust. Mary would pay her back when they came back to England, but it would leave her with the nasty feeling that there was nothing to fall back on if an emergency cropped up.

When she got home that evening Louisa met her with scarcely concealed excitement. 'I say,' she began before Emily could get her coat off, 'I was out with Tracey'—Tracey was the girl across the road with whom she sometimes went out—'well, we were just going to cross the road when this fab car pulled up to let us go over—a huge silver thing, Emily, you never saw anything like it—well, there was this terrific man sitting at the wheel...' She broke off to exclaim: 'Why didn't you tell me, Emily?' And not waiting for an answer: 'And Tracey said that he was the visiting professor at the hospital and when I asked her where, she said Ear, Nose and Throat Wards— you never said a word...'

'Well, why should I?' asked Emily reasonably. 'You're not a bit interested in hospitals or nursing. Besides, he's twice your age.'

Louisa stared at her, her great blue eyes narrowed. 'I like older men—to think that I'm going away and all this time he was here!' She pouted prettily. 'Darling Emily, couldn't you arrange for me to meet him? After all, you work for him.'

'Look, Louisa, he's hardly noticed me—he says

good morning and asks for things, but that's all—I mean, we're not even acquaintances.' She remembered the meeting on the bridle path and decided to say nothing about it.

'Anyone else would have got to know him,' grumbled Louisa. 'What about that special patient you had—didn't he look after him?'

'Yes.' Emily went past her sister and put on the kettle; a cup of tea might help matters.

'And you nursed him, didn't you? And do you mean to say that he never spoke to you?'

'Only to tell me to do things or ask about something to do with the patient.'

Louisa tossed her head. 'You're no use at all, Emily; I believe you're scared stiff of him.'

Emily considered the matter. 'No, I don't think so, why should I be?' She warmed the pot and spooned in the tea. 'How are the twins? Is William better? I'll go up and have a look in a minute.'

'They're fine. Emily, does this doctor...'

'He's a surgeon—a professor of surgery, actually.'

'Does he work at the hospital every day? Where does he live?'

Emily sighed; Louisa looked fragile and unable to say boo to a goose, but actually she had a will of iron and the strength of whipcord. 'He comes most days, but only for rounds, when he's operating and I haven't the faintest idea where he lives.'

Louisa eyed her curiously. 'Don't you want to know?'

'No—why should I?' She poured the tea. 'And how would I find out, for heaven's sake?'

Her sister didn't answer and Emily, not looking at her, didn't see the thoughtful look on her pretty face.

She was free the next day and she was surprised and touched when Louisa, over breakfast, offered to wash up and tidy the house while she dealt with the twins. 'And I'll wash up after lunch, too,' went on Louisa, 'if you wouldn't mind taking the twins for their walk while I nip down to Marks and Spencer's for some tights.'

Emily agreed; she hated washing up, and bathing and dressing the twins was much more fun than Hoovering round the house and dusting. The day passed pleasantly; she was out soon after lunch, the twins tucked warmly into their pram. But today she decided not to go along the bridle path but into the park. It looked bleak under the November sky and there weren't many people there, but she had remembered to bring some crusts for the ducks in the pond and they spent five minutes watching them gobble them up. She got back home later than she had meant to, but Louisa wasn't back; she sat the twins in their high chairs, made their Farex, coddled eggs and put orange juice in their feeding cups, laid the table for their own tea presently, and sat down between the pair of them. She was spooning food into small alternate mouths when she heard the key in the front door and called: 'I'm in the kitchen, we'll have tea when you've got your coat off.'

The kitchen door opened with a flourish and Louisa

came in and just behind her, Professor Jurres-Romeijn.

Emily paused with a spoonful of Farex poised in front of an impatient William's small mouth. 'Good lord,' she exclaimed, 'however did you get here?' she added a hasty, 'Professor.'

He didn't answer her at once but stood staring at the three of them sitting on the other side of the kitchen table. There was a gleam of amusement in his eyes although he spoke gravely enough. 'I stand corrected,' he murmured, 'but Claire is very like you, you know.'

Emily shot him an indignant glance. 'You thought she was mine?'

'Yes.' He smiled suddenly and with charm and her own mouth lifted at the corners. 'Twins, I see...' It wasn't quite a question, but she answered him as though it was.

'Yes, my elder sister Mary's—while she and her husband are abroad.'

'Ah, yes, I should...'

He was interrupted by Louisa, who hadn't had a chance to utter a word so far and was getting impatient. 'I fell down right in front of Professor Jurres-Romeijn's car, Emily, just outside the hospital, and he brought me home and do you know, he knows the street the flat's in...' She paused to smile at him and Emily thought how very pretty she was, standing there with her bright hair curling round her flushed face, her eyes sparkling.

She asked mildly: 'Did you hurt yourself?' and popped the Farex into William's mouth at last.

'Only just a very little—my ankle. But it's nothing to worry about.'

Claire, anxious for the rest of her tea, screwed up her face and let out a great howl and the Professor moved round the table, picked up a spoon and offered coddled egg. While Claire munched, Emily said: 'My goodness, that was smart work. Have you children of your own, Professor?'

'No, but any number of godchildren.'

'He's not married,' said Louisa happily, and the Professor's mouth twitched.

'I daresay I'm a confirmed bachelor. Does this moppet have to eat all this gluey stuff?'

Emily ladled more food into William. 'It's Farex and awfully good for them. Yes, she'll eat the lot, but don't bother, I can manage the two of them quite easily.'

Louisa had taken off her coat. 'Is there a fire in the sitting room?' she wanted to know, 'because if there is we could have tea there?' She smiled at the Professor. 'You'll have a cup of tea, won't you?'

He glanced at Emily, who took no notice. 'Thank you, I should like that, and perhaps I should look at that injured ankle.'

'Oh, that's almost better,' said Louisa airily. 'Come into the sitting room.'

'Why not here,' he asked mildly, 'then we can finish feeding these two.'

'Oh, Emily'll see to them...'

Emily took the hint. 'Yes, of course I will. You see to the tea, then, Louisa.'

The Professor got up and accompanied Louisa out of the room and Emily, straining her ears, could hear them laughing and talking and the tinkle of the best tea cups and saucers being got from the cupboard. Presently Louisa came into the kitchen and put on the kettle and Emily started to clear up the twins' tea. 'Can't you put them in their cots for half an hour, Emily?'

Emily had a wriggling infant under each arm. 'No, you know I can't. I'll have tea later.'

She went upstairs and got the babies ready for bed and tucked them into their cots. When she went downstairs the Professor had gone.

'He asked me to say goodbye,' said Louisa. 'He ate three of your scones; I told him I'd made them.' She looked around the small, shabby room. 'This is a dump, Emily, I wonder what he thought of it…'

'Does it matter?' Emily poured herself a cup of cool tea. 'Did you really hurt yourself, love, or did you plan the whole thing?'

Louisa giggled. 'What do you think?' She went on excitedly: 'He said he hoped I'd go out to dinner with him one evening. Emily, he's absolutely fab and I don't care if he is twice my age and he's got that gorgeous car. He said he couldn't believe that you were my sister.'

'I don't suppose he could,' observed Emily dryly. 'Did you get your tights?'

'Tights? Oh, that was just an excuse. I say, Emily,

do you suppose he'll take me out when I'm in London?'

'Probably, if he's there too.'

'Didn't you know?' asked Louisa. 'He's got a flat there—he drives up and down each day. He lives in Holland, but he's over here a lot.' Her eyes narrowed. 'I bet he's rich.'

Emily picked up the tray. 'Look, love, don't get carried away; you might never see him again.'

It was just as they were going up to bed that Louisa suddenly asked: 'I say, what was all that talk when we came in—all about him standing corrected and how like you Claire was and you said something about him thinking that she was yours...' She gave a sudden shriek of laughter: 'Emily, he thought you were the twins' mum...oh, how could he? I mean, you don't look like anyone's mum, and however did he think you could work all day and look after them as well, and run a house too?'

'Men aren't very practical about such things, and anyway, I told him that I had you to help me.'

'When?' Louisa frowned. 'I thought you never spoke to him.'

'I met him the other afternoon and I had Claire with me in the pram, so it was natural enough for him to think she was my baby, I suppose.'

Louisa had regained her good humour. 'Oh, poor Emily, I bet you blushed!'

'I can't remember,' observed Emily, remembering only too well that her face had been like fire for minutes on end.

She spent a long time at her dressing table before
she got into bed, experimenting with Elizabeth Arden.
She had never been very good at putting on make-up,
but even with her inexpert hand, she thought she
looked a great deal better. She couldn't use it as lavishly when she was on duty, but there was the hospital
ball in ten days' time; no one had asked her to go
yet, but if they did, she would; she had last year's
flowered crêpe at the back of the wardrobe; better
still, she would use the money she had saved for a
new pair of high boots and buy a new dress, something really fashionable. She tumbled into bed and lay
happily deciding exactly what she would buy—pro-
viding, of course, that she got asked.

Wonder of wonders, she did get asked. Sammy
Bolt, one of the laboratory assistants, stopped her on
the way to the canteen and invited her to partner him.
She was so surprised that for a minute she didn't say
anything. For one thing she didn't like Sammy much;
he was a long-haired, trendy type with a reputation
for chatting up the nurses, not at all her sort. On the
other hand, it would be wonderful to have an escort.
She thanked him gravely and he gave her the wide
smile which he considered the girls fell for. 'OK, I'll
meet you at the front entrance at eight o'clock.'

'Yes, all right.' She added awkwardly: 'Thank you
for asking me. I must go to the canteen now, I'm late
already.'

And over dinner, when she told her friends, she
added: 'I can't think why he asked me...I mean, me!'

Her friends were as puzzled as she was; Emily was

a dear and well liked, but hardly sexy, and Sammy was a bit of a tearaway. They wouldn't have been puzzled if they could have heard him boasting to his particular bunch of cronies that he had won the bet he had made with one of them; that he'd get the staid Nurse Seymour to go to the ball with him. 'And I'll lose her the minute we get there,' he promised. 'I've never won a fiver so fast!'

But Emily, blissfully unaware of that, worked through the rest of her day with a tiny corner of her mind centred on the new dress she would buy and the impact it would have on everyone who saw it. Something dashing and a bit daring so that everyone would look at her twice. And that included Professor Jurres-Romeijn.

Cycling home later, she allowed the whole of her mind to centre on the important matter of the dress and arrived with her head stuffed with a splendid muddle of daydreams, instantly shattered by Louisa, who met her at the door with an ecstatic: 'Emily, he's taking me to the hospital ball—Professor Jurres-Romeijn! He said he hadn't anyone to go with and would I like to go and I said yes—only I must have a new dress—and sandals and a wrap.' Her pretty mouth trembled: 'I must, I must—I'll die if I can't!'

A little flicker of rage twisted Emily's insides and was instantly doused. Louisa was her sister and as pretty as a picture and she deserved all the fun she could get while she was young. The flowered crêpe would have to do—it wasn't as though anyone would notice her, thought Emily as she said in a steady voice: 'I'll see what can be done, love. How much would it all cost?'

'I've seen a dress,' Louisa was all smiles now, 'blue organza—quite super.'

'Yes, but how much?'

'Sixty pounds.' She wasn't going to tell Emily eighty because that sounded too much.

To Emily sixty pounds was bad enough. 'You'll have to get sandals from your allowance—there are plenty of cheap ones and no one will see them under a long dress.'

Louisa looked mutinous but agreed quickly. 'Tracey will lend me that white shawl her mother brought back from Madeira. Oh, Emily darling, won't it be heavenly? I mean, he's so good-looking and I'm sure everyone will be jealous…'

Emily didn't mention Sammy's invitation; it hardly seemed the right moment. She wept a bit in bed that night; the crêpe, brought from the recesses of the wardrobe, looked limp and old-fashioned and its colour did nothing for her. She could cry off, she supposed, but her friends would want to know why. Before she went to sleep, she got out of bed and took another look at the crêpe. It was awful!

She had a free evening on the day of the ball, and because she had had a busy day she was tired and a little peevish by the time she got home. Louisa was having a bath and the twins were screaming their heads off in their cots, so that Emily had to see to them first. By the time she had settled them again,

Louisa had come downstairs, wrapped in a dressing gown, her hair piled on top of her head.

'I had my bath early,' she explained, 'so the water will be hot enough for you—sorry about the twins, they were all right when I left them. Mrs Crewe's coming at seven, isn't she? She'll give them their supper.'

'They have their supper at six o'clock,' said Emily crossly. 'Really, Louisa, you might have got it ready.'

'How could I? I've got to get myself dressed, haven't I? He's coming at eight o'clock, and I've got my nails to do…'

Emily put on the kettle. A cup of tea might restore her good humour. She wished now that Sammy was coming to fetch her instead of her having to have a taxi back to the hospital, but at least she'd be gone before the Professor arrived for Louisa. She had hardly seen him during the last few days and he hadn't said a word to her about inviting Louisa. But then why should he?

The tea restored her to a certain extent. She fed the twins, left them in their high chairs while she did her nails, washed her hair and got her things ready before putting them into their cots and having her bath. The water wasn't hot—it took ages to heat up and now it was tepid, but at least it meant that she didn't waste time over it. In her dressing gown she did her face carefully, putting on a little too much of everything in her efforts to look like all the other girls, brushed her shining clean hair smooth and put it up, then went downstairs to let Mrs Crewe in. She spent ten minutes showing that lady where everything was and introducing her to William and Claire, then went away to put on her dress.

She wasn't going to be the belle of the ball, that was for certain; no amount of pressing could conceal its faintly dowdy air. Its round neck, unfashionably modest, needed something to detract from it; the silver locket on its thick chain which she had had from her grandmother years ago. She went to get it and frowned when it wasn't in its usual place. Surely Louisa wouldn't have taken it to wear...she crossed the bare little landing and opened her sister's door.

Louisa was standing in the middle of the room. She looked quite beautiful in the blue organza dress, her hair falling round her shoulders in curls, her face exquisitely made up. In her hands she held a pair of silver sandals—expensive ones—and on the bed was a silver kid evening bag, lying on top of a silver gauze shawl.

'Louisa...' began Emily, then stopped while she took it all in. 'Those sandals—they must have cost the earth—and that bag and the shawl. Where did you get the money?'

Louisa looked scared and then defiant. 'I don't see why I should have to wear cheap sandals or borrow Tracey's silly shawl. I bought these...'

'I can see that. What with?'

Louisa turned to face her. 'I sold your silver locket...'

Emily's wide soft mouth opened with shock. 'My locket! But it's mine, you couldn't sell it!'

'Well, I did—what's the use of it to you, and I had to have the right things. I can't bear cheap clothes… You grudge me everything, just because you're not pretty, you're trying to turn me into a dull creature like you.'

Emily didn't answer. She was hurt and bewildered and wildly angry and later, when she felt better about it, she'd have something to say to Louisa. 'How much did that dress really cost?' she asked quietly.

'If you must know—eighty pounds.'

'And how much did you get for my locket and where did you sell it?'

'I got eighty pounds for it, at Wetherby's in the High Street.'

Emily turned on her heel and went back to her room, picked up her winter coat and went downstairs after peeping at the twins, sound asleep.

'I don't expect I'll be very late,' she told Mrs Crewe. 'You sure you'll be all right?'

The older woman smiled at her. 'Of course, Emily. You go along and enjoy yourself. I used to love the annual ball when I was your age.' She looked past Emily. 'Where's Louisa? Aren't you going together?'

'Professor Jurres-Romeijn is coming for her at eight o'clock. I'm going now—there's the taxi outside—I'm meeting Sammy at the entrance.'

Mrs Crewe didn't think much of Sammy, but she wasn't going to spoil Emily's evening by saying so. 'Well, have fun, my dear. I'll see you later.'

Sammy was waiting just inside the hospital entrance and Emily took instant exception to his pink frilled shirt and the way his long hair hung over his collar, but neither that nor his laconic greeting were going to spoil her evening. She greeted him with calm friendliness and went away to take off her coat. The surgeons' dining room, turned into a temporary cloak-room, was full of women and as far as Emily could see in one hasty glance round, they were all dressed in the height of fashion. No one had a neckline like hers, they all plunged wildly or had no neckline at all. She greeted some of her friends, peeped into the mirror and went back to the entrance.

Dancing was in full swing. Sammy led her straight on to the dance floor, greeting his friends as he went, and began weaving and twisting, not bothering to see if she was following suit, but, frumpy dress and the wrong make-up notwithstanding, Emily followed very nicely; she was a born dancer and presently Sammy paid her the compliment of saying so. 'Though looking at you, no one would know,' he assured her.

She beamed at him, her cheeks pink with pleasure and exercise, which was unfortunate as she had applied Elizabeth Arden blusher rather too lavishly and during the interval, after Sammy had brought her a glass of cup—the only drink the Principal Nursing Officer would allow during the dancing—the pink became red.

'Like it?' asked Sammy slyly, and gave her another glassful, and the moment she had downed it, pulled her back on to the dance floor. The evening, thought Emily, in a pale pink haze, was being fun after all and why had she been worrying, anyway? Everything was wonderful. She began to sing to the music and only stopped when Louisa and the Professor, caught up in the crush, appeared alongside her. She only paused long enough to say 'Hullo' before she turned her back on them.

She had another glass of cup presently and then somehow Sammy disappeared, leaving her to stand on the edge of the floor, still feeling carefree and not very worried. Presently she saw him with a young girl with fiery red hair and an outrageous dress. They passed close to her and Sammy looked at her as though he hadn't seen her before. She couldn't see the Professor or Louisa and feeling conspicuous, she sat down, half hidden by a potted palm. She felt very warm and she supposed it was the heat and the noise which made her feel so peculiar.

The Professor had seen her, though, and kept his eyes on her while half listening to Louisa's chat. But suddenly he was all attention; Louisa, convinced that she had his admiration and was enslaved by her pretty face, was telling him about the locket. 'I think it was rather clever of me to have thought of it,' she observed smugly. 'I simply had to have some new clothes and Emily didn't give me nearly enough money.'

The Professor's voice was deceptively soft. 'Did she not? Do tell me about it.'

The telling lasted until the dance was over, when the Professor, acting with bland speed, introduced Louisa to Tom Spencer, excused himself with a practised murmur and made his way to where Emily was sitting.

She was in the act of drinking from the glass Sammy had thrust into her hand as he went past her, the redhaired girl on his arm. She wasn't thirsty any more, but it was something to do. It was a bit of a surprise when it was taken from her hand and the Professor said gently: 'I shouldn't if I were you. It's supposed to be a harmless cup, but some joker poured several bottles of vodka into it.' He studied her red face, looking a little strange now by reason of the blusher competing with her own flushed cheeks. 'How many glasses have you had?'

She stared up at him. He looked a little woolly round the edges and she had a strong wish to get up and dance with him whether he asked her or not.

'How many?'

'Three—and some of this one.'

'God, you're half stoned,' remarked the Professor edgily. He caught her by the hand and heaved her to her feet. 'Come along, we're going to get some black coffee into you.' He looked round him. 'Where's that punk type you came with?' He added strongly: 'And why in heaven's name did you come with him?'

'No one else asked me,' said Emily.

He tucked her hand under his arm. 'I'm getting too old for this kind of thing,' he observed. 'We'll find somewhere quiet—you can sleep it off if you want to.'

He was walking her briskly round the edge of the

ballroom, but she stopped to look at him. 'Oh, but you can't do that—what about Louisa?'

'Louisa is quite capable of looking after herself—which is more than can be said of you. Come along.'

She didn't feel able to do much about it; he took her through a door and down a passage and into the consultants' sitting room. There was no one there, but the Professor pressed one of the wall bells and when a waiter appeared, asked for a tray of coffee. When it came he glanced at Emily, sitting back untidily in a too big armchair, and poured out two cups.

'Drink that,' he commanded, 'and when you've finished it, you'll drink another.'

She sat sipping the scalding drink and half way through said: 'I've rather a bad headache.'

'The vodka. It'll wear off.' He was sitting back in his own chair watching her. Presently he refilled her cup and asked: 'Why are you wearing such an unbecoming dress when Louisa is decked out in the latest fashion? Have you no money?'

At any other time she would have been furious at his daring to ask such a question, but somehow it didn't matter now. 'Not enough for both of us.'

'I have a sister of my own,' he observed suavely, 'so I'm not entirely ignorant of girls' clothing...'

'And I expect you've had lots of girl-friends,' remarked Emily; the black coffee was winning, but the vodka still had a kick in it.

'Any number. Which leads me to observe that she is also wearing expensive sandals—I imagine her outfit cost upwards of one hundred and fifty pounds or so. Surely you could both have had new dresses for that?'

'Oh, yes, of course, but Louisa had set her heart on this particular dress, you see, and I—I didn't mind—well, not very much.'

The Professor snorted. 'You're lying,' he said genially, 'but since your motives are good I'll not dig deeper.' He smiled suddenly. 'I don't need to, anyway.'

A remark which meant very little to her, although she was beginning to feel more normal now although she had to admit to herself, not at all happy.

'Shall I find your partner for you?' asked the Professor. 'Not that you're in any condition to dance.'

She shook her head. 'No, thank you—he's dancing with a girl with red hair—she's very pretty.' Two tears overflowed and ran down her cheeks—the vodka having its final fling. 'I'm quite all right now, thank you. I'm sure you must want to go back to the ballroom.'

The Professor stretched out his very long legs and contemplated the black patent pumps on the end of them. 'No, I don't want to go back—I like dancing in moderation and with the right girl. I'm going to take you home.'

Emily sat up. 'Oh, no, you're not,' she said fiercely, 'it's only eleven o'clock, I can get a taxi. Besides,' she tossed her head, 'I'm not sure that I want to go yet.'

'You're not capable of being sure of anything at

the moment,' observed the Professor. 'You're going home.'

He took her down back passages to find her coat, helped her on with it, then went through a side door to where the Jag was parked. She curled up beside him, sniffing at the pleasant mixture of cigars and leather.

'You're very kind,' she said it carefully, because the words tripped her tongue.

'I can remember being very unkind to you, Emily.' He didn't look at her as he drove the big car through the quiet streets.

She said in a small voice: 'Oh, is that why you're taking me home now?'

'No. Mrs Crewe is there, I understand?'

Emily nodded in the dark. 'I said I'd be back by one o'clock.'

They didn't say any more but drove the short distance in silence until he drew up outside the house, where he took her latch-key from her, opened the door, pushed her gently into the narrow hall and came in after her, filling it to capacity.

'It's all right, Mrs Crewe,' he called softly. 'I've brought Emily back.'

Mrs Crewe put her head round the sitting room door. She didn't make any remarks about how early it was or what had happened, but said instantly in her comfortable voice: 'I'll put the kettle on—we'll have a cup of tea.'

The little room looked shabbier than ever, the worn covers of the chairs and the elderly carpet highlighted by the bright fire. Emily took off her coat and sat down and the Professor sat down opposite her.

'Feeling better?' he wanted to know.

'Yes, thank you; I've got a headache...'

'That'll be all right after a good sleep. I'm going to help Mrs Crewe.'

The kitchen was even shabbier than the dining room, its shelves filled with cheap saucepans and a miscellanea of china. He went and stood by Mrs Crewe, who looked up at him questioningly.

'I'll take you home presently,' he told her, 'but first a cup of tea, I think.'

'What went wrong, Professor?'

'Sammy deserted her, and some fool had laced the fruit cup with vodka. Emily's had three glasses of it.' His fine mouth twisted a little.

'The poor kid,' said Mrs Crewe warmly, 'what she puts up with is no one's business,' and added hastily, 'Of course, it's her business—I shouldn't have said that.'

'I guessed something of the sort. Shall I carry the tray in?'

The Professor seemed in no hurry to go. He stayed until long after midnight, waiting with Mrs Crewe while Emily went up to her room and got ready for bed.

When she came downstairs again, her hair in a smooth curtain around her shoulders, wrapped in a dressing gown, bought more for its practical warmth than its glamour, he got up and leaned against the door while she and Mrs Crewe exchanged a few part-

ing words. He seemed totally uninterested, his gaze
fixed on a particularly revolting picture of a clutch of
dead pheasants and a bunch of grapes which hung on
the wall. Emily, glancing up, thought that he was
bored and longing to be gone; she made short work
of her good nights, thanked them both for their kindness and saw them to the door. But here the Professor
paused. 'No, go upstairs to bed,' he ordered her, 'and
call out when you're in it; it's the best place for you
for the time being.'

She couldn't but agree with him; she went upstairs
meekly enough and climbed into bed and obediently
called that she was there. Only then did he usher Mrs
Crewe out and shut the door behind him. Emily lay
for a while in the quiet little house, going over her
evening. It hadn't been a success; indeed, it had been
a miserable fiasco and how she would ever look the
Professor in the face again she didn't know. And there
was the question of the locket to settle with Louisa.
Tomorrow was going to be a perfectly beastly day.
She frowned above tight shut eyes and slept, never
hearing the Professor and Louisa coming in more than
an hour later. It might have comforted her to have
known that he did no more than open the door for her
sister, bid her a pleasant goodnight, and get back into
his car.

CHAPTER FOUR

EMILY NEED NOT have worried; when she went on duty the next day it was to be told by Sister that Professor Jurres-Romeijn had gone back to his own country.

Emily felt a curious sinking sensation. 'For good?' she asked.

'No, no, some date he had with someone or other—a girl-friend, most likely—he's not married, you know.' She glanced at Emily. 'You look a bit under the weather, Staff—too much dancing last night, I suppose.' She didn't wait for Emily to reply but went on briskly. 'Go and see to Mr Taylor, will you. He's very nervous of his tube—try and explain to him...'

She dismissed Emily with a nod and bent her head over her paper work once more.

Emily hadn't seen Louisa before she left for work. She had seen to the twins, given them their early morning feed, eaten a hasty meal herself and then nipped quietly into Louisa's room with her alarm clock, set for half past eight. The twins wouldn't sleep after that, even on full tummies, and Louisa would probably not wake. It was a pity, Emily thought worriedly, that she wouldn't be home until after five o'clock, Louisa would be tired after the ball and perhaps impatient with the twins. But she had to dismiss any doubts from her mind and get on with her work. The wards were full and there would be a theatre list tomorrow; patients had to be prepared, reassured and advised as to how they should behave after the operation.

Emily went through her day with her usual calm good sense, not allowing any private thoughts to intrude into it. Only as she was cycling home did she let her mind roam. Louisa would be cross, she felt sure. After the excitement of the ball, the dull routine of her day would have irked her, the necessity of feeding and bathing the babies, taking them for a walk in their pram, doing the household chores, would have brought on one of her bad moods. She had had them as a child; when she found that she wasn't to have her own way, she had sulked and cried and made life miserable for everyone, until, very often, she had been given in to. Emily heaved such an enormous sigh that she almost fell off her bike. It was to be hoped that the Professor had been so charming that Louisa was still under his influence.

Which to a certain extent was true. Louisa, after a brief grumble about her hard day, launched herself into an account of her evening which lasted while Emily took off her things, made the tea, went to see the twins, and came downstairs again. They shouldn't have been in their cots as early as they were, but as Louisa explained, she was so tired herself that she had put them there in the hope that they might sleep until their feed was due. 'And I took them out this afternoon,' she said virtuously. 'Although I could hardly put one foot in front of the other.'

Emily made soothing noises, poured tea and surveyed the evening ahead of her. No washing had been done and the twins would want their six o'clock feed very shortly; there was no sign of supper either. She drank her tea slowly, toasting her feet in front of the fire, then set about methodically putting things to rights. The washing machine was loaded, the babies' feed prepared, and the potatoes peeled and in a saucepan before William let out a howl followed all too quickly by Claire. Emily nipped upstairs, changed them and whisked them downstairs and into their high chairs. 'You do Claire, I'll see to William,' she told Louisa, still lounging by the fire. 'And it's a pity you didn't put the washing machine on a bit earlier in the day—nothing will dry overnight.'

Louisa pouted. 'What a cross old maid you're getting, Emily,' she observed. 'No wonder you never get asked to dances and parties.'

Which remark was so unfair that Emily could think of nothing to say to it. But later, when the babies were safely tucked up and the supper was cooking, she confronted her sister.

'The locket,' she said. 'You'll have to get it back, Louisa.'

'How can I? I haven't a penny—my allowance doesn't come for another week, and I need some clothes if I'm going to London. Really, Emily, you ought to be glad that I was able to fit myself out so well.'

'Never mind your new clothes—you'll go tomorrow and ask them to keep it until you can fetch it.' Emily wasn't often cross, but she was now. Louisa gave her a doubtful look and then said reluctantly:

'Oh, well—all right, though I do think you're mean.'

And later, in bed Emily wondered uneasily if she was mean, perhaps she was becoming old-maidish, even though there wasn't supposed to be any such thing nowadays. When Mary was home again and the twins had gone, she would give up the horrid house they were living in, go back to London and get a job at her old hospital, find a small flat close by and have some fun. She was a bit vague about what sort of fun, but it involved buying some pretty clothes and having a holiday and going to a trendy hairdresser.

She woke quite cheerful, her daydream still very much alive in her head so that the ward wasn't irksome at all and even Sister, in a bad temper all day, couldn't quite destroy it. She cycled home through the bleak evening making rather wild plans for the future, interrupted much too frequently by speculations as to when the Professor would return. Why he should be so entangled with that same future, she had no idea, only when she thought about her new wardrobe and all the parties she would go to he seemed, quite naturally, to be with her.

She opened the house door, still in a dreamy state,

and had her euphoria blown to smithereens at once. Louisa poked her head round the kitchen door.

'There you are. I've some bad news for you, Emily, and you might as well know it at once. The locket's sold. It was sold as soon as the shop opened this morning, and that silly man I asked about it wouldn't tell me who'd bought it.'

Emily stared at her unbelievingly. 'But it can't be—who could have wanted it? Was it in the window?'

Louisa shrugged. 'How should I know? Anyway, it's gone and there's nothing we can do about it, is there?' She glanced at Emily and then quickly away. 'Renier thought my outfit was lovely.'

'Renier?' Emily was brooding over her lost locket.

'The Professor, silly. Oh, Emily, don't you ever bother about anyone? Did you see him today?'

'He's in Holland.' Emily picked William up from his playpen and started to tickle his small fat chin.

Louisa's face dropped. 'He didn't tell me...'

'Why should he? You're a girl he took to a dance, Louisa—nothing more.'

Louisa's lovely eyes narrowed. 'I've every intention of being much more. Just you wait until I've done my modelling course and got myself some decent clothes.' She let out a gusty sigh. 'Oh, just you wait, Emily!'

Emily was too cross to answer. She tucked William under one arm and went into the kitchen to put the kettle on.

She went to the jeweller's the next day, but he

wasn't prepared to tell her who it was who had bought he locket; even when she explained that it was all a mistake, that her sister had sold it because of a misunderstanding. The manager was regretful but quite adamant. Emily, a mild-tempered girl on the whole, went home in a filthy temper, all the worse because she couldn't give vent to it until the twins were in bed and asleep, and then Louisa, sensing the storm which was brewing, declared that she had promised that she would go to the cinema with Tracey and tore out of the house just as Emily was on the point of unleashing her rage.

It was two days later that she saw the Professor again. She had had a frustrating day at the hospital; nothing had gone right, the tonsils in the Children's ward had all behaved badly, screaming and raging and being sick, and she had become worn out with persuading them to be good and feeding them ice cream and cuddling them when they cried. Sister, who wasn't keen on children, always left Emily to deal with tonsil day.

The weather was as gloomy as her mood as she got out her bike and started off home, despite the fact that Sister had allowed her to go home early. As she wheeled her bike through the gate she was surprised to see that there was no light on anywhere. She couldn't remember Louisa telling her that she would be out as late as this with the twins, unless she had taken them out to tea with one of her youthful friends. Emily unlocked the back door and went into the kitchen to find the house quiet. There was no note and no one answered when she called. More puzzled than worried, she took off her outdoor things and looked into the sitting room, but there was no one there either—perhaps Louisa had left a message in her room. She went upstairs to see. Louisa's room was untidy; it always was. Her own, in contrast, looked bare. Frowning now, Emily went back on to the landing. She must have missed a note downstairs somewhere. The door of the twins' little room was shut and almost without thinking, she opened it and looked inside. The babies were in their cots, apparently asleep.

Only they weren't asleep. They were unconscious—out cold—their small hands and feet icy, their pupils not reacting, their breaths so shallow she could barely see that they were breathing. An icy hand clutched at Emily's heart and the wish to give way to panic was so great that she was forced to close her eyes for a moment—long enough for her calm good sense to take over. She looked round the room rapidly; there might be some clue. And there was; on the mantelpiece there was a small bottle of Seconal.

During the next seconds her mind registered two facts: the tablets were out of reach of the twins, and the bottle was tightly stoppered; and that Louisa had grumbled on the previous evening because she had wanted to go to a late afternoon fashion show at the Town Hall and Emily had told her that it couldn't be done because she herself wouldn't be home until half past five at the earliest.

Even while her mind was busy, so were her capable

hands; taking pulses, feeling the small bodies for the clamminess and the chill. At least their breathing, although far too shallow and light, was unhampered, at least for the moment, and they hadn't been sick. She thanked heaven for that and at the same time tried to think what was best to be done. She gave them one more anxious look and started down the stairs at a run. She was almost at their foot when the front door bell rang.

She was across the little hall in a flash to open it and let out a great gusty sigh of relief when she saw who it was—the Professor, his powerful frame looming large in the poky porch.

Emily put out an urgent hand and clutched his sleeve. 'Thank heaven it's you!' she exclaimed in a small scream. 'The twins…'

He bent his head and came through the door, closing it behind him so that in the narrow passage they were jammed close together. 'They're ill?'

'Yes,' she moved towards the stairs, 'oh, you must hurry—they're up here…'

He was right behind her as she galloped up the stairs and at the bedroom door he lifted her aside with one hand and went past her to the cots.

It seemed an age before he lifted his head from examining the babies, although it wasn't more than a minute. 'Coma,' he said. 'How on earth…there's no gas in the room?'

'No…I think they must have had…'

She didn't finish because he had already seen the little bottle for himself.

'Seconal.' He flashed her a look. 'Do you take sleeping tablets?'

'No—I…'

'They must go to hospital at once—my car's outside.' He began to wrap William in a blanket and Emily went to do the same for Claire. The Professor glanced up briefly and she was horrified at the icy look in his eyes; his voice was ice too. 'You've been on duty all day?' And when she nodded: 'Is this how you keep them quiet? Dope them? Only this time your hand slipped…'

He pushed past her and started downstairs and Emily stood, shocked into stillness by his words. Her face was chalk white and she was shivering with fright and cold, but she followed him, climbed into the car without a word, received William's still little body on to her lap where Claire already lay, and sat still speechless while he raced through the dull streets to the Accident Bay, where he flung open the door, urged her to be quick and went inside with William. There was help immediately, of course. The twins were laid gently down and their small stomachs washed out while their noses and mouths were cleared to prevent their lungs collapsing. Half way through the Professor turned round and saw Emily, standing like a frozen statue, just behind him.

'Go away,' he told her harshly.

She gave him a look of loathing. 'No. I'm staying.'

And stay she did, keeping as close as she dared while the Professor, the Casualty Officer, an anaesthetist, her friend, Staff Nurse O'Brien and a student

nurse worked their hardest. William recovered first
and only the Professor's large arm prevented her leap-
ing to gather him in her arms. His 'Stay where you
are, Nurse Seymour,' was uttered in a tone of voice
which would countenance no disobedience, and common sense told her that he was quite right. William
wasn't going to be himself for a little while yet; he
was wrapped up carefully and borne off to the Children's ward while they bent over Claire. She re-
sponded presently, too, but only after the Professor
had ordered an injection of Megimide. Emily watched
her carried away to join her brother, glanced at the
Professor, giving instructions to the Casualty Officer,
and at Bernadette O'Brien and her nurse, clearing up
the mess, and edged to the door. No one was going
to stop her going to Children's and staying until the
twins were perfectly recovered.

She was actually at the door when the Professor's
voice halted her. 'I should like to speak to you,' he
warned her, and when she took a tentative step back-
wards: 'Now.'

In a voice which no one else there could hear, he
said: 'Now I should like to know more about this
most regrettable happening. How many tablets did
you give? And have you done it before?' She hesitated and he added: 'We will go into the entrance; we
shan't be disturbed.'

So she went into the bare, short corridor which
opened directly on to the ambulance bay. It was dark
and cold and she shivered, trying to hide it.

'Now...' prompted the Professor.

She hardly heard him. 'Will they be all right?'

His eyes were still cold, but his voice was kind enough. 'Oh, yes—I imagine that they had only been in coma for an hour or so and they're healthy little creatures. They'll have to stay a few days to make sure that they haven't got pneumonia.'

She nodded, too miserable to speak, but he reiterated: 'Now, if you please, Nurse, let us have the facts.'

'Well—' began Emily, and stopped. He would probably not believe her if she told him the truth; in fact, he might possibly think that she was blaming Louisa because she wasn't there to defend herself. Try as she could, she couldn't think of anything plausible to say.

But she didn't need to say anything; a taxi stopped in the bay and Louisa tumbled out and rushed into the corridor. She saw Emily at once, but not the Professor, who had gone to lean up against a wall.

'Emily—oh, Emily—Mrs Turner saw you and told me. Oh, Emily, I never meant to give them too much—I just thought that if they had some in their feed they'd go to sleep and I could go to the fashion show. I did so want to go and I didn't think it would matter, only the show lasted longer than I thought it would and you got home early, didn't you?' She started to cry. 'I'm so upset, I feel quite ill.'

'The twins feel quite ill too,' said the Professor quietly.

Louisa turned in a flash. 'Renier—I didn't know you were here, too.' She went close to him and put a

hand on his arm. 'I think I'm going to faint—I can't
stand being upset. Emily will tell you, I'm very sensitive…' She smiled at him through her tears. 'Please
will you take me home?'

His thick eyebrows lifted. 'I've no intention of
leaving the hospital until William and Claire are completely recovered.' He took her arm and walked her
down to the bay where the taxi was still waiting, put
her inside, said something to the driver, and watched
it drive away. Long after it had disappeared he stood
there, apparently absorbed in the dreary view of the
hospital yard before him, so that Emily started to walk
away. Perhaps he was so sick of them both that he
wanted nothing more to do with either of them. He
was beside her before she had taken a couple of steps.
His first words startled her.

'I find it difficult to believe that you and Louisa
are sisters.'

She felt lightheaded with relief because the twins
were going to be all right. She could think of nothing
else. 'Lot's of people say that—we aren't a bit alike;
she's so pretty.' Her voice held no envy, rather a pride
in having a lovely sister.

'I wasn't speaking of looks. I judged you harshly,
Emily, and I'm sorry. I hope you will forgive me—I
should have known better. My only excuse is that the
sight of those two babies angered me so much.'

They had stopped by the door leading to the Accident Room and even if Emily had wanted to go
through it, she wouldn't have been able to; the Professor was blocking her way. She looked up at him,

at his rather arrogant good looks and his blue eyes, now strangely friendly. 'That's all right,' she said a little gruffly. 'I was angry too, I know how you felt.'

He held out a large, beautifully kept hand and she shook it solemnly, but when she went to withdraw it, he held it fast. 'The twins will be all right. We'll go and have something to eat and then you shall see them before you go home.'

Emily was ravenously hungry and she had the sure feeling that if he said the twins were going to be OK then they would be. 'I'm not dressed for going out,' she pointed out.

'Nor am I,' he declared blandly, a palpable falsehood, if ever there was one. 'There's a nice little pub at Cushford'—Cushford was a village a mile or so away down a side road. He noticed for the first time that she was wearing a sweater and skirt; there had been no time to put on her coat. 'Borrow a coat from someone—a hospital cloak will do…'

Emily didn't like to point out that the wearing of hospital cloaks more than five hundred yards from the hospital was forbidden and it didn't seem to matter, anyway. She begged Bernadette O'Brien's cloak from her and waited while he had a final word with Mr Spencer, who had just arrived.

It was bitterly cold by now and she was grateful for the cloak as they got into the car. The Professor plunged his hand into a compartment under the dashboard and handed her a pair of gloves. 'Put those on.' His glance took in her still white face and shaking mouth. 'You'll feel much better when you've had a meal.'

She thanked him and then suddenly remembered Louisa. 'Oh, I really should go home,' she declared. 'I mean, poor Louisa's all alone and she's so upset.'

'Not, I think, as upset as you are, Emily—she's made of different stuff, I fancy.' He glanced at his watch. 'We shan't be long, you know, by the time she's made herself a cup of tea and got herself sorted out, you'll be home.'

If she had been quite herself, she wouldn't have believed him for one minute, but she wasn't quite herself.

The pub was small and cosy with a pleasant fug of tobacco smoke and beer. The Professor led her through a little door at the back where, surprisingly, there was a minute restaurant, most of which was already occupied. He sat her down in a vacant chair and went away again to return with the pub owner, a thin, sad-looking man who when he smiled didn't look sad at all. He offered Emily the menu, received the Professor's order for drinks and went away again, whistling under his breath.

The menu was quite varied and full of such wholesome food as steak and kidney pudding and two veg., roast pork and apple sauce, and T-bone steak.

'Steak and kidney for you?' suggested the Professor, and Emily, who seldom had the time to make one herself, agreed happily.

'And for pudding?' urged her companion. 'The treacle tart sounds good.'

Treacle tart was loaded with calories; it was all very well for the Professor, he had a vast person to keep nourished, whereas she was already slightly plump. When she hesitated he said: 'You've used up every scrap of energy in the last two hours or so; you'll need to replace it, you know.'

She did that with pleasure, eating every scrap of food on her plate, as well as drinking the sherry she was invited to drink first, and the excellent claret which accompanied the steak and kidney pudding.

If she had stopped to think about it, she would have been surprised to find that she felt quite at her ease with the Professor, who chatted about this and that while stowing away a huge meal. It was only as they were drinking the excellent coffee that Emily said suddenly:

'Oh, lord—haven't we been here a long time? Supposing the twins…'

'Don't panic. I left this phone number with Spencer; he would have telephoned if he needed me.' His smile was kind. 'We'll go when you want to.'

The twins were doing fine, both sleeping, a normal colour once more, their breaths even and deep.

'No pneumonia there,' the Professor assured Emily, 'but we'll keep them in for a few days. When do you have your next days off?'

'At the end of the week—Friday and Saturday.'

'You shall take them home on Friday morning. And now if you're ready, I'll drop you off on my way home.'

But when they reached the little house he got out

too and opened the door for her and, uninvited, followed her inside. Louisa was in the kitchen. She was
wearing a new dressing gown Emily hadn't seen before, and her hair was hanging artlessly round her
shoulders. Her pretty face was the picture of woe and
as they went in the tears began to spill out of her blue
eyes. 'Emily,' she rushed at her sister and flung her
arms round her, 'I'm so dreadfully sorry—do forgive
me! You know I'd never hurt the twins and I didn't
know the Seconal would hurt them—I mean, I only
went to sleep when I was given them because I was
worried when we came here.'

Emily kissed a cheek and unwound Louisa's arms
gently. 'It's all right, love, the twins are fine, they'll
be home in a few days.'

Louisa gave a choking sob and peeped at the Professor from under her long, mascaraed lashes. He was
watching her with such interest that she left Emily
and went to him, putting a hand on his arm. 'Renier,
you don't hate me, do you? I know I've been a silly
girl, but I'm not clever like Emily.' She wiped a tear
away with a finger and smiled enchantingly at him.
'I hope you still want to take me out when I come to
London.'

'What man could resist such an invitation?' The
Professor's voice was all silk and Emily glanced at
him uncertainly. Then her face cleared, for he was
smiling at Louisa and patting the hand on his sleeve.
Perhaps he was getting serious about Louisa; it
seemed absurd, but such things did happen, Emily
told herself, and felt suddenly forlorn.

He went shortly after that, bidding her a casual good night and smiling again when he looked at Louisa. He didn't say when he was going to see her again, though, and Emily was treated to a nasty attack of tantrums when he'd gone.

She saw the twins every day, cutting short her meal times, visiting them on her way on and off duty, in the morning before she went on the ward, in the evening before she went home. They flourished, making the rapid recovery small children and babies so often do, and never once did she see the Professor. He was there in the hospital because one of her friends had taken a case to theatre and he had been operating, and she had seen his car parked in the forecourt. It was extraordinary that, disliking him as she did, she should miss him. Perhaps because the dislike was overshadowed by her gratitude. She was surprised that Louisa never spoke of him; she was very quiet, and doing far more housework than she usually did, so that Emily made no objection when she asked if she might go to the cinema with Tracey. Emily, watching her go, thought that she had dressed rather too well for such an ordinary outing, but Louisa was mad about clothes; perhaps she was trying out some new ideas

Louisa had told her not to stay up for her. 'I expect Tracey will ask me back for a cup of coffee afterwards,' she pointed out, 'and it's only just across the road.' So Emily went to bed with a book and thought about the twins and Mary and George and started making her plans once more. They were rather foolish ones, perhaps, but pleasant. It was surprising that in a daydream one was always so pretty, so attractive to men. She dropped off presently and didn't hear Louisa coming in much later. The Professor dropped her off at the door, turned the car silently and sped back to London.

He was at the hospital the next day, though, and Emily, trotting briskly to and fro about her many jobs, was brought to a halt by his cheerful 'Good morning, Staff Nurse.' And since he was standing in front of her, she had perforce to stay where she was.

She gave him a polite good morning in return and made to go on, but edging round his vast frame was undignified, so she said: 'The twins are coming home tomorrow morning.'

The Professor's eyes twinkled. 'Yes, I did know.'

She blushed. 'Oh, of course, you said they could, didn't you?'

'Louisa gave you my message?'

She gazed at him with astonished eyes. 'Message? No—how could she?'

'Easily enough.' He was staring at her hard. 'I took her out last night.' He frowned. 'She told me that you knew I was taking her to see that new film in the West End.' And then: 'No, don't trouble to think up an answer, I can see for myself that she didn't.' He frowned down at her. 'There was no intention of secrecy, Emily—she begged so prettily to be taken I hadn't the heart to refuse.' The frown disappeared and he smiled. 'I didn't want to refuse, anyway.'

Emily conjured up an answering smile. 'You make

me sound like an elderly aunt! Why should I object to Louisa going out?' Suddenly her calm deserted her. 'And she can make what friends she likes,' she said peevishly, 'I'm not in the least interested—not in any of them.' She gave a small snort. 'And now, if you don't mind, Professor, I have some treatment to do.'

She flounced away, her head very high, and he watched her go, a quite different kind of smile tugging at his mouth now.

She had it out with Louisa later; once the twins were back there would be no chance. And for once she took no notice of Louisa's tears and cries that no one understood her. 'You just listen to me,' said Emily briskly. 'I've never stopped you going out with anyone yet, you've gone to London when you've wanted to, you've had plenty of freedom, so there was no need for you to lie about going out with Professor Jurres-Romeijn. I can't think why you did.'

Louisa had stopped crying; it was a waste of time. 'I thought you might be jealous,' she said softly.

Emily stared at her across the kitchen. 'Me? Jealous? Whatever for?'

'You always say you don't like him, but I think you're stuck on him.'

'Louisa, you must be out of your mind—I don't even like him! He's been wonderful with the twins and he's pleasant to work for, but he's not my sort, now is he?'

'Not really. I mean, he's so handsome and elegant, and he must be rich, too. He likes pretty girls, he told me so.'

'All men like pretty girls,' said Emily dampen-
ingly.

'Would you be surprised if I hooked him?'

'Yes, I would,' said Emily thoughtfully. 'Oh,
Louisa, don't try—he's not for you.' The Professor
was the last man on earth to allow himself to be entangled with a girl like Louisa because he was quite
aware of what she was up to, to start with. Probably
he was amusing himself immensely, but he'd never
be caught. He would want to do his own catching.

Louisa laughed. 'You're so hopelessly behind the
times, darling.' She danced off upstairs and left Emily
to get the supper.

And the next morning, when the Professor drove
her and the twins back home, she could find no clue
as to his feelings towards Louisa. Indeed, it seemed
to her that he treated her rather as a good-natured
uncle might treat a favourite niece, but that might be
deliberate. The twins were put in their playpen, ad-
mired and played with, given a rusk to bite into and
allowed to crow and shout to their hearts' content
while the three grown-ups had coffee. Emily was almost silent, although she did her best to join in the
lighthearted conversation the other two were having.
It was a relief when the Professor got up to go, re-
minding her that he had another pharyngectomy in
two days' time. 'And I shall want you to special him,
Emily, just for the first two days—Mrs Crewe will do
the night duty.'

On this business-like note, he took himself off and
Louisa said snappily: 'He might at least have sug-

gested another evening out—perhaps he didn't like to in front of you.'

'Very likely,' said Emily.

The days fell into step once more. The pharyngectomy was a success, the twins throve and Louisa counted the days until she should be gone. It was getting towards Christmas, too, but she had shown no sign of wanting to come back to spend it with Emily and the twins. Emily prudently asked for a week's holiday, as no one would want to babysit over Christmas; Sister didn't like her not being on duty then, but when Emily explained she agreed at once, merely commenting that surely Louisa would want to be with her family at such a time. 'Well, if she changes her plans, I'll let you know, Sister,' Emily promised.

She stopped on the way home that evening and bought some paper chains and ornaments for the tree she intended to have; the twins would notice them and so, for that matter, would she. One made Christmas, even for two babies.

CHAPTER FIVE

LOUISA HARDLY MENTIONED the Professor during the next few days. She was sorting her clothes, preparatory to moving up to London, and Emily found her more than usually helpful around the house. 'She's only a child still,' thought Emily lovingly, watching Louisa's golden head bent over William and his tea. So it was a bit of a shock when the doorbell rang later that evening and the Professor loomed in the porch. 'Is Louisa ready?' he wanted to know.

Emily stood back so that he might pass her. 'Well, she's up in her room—I don't know...'

'Well, she doesn't have to dress up, does she?'

'I wouldn't know.' She tried to make her voice sound casual, but it came out quite wooden.

He sat down in one of the shabby armchairs by the fire. 'You didn't know.' It was a statement, not a question. 'Louisa asked me—she left a note at the hospital—if I would mind dropping her off at her flat as I went home as she had to meet someone there. She said that the someone would bring her back.'

Emily perched on the chair opposite his. 'Oh—no, I didn't know. I expect Louisa forgot to tell me.'

A statement which Louisa, her limpid gaze on the

Professor, bore out when she came downstairs. 'I'll be back quite early,' she told Emily. 'One of the girls' boyfriends is bringing me back. I borrowed your scarf—you don't mind, do you, darling?'

Emily saw them to the door and shut it quickly behind them, which was a pity, for she missed Louisa's: 'Such a pity we haven't had supper yet, and I'm starving.'

'I have a dinner engagement,' said the Professor as he opened the car door.

And Emily, left alone, washed up the supper dishes which Louisa seemed to have forgotten, then got out the paper chains and began to paste them together. She wasn't very good at it and after a little while she gave up and just sat, doing nothing at all.

Louisa was going in three days' time. Emily had arranged to have her two free days then so that she could get the twins organised. She still had to make final arrangements with Tracey's mother, who had said that for the time being at least she would look after the twins during the day while Emily was at the hospital. It was by no means an ideal arrangement and she wasn't quite sure how she was going to afford it, but it would have to do for a little while. There was a chance that one of her friends at the hospital would move in with her, sharing the expenses of the house and looking after the twins when she wasn't there, but that had to be worked out. It would mean getting their off-duty arranged so that they were never off at the same time, but at least it meant that for four days of the week when they each had their two days free the babies would be looked after.

Emily closed her eyes. Life, just lately, had become difficult and there seemed no point in it, somehow. The front door bell sounded softly and she got up to answer it. It was too soon for Louisa, but it must be someone who knew her and that the twins would be asleep.

Mary and George were standing side by side in the porch. Emily blinked, gave a little choking laugh and flung herself at Mary. 'Oh, my dears,' she gasped, 'if only you knew how wonderful it is to see you! Come in, do.'

They all went into the sitting room and stood looking at each other until Emily burst out: 'How did you get here? Oh, it's such a lovely surprise—couldn't you let me know? Are you back for good? Would you...'

George flung a brotherly arm round her shoulders. 'Hey, hang on—one question at a time! But first, how are the twins?'

'Upstairs and asleep and fighting fit.' She looked at Mary. 'Would you like to see them first, before we talk?'

Mary nodded, and they all crept upstairs to stand round each cot, staring down at first William and then Claire. When they were downstairs again Mary said: 'It must have been pretty grim for you, darling. Where's Louisa?'

Emily was draping coats and scarves over chairs.

'She's up in London for the evening—she's moving to a flat with three other girls, in three days' time.'

'And how were you going to manage?' George wanted to know.

'Well, I've almost fixed up with one of the nurses at the hospital to move in here with me and help me look after the twins, only it takes time to get the off-duty right, so a lady across the road had promised to have them while I worked, just for a few days—I've got a holiday over Christmas.'

Mary was looking round her. 'Darling, you've had a dreadful time! Of course there hasn't been enough money, has there? And this crummy little house…' She crossed the room and put her arms round Emily. 'You're a dear girl and we shan't forget it. We thought, when you wrote and said you'd moved here, that everything was all right—you never said…but then you never do. Well, that's over now. George is to work at the Birmingham Head Office and they've offered us a house in the country close by—a kind of reward for poor George getting caught up in all that mess. We'll tell you about that later. So you'll be free to go back to London, my dear.'

Emily smiled. A bit of her daydream was going to come true, anyway, and she could start making plans now in good earnest. 'We've not liked it much here, but it was healthier for the twins—there are some quite nice walks…'

'Have we had supper?' asked George.

'Oh, I'll put the kettle on at once,' cried Emily. 'I'm so sorry. Will tea do and—and toasted cheese?'

George got up. He was a nice-looking man and very calm and leisurely in his manner. 'Fish and chips,' he declared. 'Just tell me where to get them, and a bottle of something from the pub.' He was already at the door. 'Get out the knives and forks and a corkscrew, I'll be with you in no time.'

When he'd gone Emily asked: 'Was it awful, Mary? Not getting letters from you—only that funny one saying you were delayed...'

'Well, it wasn't very pleasant, but you know George, my dear, he never loses his head and he knew that if he just sat tight someone would give way somewhere. His Head Office smoothed things over finally and we got back this afternoon. We had to leave a good deal behind and there won't be anyone going in his place, but we're home again. I worried about the twins, of course, but I knew they'd be safe with you.'

Emily built up the fire and wondered if now was the time to tell Mary about the overdose, then decided that it wasn't. For one thing Louisa wasn't there and it savoured of sneaking behind her back, and for another, Mary and Louisa didn't get on very well. 'You'll spend the night, of course. There's no spare room, but I'll make up my bed and sleep with Louisa. I've a day off tomorrow, isn't it lucky?'

'Lovely—we've a lot to talk about and to do. I hope the twins remember us. And we won't stay here, darling, you've enough on your plate as it is. There's an hotel here, close by, isn't there? We'll sleep there and come round directly after breakfast, then I can bath and dress the babies and take them off your hands.'

George came back with the food then and a bottle of wine tucked under one arm, and no one talked seriously after that. They were still sitting round the table when Louisa came back. She must have seen that the lights were still on for they could hear her, while she was still in the hall, complaining that there was no need for Emily to wait up. 'I'm not a child,' she declared as she flung open the door, to stand with her pretty mouth open.

'Mary—George, what's happened? How did you get here? Oh, how lovely, now you can have the twins. It's been such hard work…'

Mary went over to give her a rather perfunctory kiss on the cheek. 'Who for?' she asked. 'I can guess who did the lion's share of the work. I hear you're taking yourself off to London.'

Louisa went to embrace George without answering at once. 'Well,' she declared after a minute, 'I have my future to think of, and when I'm a famous model you won't talk like that to me!'

Mary didn't answer her, and Emily began to talk about something else. Her two sisters had never got on very well and to quarrel on their first evening together for months would be too awful. She plunged into plans for the next few days and Louisa presently drifted away to her bed; no one was particularly interested in her flat, not just at that time, and she was really only happy when the attention was centred upon herself. The hazards Mary and George had passed through left her cold.

But not Emily. She listened, enthralled, while George, in his calm voice, recounted the happenings of the last few months. 'And glad we are to be home again,' he finished.

It was after midnight when they left, with the promise that they would be back early in the morning. Emily went to bed happier than she had been for months. The mantle of care she had been wearing had slipped from her shoulders and much though she loved the twins, she would be free to lead her own life once again. She slept like a log and was up early to see to the twins and eat her breakfast. Of Louisa there was no sign and when she went into her sister's room with a cup of tea, Louisa only grunted and turned over.

Mary was getting ready to bath the twins and Emily was washing up when the door bell was pealed with vigour. 'That'll be George,' said Mary, and went to the door.

She came back after a few moments, looking puzzled and amused. 'There's a man at the door,' she observed. 'He's enormous and very good-looking, and he says he's come to see the twins.'

Emily blushed and hated herself for it. 'He's a surgeon at the hospital—at least, he's a professor. He—he knows the twins…' She wiped a cup with care and went on: 'There's something I haven't told you, Mary, but I suppose Louisa should do it, but then you'll be angry…'

'If someone doesn't tell me something soon I shall be very angry! What's the mystery, love?' Mary gave Emily a quick glance and went back into the hall, to reappear a moment later with the Professor at her heels.

Emily introduced them, acknowledged the Professor's bland good morning with a brisk nod and waited for someone to say something.

'I feel in my bones that the twins have been ill,' said Mary, eyeing the Professor. 'Perhaps you'll tell me about it.'

'Certainly, Mrs Brooks, but I think, as Emily suggests, Louisa should be here too.'

Emily went to the bottom of the stairs and called her sister. It was a very small house, with thin walls, so Louisa must know by now who was downstairs. Apparently she did, for presently she joined them in the kitchen, wearing the new dressing gown and with her hair arranged just so. She had got her make-up on too, Emily noticed.

She smiled at them all, a wistful smile which her two sisters had seen on many occasions, and ignored now, and strangely enough, so did the Professor.

'Your sister must be told about the twins,' he observed in what Emily described to herself as a family doctor voice. 'Emily and I both think that you should do the telling.'

Louisa tossed her head. 'Of all the stupid fusses about nothing!' She pouted prettily at him. 'I thought we'd all forgotten about it—after all, they're none the worse.'

'They could have died,' stated the Professor flatly.

'And if someone doesn't tell me at once what all this is about, I shall scream,' said Mary. 'What did you do, Louisa?'

'There, you see?' cried Louisa, and went to stand by the Professor, as though he would protect her from heaven knew what. 'I'm accused of something no one knows anything about!'

She waited, but since no one spoke she went on sulkily. 'Oh, all right, I gave the twins something to make them sleep while I went to a dress show and it was too big a dose.' Her voice rose. 'Well, how was I to know? They'd been crying all the morning, and I was fed up.'

Mary had gone quite white. 'And what happened? No, not you, Louisa, I suppose you were safely out of the house.' She looked at Emily.

'I found them when I got home; I was just going to telephone the hospital when Professor Jurres-Romeijn came to see Louisa. He took them—us—to hospital in his car and they were perfectly all right after they'd been treated. They stayed in for three days and the Professor looked after them.' She added: 'He's very clever.'

The Professor's mouth twitched although he remained silent, leaning against the kitchen table with his hands in his pockets. It was left for Emily to say: 'You don't have to worry, Mary, they're absolutely fit again.'

Mary said slowly: 'Thanks to you and Professor...

I've forgotten your name—but no thanks to Louisa. I won't forgive you, Louisa.'

Louisa took refuge in another burst of tears and this time it was the Professor who said: 'If you want to go into town, I'll wait and give you a lift, Louisa, but be quick.'

She stopped crying at once, flashed a triumphant look at her sisters, and disappeared upstairs.

When her bedroom door closed Mary asked: 'You think I'm being hard on her, Professor?'

He shook his head. 'No, I think you have shown remarkable restraint. May I take a look at William and Claire now I'm here? And perhaps when your husband is free, we might all three have a chat.'

She gave him a thoughtful look. 'Yes, of course, I'd like that—so would George.' She smiled suddenly. 'I'll just pop upstairs and get them ready—will you come up or shall I bring them down?'

'I'll come up.'

When she had gone Emily said: 'Thank you, Professor,' and he nodded understanding. She was thanking him for offering Louisa a lift; her young sister's ego had been sadly mauled and he had given it a boost again. Perhaps he was annoyed at the way Mary had spoken to Louisa; if he had fallen in love with her, he wouldn't like her to be upset, even if Mary had been justified. Emily pondered that as she hung the tea towels to dry.

He didn't answer her, only nodded again carelessly and went upstairs to where Mary was waiting for him. He came down presently, remarking that the twins

were as fit as they could possibly be and that doubtless he would be seeing her before long, and refusing
the cup of coffee she offered to make, collected an
impatient Louisa and went.

'He's nice,' observed Mary, coming downstairs
again. 'Knows how to handle children, too. Do you
work for him all the time?'

'No—he has some cases on the ward, though, and
I specialled one of them for him.'

'So how did Louisa get to know him?'

Emily was standing by the stove, watching the kettle boil. 'She fell down in front of his car.'

'Don't tell me—she hurt her ankle, so he brought
her home…'

'How did you know?'

'Emily darling, it's one of the oldest tricks in the
world, though I don't fancy that he fell for it—probably it amused him at the time.'

'He fancies her.'

'Who wouldn't? She's very pretty.' Mary went to
stand by Emily and threw an arm round her shoulders.
'You've had a rotten time,' she said warmly, 'although you'll never admit it. Well, George is going
to pay you back every penny of what we must owe
you and if you feel like it we'd love you to come and
stay with us—unless you want to go back to London
at once.'

'Well, it's sweet of you both, but I'd love to get
back to London—I've two weeks' holiday due, so I
only need to stay here another two weeks. I ought to
be able to get a job by then and I can live in until I

have the time to find a bed-sitter or perhaps share a flat.'

'But that's almost Christmas!' Mary protested.

'It's a whole month till then. May I come and stay with you in the New Year, as soon as I can get a week's holiday? I shall miss the twins.'

She made the coffee and put the pot on the table with two mugs.

'You won't miss being at this hospital, then?'

'No, not really, I've made some friends, but I've not had much chance to go out.'

George came in then and presently the twins woke up from their morning nap and Emily, leaving the little family together, dressed carefully and took a bus to the hospital. Day off or no day off, she was going to hand in her notice.

It was easier than she had expected it to be. The Principal Nursing Officer was understanding when it had all been explained to her; she would be able to leave in just two weeks' time. Emily went back through the wide, modern corridors to the entrance, telling herself that she should feel on top of her world, and yet somehow she didn't want to go. She couldn't think why. At least not until she came out into the entrance hall and saw the Professor standing there, talking to Mr Spencer. He was standing half turned away from her, his grey head bent thoughtfully as he listened to his companion, and at the sight of him, large and elegant and remote, she knew why she didn't want to go away. She wouldn't see him any more if she did, not that she had ever seen a great deal of him, but even a glimpse each day would be better than never... And how like me, thought Emily on a soundless sigh, to fall in love with someone I'm never going to see again, and who's never taken any notice of me at all...

The Professor turned his head and looked at her. There was no expression on his face, but he said something to Mr Spencer and walked across the entrance hall to her. 'You look excited, has someone just offered you a Sister's post or have you come up on the pools? Is it not your day off?'

She hadn't told him that, but perhaps Louisa had. She said, carefully not meeting his eye: 'Neither. I've just given in my notice.'

She didn't see the sudden lift of his eyebrows and his voice was as casual as before. 'Going back to London now that your sister is back?'

'Yes.' For the life of her she couldn't think of anything more to say.

'It's more than that,' he said slowly. 'You look as though someone had lighted a torch inside you.'

Her eyes flew to his face and her own reddened. 'No,' she managed, and meant 'Yes—you.'

'Going home?' he wanted to know. 'I'll drop you off.'

'Oh—well that's very kind of you, but I...'

He interrupted her. 'Emily, what have I done?'

'Done? Nothing, it's just that it's good for me to walk.'

He glanced out of the glass doors. 'In blinding rain and a howling gale? How did you come?'

'On the bus.'

He turned her round and fell into step beside her. 'I should like to meet your sister's husband,' he observed as he opened the Jag's door and popped her in.

So there was nothing to do for it but invite him in when they reached the house, to find George and Mary and the twins all together in the sitting room. Mary smiled at them as they went in. 'There you are—did you give in your notice, darling? And when can you leave? Have you telephoned for an interview at your old hospital?' She got up. 'Professor Jurres-Romeijn, do sit down—this is George, my husband. Darling, the Professor saved the twins' lives.'

'I think you will have to include a number of other people in that statement.' The Professor smiled back at her and shook George's hand and Mary repeated:

'Well, darling, you haven't answered any of my questions.'

Emily hadn't wanted to, not in front of the Professor, but there was no way out. 'Yes—and I can leave in two weeks, because of my holidays, you know, and I haven't telephoned yet. I haven't had time…'

She cast off her hat and coat, said: 'I'll make some more coffee,' and went away to the kitchen. It was ridiculous; this might be her last chance of seeing the Professor outside the hospital and here she was running away. She filled the kettle and thumped it down on the stove and lighted the gas, feeling bad temper and frustration and misery inexorably mixed together inside her.

The Professor had Claire on his knee when she returned to the sitting room, while William perched on his father's lap. Mary was sitting back, doing nothing and looking pleased with herself. 'When is Louisa coming back?' she asked idly. 'Is she out for lunch?'

The Professor's quiet: 'Yes, she's having it with me,' sent Emily's heart, already in the depths, plunging just as far as it would go. But she schooled her face to polite interest, no more, as she handed round the coffee. 'It'll be very quiet here without her,' she observed to the room in general.

Mary shot her a glance. 'You'll want all your time to pack up and settle the house. Will you put the furniture in store? George will see to that for you.'

'Well, yes—I'd better, until I find somewhere to live.'

'And get a job?' questioned the Professor softly.

'Yes.'

The Professor fixed her with a compelling eye. 'By some extraordinary coincidence I had a letter from Doctor Wright this morning; he has already accepted an invitation for him and Mrs Wright to spend Christmas with me at my home in Holland and he asked me if there was any chance of you being free to accompany him. Mrs Wright is nervous of him travelling…do you by any chance drive?'

Emily's voice came out in a surprised squeak. 'Yes, I do.'

'Splendid—Mrs Wright doesn't like the idea of driving so far and Doctor Wright isn't quite up to a long journey, although he potters locally, I believe.'

He smiled persuasively. 'A couple of weeks of your time, Emily? A change would do them both good—they've been through a good deal.'

'I haven't driven a car for ages—and I don't know Holland.'

'I could arrange for someone to take you out on one or two runs easily enough, and Holland is a good deal easier than England—no hills, wide roads, short distances between towns.'

Emily didn't reply. It seemed like a miracle that she would actually be with the Professor at his home. Things didn't happen like that in real life; there must be a snag. Perhaps she would be expected to stay at some nearby hotel...

'I should be delighted to have you as my guest,' said the Professor with uncanny insight.

'Well...' She looked at Mary and found her smiling and nodding and George, as usual, looked calmly complacent; nothing ever disturbed George.

'You go, darling,' urged Mary, 'it'll make a nice change from the twins and give you time to decide about the next job.' She added cunningly: 'George could get on to finding you a flat while you're away.'

'But I haven't even written to the hospital yet...'

'Do it today, then, and if there isn't a vacancy you can try somewhere else.'

'Of course, if you don't care to do it,' murmured the Professor, 'I'll let Doctor Wright know. Unfortunately I shan't be able to come over and fetch them.' The Professor's voice, quiet and deep and unhurried, managed to sound accusing, nonetheless.

There was a silence until he spoke again: 'Perhaps you have a reason for refusing?'

Of course she had a reason, thought Emily crossly, and a fine thing it would be if she bleated out that she wanted to go, but having to see someone one loved each and every day for a fortnight was rather more than one could hope to stomach.

'Emily, you're being a twit,' said Mary roundly. 'You know you want to go—such a nice change from all those hospital wards and the babies.'

'Very well,' said Emily, and watched the Professor's face relax. 'You'll be late for lunch,' she reminded him, 'and Louisa hates being kept waiting.'

For a fleeting moment he looked frighteningly ferocious. 'I seldom forget dates with pretty girls,' he told her silkily, and at the door:

'I'll let you know details very shortly.'

Mary, coming back from showing him out, glanced at Emily quickly. 'One would imagine, seeing you two together, that you don't like each other; that's absurd, of course.'

'Why is it absurd?' Emily was busily collecting coffee cups and loading them on to a tray. But Mary didn't answer.

The following day George and Mary and the twins went; Emily saw them off with mixed feelings; she was going to miss the twins dreadfully but it would be wonderful to be on her own. They had made her promise to go and stay with them just as soon as she could, and George had given her a nice fat cheque, waving aside her protests with an airy: 'You've

earned it, old girl; it was the one thing that made life
bearable, you know; we didn't have to worry about
them because we knew you were looking after them.'
He gave her a hefty pat on the shoulder. 'Now go and
rig yourself out and have a splendid Christmas. And
remember you're coming to us just as soon as you
can. I'll look out for a flat for you—there's someone
I know in town who'll help there. Give me enough
notice and I'll get your furniture out of storage before
you get back.'

The house seemed quiet and cold when they'd
gone. Louisa had gone up to London again, taking
some of her things with her; tomorrow she would be
gone too. Emily, who was on duty at two o'clock,
made herself a sketchy lunch and went to fetch her
bike. She would have liked to have made arrangements to get the furniture collected and stored, but
until she heard from the Professor, there was nothing
she could do about that. She'd start packing up tomorrow, she decided as she climbed the staircase, and
then didn't give it another thought; Sister was going
off duty for the rest of the day and there was the
report to listen to and then a surprising message from
the Office to say that she was to report for night duty
on the following day. That meant that she would have
to go on duty at eight o'clock in the morning and
work until after lunch and then go on duty in the
evening. Half way through the afternoon it struck her
that she wasn't likely to see the Professor; he did his
rounds during the day. She caught her breath at the
thought of not seeing him, she had been counting on

that even though she knew it was pointless and hopeless. It was going to be bad enough actually being in
his house and seeing him every day for a fortnight—
it would be heaven too.

There was no sign of him during the afternoon and
his car wasn't in the forecourt when she went off duty
at eight o'clock that evening.

She went home feeling worried. Supposing he had
changed his mind and didn't want her to go to Holland after all? She was still worrying as she went into
the house, to find Louisa there, drying her hair in front
of the fire.

'Oh, hullo, you're back,' said Emily unnecessarily.
'Mary and George and the twins went this morning
just after you'd gone. It's been funny without them.'

Louisa mumbled something and Emily asked, turning the knife in the wound: 'Did you have a nice
lunch yesterday?'

'Lunch? Oh, yes—Renier's a smasher when it
comes to going out. Jack brought me back this afternoon…'

'Do I know him?' asked Emily cautiously, and set
about frying eggs and bacon. She was famished and
there was no sign of any supper.

'No—he's Ann's brother. Ann's one of the girls at
the flat. He's absolutely fab!'

'I thought you liked older men?'

Louisa peered at her through her wet hair. 'Oh,
they're all right for a free meal, but Jack's more fun—
not that you'd know.'

Emily cracked an egg into the pan. 'I thought you were a bit gone on Professor Jurres-Romeijn.'

'Well, he's rather gorgeous and he's rich, but I'm never quite sure what he's thinking.' She went back to towelling her hair. 'I haven't had supper yet, will you do me an egg? I thought I'd go in the morning. Jack's coming for me.'

'All right, love. I'll be at the hospital, I'm to go on night duty tomorrow.'

'Again? Lord, what a life you do lead! Are you going to stay here or go to Mary's?'

Emily thought it prudent not to mention her trip to Holland; after all, she hadn't heard any more about it. 'I'm going to store the furniture and get a job in London—I think my old hospital might give me a post again.'

Louisa wasn't very interested. She began to talk about the model school and the fun she was going to have. 'And heaven knows I deserve it,' she declared, 'life's been so dull here. I can't wait to get to London. We must meet sometimes when you've found yourself somewhere to live. I won't ask you to the flat, I don't think you'd like the girls much—I mean, they're younger than you and two of them are models already.' She got up and went to look at herself in the mirror over the fireplace. 'I haven't paid you any housekeeping for last month, have I? I can't spare it, Emily, I simply had to have some shoes I saw— they're black patent and I really need them.'

Emily fished around in her handbag. 'That reminds me, here's something towards them.' Two five-pound notes, all she had until she went to the bank and cashed George's cheque. Louisa took them with a careless: 'Oh, thanks—I can always use bread.' She turned round from her inspection. 'Well, I'm off to bed, you've no idea how tired I am.'

And Emily, on her busy feet since early afternoon, had a very good idea. She was tired herself, but the supper things had to be cleared away and breakfast put ready. 'See you in the morning before I go?' she asked.

'For heaven's sake, don't wake me at that ghastly hour! Let's say 'bye now.'

Emily let herself out of the house in the early morning into a dark cold street. She had half hoped that Louisa might have got up to see her again, but there had been no sign. There was no sign of the Professor either, so she went home again at two o'clock wondering what was best to do. But there was a good deal to do and she had the rest of the day in which to do it. She cleared Louisa's room, cleaned the house, had a meal and a bath and went back to the hospital. The evening was even worse than the morning had been. She thought longingly of her bed and hoped the night would be a quiet one.

As it happened it wasn't too bad; there had been no operation cases that day and none of the patients were dangerously ill. All the same, she was kept occupied, answering bells, re-packing dressings, giving drinks and bedpans, prepping two cases for theatre in the morning. She was glad that she had a good junior nurse on with her, inexperienced but sensible; it was her first night too, but she was willing and anxious to do the right thing, and she had a sense of humour, something one needed with several elderly ladies all convinced that they were dying and demanding attention.

If every night is going to be like that one, thought Emily, dragging tired feet down the staircase, it won't be too bad. She put a hand up to her cap and tweaked it straight. She had lost a pin but she couldn't be bothered to do anything about it now—something she regretted as she reached the ground floor and found the Professor at the bottom watching her.

'You look the worse for wear,' he told her briskly, and although her heart had taken a great happy leap at the sight of him, she said quite crossly: 'Well, I've been on duty all night and I'm very tired.'

'And cross.'

'And cross.' She glowered at him because he looked so elegant and well-rested and she, who would have given the world to have impressed him, looked like something the cat had brought in.

'I've a letter for you from Doctor Wright, you can read it later. You leave on the twelfth of December, don't you?' And when she nodded: 'Good. You're to go to Doctor Wright's home on the morning of the fifteenth and drive them over to Holland. When are your nights off?'

Emily made her tired mind work. 'Three nights from tonight.'

'There'll be a man with a car from Dent's Garage outside your house at three o'clock in the afternoon on your first free day and on the two succeeding days. Is that all right?'

She gave him a bewildered look and he said patiently: 'You're to drive around a bit and get used to it again. Now go home to bed, you're not fit for anything else.'

She turned away, wanting to burst into tears for no other reason than that she looked a mess and he had no patience with her. She hadn't taken two steps before he'd caught her by the arm and turned her round to face him.

'You poor small creature,' he said gently, 'I've no right to talk to you like that—I'm sorry. Tell me, where will you go when you leave here?'

She blinked. 'I don't know. I hadn't thought about it because I didn't know, did I?' She wasn't accusing him, only stating a fact.

'Louisa?'

'No—no, there wouldn't be room, besides…' She stopped and finished: 'She'll be so busy. I'll find an hotel.'

'I've friends living close to me; they'll be glad to put you up. I'll take you up to town when you leave.'

'Oh, but I couldn't…'

'Don't be a silly goose. Now go home to bed.'

Emily went, already half asleep and a bit muddled in the head as a consequence but content because she was going to Holland. That was a fact, and what was more, the Professor seemed to have arranged things very nicely for her. She wondered what his friends would be like, and was she supposed to pay for bed and breakfast? She was pondering this when she fell asleep.

CHAPTER SIX

THE DAYS AND NIGHTS flew by and it was lucky that the nights weren't too bad, for there was a good deal to do before she went to bed each morning. She had arranged for a warehouse to store the furniture and they were to come for it on the day before she was due to leave and although that was still ten days away, there was a good deal of packing up to be done. And Mary telephoned most days to give her news of the twins and recount how well they were settling in. There had been a phone call from Louisa, too, an excited hasty conversation in which Emily couldn't get a word in edgeways. Life was fun, said Louisa, and she loved the model school although it was hard work and some of the girls were incredibly mean to each other. 'Not that I care,' said Louisa airily, 'it's a competitive profession. Oh, Emily, you can't think what you've missed, wasting your time in a hospital.'

Emily forbore from the obvious comment that she was hardly model material. 'I'm quite happy,' she pointed out. 'Shall I see you some time?'

But Louisa was vague about that. Not before Christmas, and certainly not at Christmas; she had so many parties lined up...

'In the New Year, then, love,' said Emily. 'I'll let you know my address when I've got one.'

Afterwards she remembered that Louisa hadn't asked her how she was managing or how she was going to move house or whether she had a job to go to. 'Oh, well, as long as she's happy,' said Emily to the room at large.

She saw nothing of the Professor, although she went a little early each evening and lingered in the morning in the hope of meeting him. He had disappeared into thin air, it seemed, and she started her nights off feeling let down. The house looked strangely empty when she reached it, most of the books and ornaments had been packed now and she had polished the furniture in the sitting room and stacked it neatly and shut the door on it, which left the kitchen to live in. She cooked herself some breakfast, then remembered that she was to take a car out that afternoon, so that she gobbled the meal, cleared away like lightning, had a bath and went to bed with the alarm clock set for midday. It meant only three hours' sleep, but she would be able to go to bed and sleep the clock round that evening.

She was dressed and ready when the car arrived, driven by a sober-looking middle-aged man who greeted her civilly enough, opened the door for her and moved into the other seat. The car was a rather elderly Rover and before she could say anything the man said: 'This is the model you will be driving, miss.' He sat back, his arms folded across his chest, and she realised that she was to take over without any more ado. She was nervous, scared stiff in fact, but after all, she had got her driving licence. She started the engine and quaking inwardly set the car going. For the first few hundred yards she was in a panic that she would do something stupid, but then quite suddenly she felt all right; there wasn't too much traffic around and her feet and hands seemed to be doing all the right things. 'Where to?' she asked.

'Turn left at the next crossroads, miss, and go through Brookmans Park and up as far as Hatfield, then go round the town and across to St Albans and back down the A6.'

She found herself enjoying it presently and although she made one or two mistakes, they were small ones, and since her companion merely grunted gently she concluded that she wasn't doing so badly. She drew up finally with real reluctance before her little house and was elated when her companion pronounced that she was quite competent to drive the car anywhere she might want to go. 'I'll be here tomorrow, same time,' he warned her. 'We'll spend an hour on the motorway and then find a quiet road so I can see you reverse and turn.'

And that went off successfully too. Emily returned to night duty feeling rather pleased with herself; she was to have one more outing, driving her taciturn companion as far as London's heart and back home again. The other day she was going to spend shopping; she had George's cheque and she hadn't had any new clothes for a long time.

She had had a letter from Doctor Wright, too, a

friendly missive saying how glad he and his wife were that she would accompany them to Holland, 'Because we wouldn't have gone on our own,' he had finished.

She had tried to come to terms with herself over the Professor too. She would have to see a good deal of him, she supposed, and although that would be a delight for her, she would have to be careful not to let him see that. She thought about him a great deal although she didn't see him, and carefully veiled enquiries as to his whereabouts drew blanks. It wasn't until her next nights off that she asked Mr Bennett from the garage if she should pay him for the use of the car and got more news of the Professor than she had expected.

'Not a farthing, miss—Professor Jurres-Romeijn settled the bill before he went. Back in Holland he is now and not expecting to come back for a few days. One of his partners is ill, so he had to go and take over for a bit. A very nice gentleman, if I might say so—not a bit like some foreigners.'

Emily did her last four nights duty in something of a panic. If the Professor had returned to his home for a sudden emergency, might he not quite easily forget that he had said that he would drive her up to town? Supposing he didn't come? Should she ring Doctor Wright, or just turn up at his house on the day that had been arranged? She would have to find a small hotel for a couple of nights. Instead of spending a glorious day shopping she should have been better employed looking for a modest bed and breakfast somewhere. Not that she regretted her day at the shops; she had had a wonderful time with just for once enough money to buy what she wanted; a tweed coat in a flattering shade of green, a jersey dress to wear with it, a well cut skirt and several sweaters and blouses, a velvet skirt from Marks and Spencer teamed with a beautifully cut top she had seen in Liberty's. She bought another blouse or two to wear with it because she couldn't afford several evening dresses—besides, she might not need them. And she spent more than she had intended on shoes. She hadn't had such lovely shoes for years…and boots, knee-high and very soft leather. There was enough for gloves and a handbag and a little felt pillbox hat before common sense told her to call a halt. On her last day, before she went on duty for the last time, she packed her case, saw the furniture out of the house and went to work. There had been no message from the Professor and by now she had stopped worrying; she would go to town and make her own arrangements until she was due to go to Doctor Wright's. Several of her friends had given her the names of small hotels where she would be able to get a room and she could fill in her days easily enough. Shops and museums, she told herself vaguely.

She had breakfast at the hospital in the morning, said goodbye to her friends and went home for the last time to the empty little house. It was a cold morning and the man was coming to cut off the gas presently. She made a cup of tea and had a bath and dressed in the new clothes, wasting a lot of time over her face and hair before going downstairs with her case. The man from the gas had been, so had someone from the Electricity Department. She locked up carefully, inspected each empty room in turn and picked up her case. She would catch a bus from the end of the street and go to the Underground; it was still quite early and she had all day to look for an hotel. She opened her bag to make sure that the list she had made out was there, just as the door bell rang.

She rushed to the door unaware of the delight showing so plainly on her face as she opened it to find the Professor, huge in his car coat, standing on the step. 'Oh, you came,' she exclaimed stupidly, and then remembered to take the smile off her face and just look polite. On no account must he ever even guess at her feelings, and he was looking at her now with lifted brows and a faint smile which she couldn't understand at all. She added, still very polite: 'I'm just ready.'

He went past her into the narrow hall. 'I imagine that you're glad to leave.'

'Yes, I am.' She saw his glance taking in the emptiness and the shabby walls. 'They took the furniture yesterday.'

'You sold it?'

She felt shocked. 'Oh, no—it's all I have. I'll furnish a flat or a bedsitter when I get one.'

He didn't answer and she hadn't expected him to; it could hardly interest him—where she was going to live next.

'You've not been to bed? You were on duty last night?'

She nodded.

'You shall go to bed as soon as we reach my friends. Come along, then, if you're quite ready.' He took her case and put it in the boot and opened the car door for her after she had banged the door after her. The key she had already returned to Tracey's mother, who was going to let the house agents have it later.

She was very tired and the comfort of the car lulled her into a half-waking state which left her head quite empty of ideas for a light conversation. But apparently that didn't matter much; the Professor seemed little inclined to talk and the journey was a short one. Pulling herself together as they slid into the West End traffic, Emily was uneasy to see where they were. This was a part of London she hadn't seen much of; tall Regency houses in quiet squares with small gardens in their centres, but perhaps they were taking a short cut.

They weren't. The Professor drew up before such a house in the centre of a terrace, got out, opened her door and helped her out too and crossed the pavement to ring a large brass bell beside a soberly painted front door. It was opened by a hall porter, who at the Professor's bidding collected her case and led the way to the back of a well appointed hall to the lift.

'I don't like lifts,' muttered Emily, and hung back a little.

Unlike anyone else, who would certainly have asked her why not, the Professor merely signed to the porter to use the lift for himself, and guided her to the stairs.

'It's the top floor,' he informed her.

'Oh—well, you need not have walked up—it's only me being silly. I was stuck in a hospital lift once, I had an unconscious patient on a drip with me, and the drip went wrong. The porter couldn't help and it seemed all day before we got out...'

'An unpleasant experience. And don't give a thought to me; I may be over my first youth, but I can still climb stairs.'

She blushed and wishing to make some amusing reply, found her head empty again.

The landing on the top floor was as richly carpeted as the stairs and the front door of the flat was a handsome one. It opened as they reached it and a small dark girl and a rather stocky man a good deal older than she both spoke at once. 'Come in, Renier—and this is Emily...'

She was shaken by the hand and led inside and the Professor disappeared with her case down a long passage. 'A drink,' cried the dark girl. 'Renier hasn't had a chance to introduce us—I'm Dolly and this is Peter—we've known him for ever, you know. Sit down, Renier said you'd be tired, so you shall go to bed presently...it's lovely having you. Peter, take Emily's coat.' She turned round as the Professor came into the room. 'We're going to have a glass of Madeira and an early lunch, then Emily can take a nap.'

'Then for heaven's sake give her a biscuit with it,

I don't expect she had much breakfast. Did you, Emily?'

They all looked at her, Peter and Dolly with a warm sympathy, the Professor with a gentle mockery. She told them no, she hadn't really, and obediently ate the biscuits offered with her drink. She was very afraid that she would go to sleep in the warm, charmingly furnished room; her companions' voices came and went in her sleepy ears until the Professor's remark that he must be off brought her wide awake. 'I've a couple of cases,' he explained, 'but I'll be clear this evening. Why not dine with me?' His eyes flickered over Emily's dress. 'Pot luck, and don't change,' he added.

'Lovely.' It was Dolly who answered for them all. 'We never see enough of you.' She leaned up and kissed his cheek and Peter said:

'So long, lad,' which struck Emily as quite inappropriate—the Professor didn't look a bit like a lad.

He was looking at her poker faced now. 'Since we're all saying goodbye so nicely…' he said, and crossed the room, plucked her out of her chair, kissed her soundly, set her down again and went away.

The other two looked so unsurprised that Emily came to the conclusion that he was in the habit of kissing girls goodbye, only of course, not in hospital. She tried to look as though she was unsurprised too and she must have succeeded quite well, for Dolly started to talk about something or other which didn't need an answer and presently an elderly woman came to the door and told them that lunch was ready.

The food was delicious and Emily was hungry, but a full stomach on top of being up all night made her so very sleepy that she almost dozed off over coffee.

'Bed for you,' said Dolly briskly. 'I'll call you at teatime—you just get into your bed and sleep until then.'

Which Emily did, barely noticing the pretty bedroom, but the bed was sheer heaven, warm and soft and smelling faintly of lavender. She was asleep within seconds.

She was wakened four hours later by Dolly's cheerful voice and the pleasant clatter of a tea tray. 'We let you sleep,' she said comfortably. 'And now eat everything up before you dress—there's a shower room through that door, by the way; you've heaps of time before we go to Renier's.'

Emily sat up and eyed the buttered crumpets hungrily. 'I ought not to—I'm too fat...'

'Rubbish, you're just right, men hate skinny girls.'

Emily drank some tea. 'Does he live far away?'

'Renier?' Dolly smiled. 'On the next floor, ducky, though he's only there when he's in England—his home is in Holland.'

Emily licked a buttery finger. 'Oh, well—I did know that he lived there, but you see we're—we're not...that's to say I don't know him well, I've only worked on a case for him.'

Dolly strolled over to the window and stood looking out into the wintry evening. 'You'll see quite a lot of him while you're in Holland, won't you?'

'Yes,' agreed Emily seriously, 'but it's not like being friends, is it? He's a professor and all that...' She felt she wasn't explaining very well, but Dolly seemed to understand.

'He's like anyone else only nicer. Most girls can't wait to get at him,' she said lightly.

'Oh, I'm sure of that, for he's very nice-looking, only sometimes he looks as though he's laughing at one. I—I think I should tell you that he thinks I'm a prim miss and p-plump, so you can see we're not friends; I'm going to Holland because Doctor Wright needs someone to drive the car and keep an eye on him.'

'You don't like Renier?' Dolly sounded sympathetic.

Emily choked on a small sugared cake. 'He's a very good surgeon,' she said, though it cost her a lot not to say more, and Dolly, who still had her back to her, frowned a little.

'Well, let's hope you get to know him better. He told us all about the twins, you know.'

'Did he? And about Louisa, too, I expect? My young sister—she's very pretty—he took her out; she's going to be a model.'

Dolly came back and sat down on the side of the bed. 'Is she? I'd rather be you, any day.'

By the time it was ready to go to the Professor's flat, Emily felt wide awake. She had done her face and hair with care and the jersey dress looked quite nice; it was a relief to see that Dolly was wearing the same dress she had had on all day. They walked down the stairs and Peter rang the bell. The door was

opened by an elderly man with a stern face who
wished them good evening and begged them to enter
in a dampening sort of voice instantly nullified by the
Professor's shout from an open door at the end of the
hall. He appeared a moment later and ushered them
into a large room very comfortably furnished with a
great many big armchairs, a handsome bow-fronted
cabinet, rows of bookshelves spilling books all nicely
highlighted by the blazing fire in the stone hearth, and
presently when they were all sitting round it, he en-
quired of Emily if she had slept and soon they were
all engrossed in the map he had produced for her to
see. 'I've marked the route for you,' he explained,
'and the Wrights know the way, but you'll have to be
careful in Rotterdam and again when you get to
Utrecht.' He looked across at Peter. 'Remember when
you two went on a grand tour of the Netherlands because you took the wrong turning? Not that Emily's
likely to do that, she's too sensible.' He took her glass
and refilled it, and she began to feel quite happy and
not scared stiff as she had expected. How silly to love
someone you don't know anything about, she thought,
watching him pouring drinks for the other two; if only
he'd laugh and joke with me like he did with Louisa.

But that, it seemed, was wishful thinking. Presently
they went in to dinner, announced by the severe man,
who surprisingly allowed himself to smile when
Dolly asked how his wife did.

'Thank you, madam, she's very well indeed; she
hopes you will enjoy the brown bread ice cream, she
remembered that you have a partiality for it.'

'Mrs Willy remembers everything,' observed their host. 'Willy, will you fetch up a bottle of champagne? It's the only thing to drink on an occasion—and this is one.'

Dolly and Peter smiled as though they understood him, but Emily, who didn't, looked puzzled. No one explained what the occasion was, though, and she forgot all about it in the pleasure of eating Mrs Willy's scallops. They had rib of beef next which the Professor carved with a neatness only to be expected of him, and then, as a concession to the ladies, lemon sorbet, served in a frozen lemon cup and accompanied by little silver dishes piled high with whipped cream.

'Any time you don't want the Willy's,' declared Dolly, 'I'll have them off you.'

'One of my oldest friends,' declared the Professor to Willy, 'and she wants to snatch my cook!'

Peter chuckled: 'Well, you could easily bring that Bep from Holland whenever you come.'

'Then who would look after this place while I'm away?' He glanced at Emily, who hadn't much to say for herself. 'Shall we go into the sitting room for coffee? What are you all doing tomorrow?' He looked at her as he spoke so that she felt bound to make some sort of a reply.

She improvised hastily. 'Oh, I wanted to go along to Fenwick's and there's an exhibition at the National Gallery I wanted to see.'

'I don't know about Fenwick's,' he told her, 'but I should like to see the exhibition. I'm free tomorrow; I'll fetch you after breakfast.'

She gazed at him with a transparent horror which set the corners of his fine mouth quivering. 'It's very kind of you, Professor, but I couldn't think of taking up your time...'

He waved away her excuses. 'I don't leave for Holland until the evening; I shall be delighted.'

'You go,' encouraged Dolly kindly. 'Personally I can only bear exhibitions if Peter's with me.'

Emily had to say yes after that, and presently they said goodnight and she accompanied her kind new friends back to their flat and after half an hour's desultory talk, went to bed. She had meant to lie in bed and worry about spending the morning with the Professor, but she went to sleep at once.

As she got into his car the next morning, she wondered where on earth he was going to park. It wasn't until he was in Brook Street preparatory to turning into New Bond Street that she mumbled: 'I don't really want to go to Fenwick's—it was all I could think of...'

The Professor gave a great rumble of laughter. 'I wondered if you meant it. And what about the exhibition? Did you think that up on the spur of the moment, too?'

'There isn't. Let's go to the Tower and look at the Crown Jewels, instead.'

They spent a delightful morning. Emily forgot about being shy, she forgot too that her companion was probably just being kind and filling in an odd hour or so of his free time. She gazed with awe at the Regalia, stared at the Yeoman Warders, peered

into dungeons and shuddered over the block, ably sec-
onded by her companion, who seemed to be enjoying
himself as much as she was. She was surprised when
he reminded her that it was almost one o'clock and
what about lunch.

'I'd forgotten—oh, dear, and I didn't ask Dolly
what time she wanted me back.'

'I told her you'd be lunching with me.'

They drove back the way they had come while she
wondered where they would go. When he stopped
outside the Connaught Hotel's dignified entrance, she
exclaimed: 'Not here? I'm not in the right clothes...'

He turned to look her slowly over. 'The clothes
seem just right to me, Emily.' He smiled at her and
her heart, which she had thought she had well guarded
against foolish ideas, flipped over and left her without
breath. 'Besides, I can park the car here...'

A reasoning which was undeniable.

And once inside she forgot about her clothes and
her probably shiny nose; it was grand and elegant, but
the Restaurant Manager who showed them to a table
was attentive and knew the Professor well enough to
address him by name. Emily sipped a glass of sherry
and worked her way through a menu which left nothing to be desired. She took so long that her companion suggested in an amused voice: 'How about
smoked salmon to start with, duckling to follow and
a bottle of claret to go with it?'

He was an easy person to be with, she had discovered that. Right at the back of her head was the un-
welcome memory of his conversation with Mr Spen-

cer, but she slammed a lid on it for the moment. Under his gentle conversation she blossomed, and by the time they had reached the sherry trifle she had forgotten everything but the delight of the moment.

It was while they were drinking their coffee that he suggested that she might like to accompany him to Liberty's and help him choose a gift for his grandmother. 'Like you, I have no parents, Emily—a brother and a sister and my grandmother, a very tart old lady whom we all adore.'

'But I don't know her tastes,' began Emily, her eyes shining at the idea of another hour or two in his company.

'I thought if we walked round we might see something.'

They decided on a frivolous chintz-covered cushion, beribboned and lace-edged, smelling delightfully of the lavender and rose leaves with which it was stuffed and by then, having wasted a great deal of time in almost every department, it was teatime. The Professor took her to the Ritz this time, where they ate cucumber sandwiches, buttery muffins and tiny, sugary cakes.

'When do you have to go?' asked Emily as she poured second cups.

'Oh, about half past six—seven o'clock.'

'But it's five o'clock now—you'll never be ready.'

'Willy will have everything waiting for me; I only have to throw my case into the boot. I've enjoyed my day, Emily.'

She looked at him across the table and just as

though he were speaking out loud she heard his voice
telling Mr Spencer: 'Am I to be fobbed off with that
prim miss…?' She went red and then a little pale,
unable to take her eyes from his thoughtful stare. 'I've
enjoyed it too,' she told him in a quiet voice devoid
of expression, and then, terrified that he would think
her even more prim than he supposed, plunged into
small talk. It lasted her until they reached his flat
again and she fell thankfully silent as they went upstairs together. In a minute they would say goodbye,
although she reminded herself she would be seeing
him again in a few days, but it might not be the same;
he would be in his home with guests and his family
around him and probably they wouldn't be alone together at all. She stopped outside his door and held
out a hand. 'Thank you for my day, Professor.'

He took the hand and kept a tight hold of it. 'I'm
hoping to pluck up sufficient courage to ask you to
call me Renier,' he told her, half laughing. 'Each time
you address me as Professor I age a year, but I do
have enough courage for this.' He bent and kissed her
on her surprised mouth and then straightened up to
ring the bell. Dolly came to the door, said hullo to
Emily, offered a cheek for his goodbye kiss, wished
him a pleasant journey and ushered Emily inside. It
was all done so quickly that Emily had no time to say
anything. Thinking about it afterwards, she concluded
that she had had nothing to say anyway. Social kissing was quite the done thing, she was aware of that,
but she found it hard to forget that the Professor was
someone she worked for and someone, moreover,

who thought nothing of going to a place like the Ritz
for his tea. What he must have thought of that
wretched little house she shuddered to think.

It seemed very lonely without him, although Dolly
and Peter were kindness itself, taking her out on the
remaining two days, and she and Dolly spent the last
morning shopping while Peter was at his office. Emily
didn't buy anything; she still had some money left
over from her salary and George's cheque, but she
wasn't sure if she would need to spend it in Holland.
But Dolly made up for them both, trying on dresses
for the parties they were bound to attend at Christmas.
They arrived back happily tired and after dinner Emily telephoned Louisa to say goodbye.

Louisa wasn't in, the girl who answered the telephone told her; she was spending the evening at the
theatre with friends, so Emily could do no more than
leave a message and hope that she would get it. Before she went to bed that night she wrote to Louisa,
to tell her that she would let her have her address
once she was in Holland. She wrote to Mary too,
saying the same thing and apologising for being so
foolish as not to have found out just exactly where
she was going. Being in love was making her addle-
pated!

Peter insisted on driving her to Doctor Wright's
house in the morning and when she protested, told
her that Renier had asked him to do so: 'Though I'll
make haste to say that I should have done it anyway.'

He bade her a friendly goodbye, just as Dolly had
done, refusing to wait and meet Doctor Wright with

the excuse that he had to get some work done before
lunch, and drove away as soon as he saw the door of
the doctor's house open. It was a pleasant Victorian
residence, very solid, with a small garden and
screened by shrubs and trees, and inside it was more
than comfortable, albeit a little gloomy by reason of
the narrow sash windows. Emily was touched and
surprised at the welcome she received from the doctor
and his wife and a little alarmed to see that her erst-
while patient wasn't looking very well. He declared
that he was feeling splendid, though, and looking forward to his visit. 'We've been before, several times,'
he explained. 'I suppose Renier gave you a map and
told you how to get there?'

They spent the next half hour poring over it and
arranging their journey. They were to go on the night
ferry from Harwich, but the doctor declared that he
didn't want to be rushed; they would leave with
plenty of time to spare; they could always go on board
early. Which pleased Emily, feeling a touch of last-
minute nerves at the idea of driving so far and on a
strange route.

'It's a piece of cake,' declared Doctor Wright, and
beamed at her when she congratulated him on the way
he had mastered his speech in such a short time. 'Not
bad, eh?' he asked, delighted with himself. 'I shall
start thinking of going back to work after Christmas.'

He rested after lunch while Emily and Mrs Wright
gossiped in the sitting room and presently, after tea,
Emily fetched the car from the garage, helped the
elderly maid to put the luggage in the boot, settled

her two passengers comfortably, and with her fingers metaphorically crossed, drove carefully out of the short drive and set the Rover's nose Harwich-wards.

CHAPTER SEVEN

THE FIRST PART of the journey went very well. Emily, once she had recovered from her initial fright, found that she wasn't scared at all. She wove her way through London's traffic and drove smoothly towards Colchester and Harwich. The car went well, Doctor Wright seemed comfortable enough in the back with his wife beside him and there was plenty of time. They embarked without waste of time and went straight to their cabins, and before they parted for the night Emily, feeling that it was expected of her, checked the doctor's pulse, made sure that he was comfortable and arranged for a light meal to be brought to them. The doctor was tired and when he was tired, his speech, never easy, became almost impossible to understand; she could see that he would be grateful to go to bed.

Mrs Wright sat next to her when they disembarked at the Hoek and Emily discovered quickly enough that she wouldn't have liked it otherwise; she could concentrate on her driving, leaving it to her companion to direct her. Rotterdam was a nightmare and once or twice she felt like taking her hands off the wheel and screaming, but Mrs Wright was a calm person. She remained unflustered, even when they took a wrong turning, and rather later than sooner they found themselves on Rotterdam's outskirts, on the motorway to Utrecht and safe in the knowledge that they could stay on it until they reached the roundabout on the outskirts of that city.

They had landed early in the morning and even though Emily had had to slow up in Rotterdam, it was still only mid-morning. She slowed, obedient to Mrs Wright's instructions, at the roundabout, and turned on to the Amsterdam motorway, then turned again presently, this time into a side road which would take them to Breukelen. They crossed the river here, to take a narrow country lane, running beside the river and empty of traffic. As Mrs Wright explained, the road on the opposite side was used for that; it went all the way to Weesp, near Amsterdam, hugging the river Vecht all the way, but not as closely as the road they were now travelling on.

Emily would dearly have loved to have stopped and looked around her. She hadn't seen much yet; Rotterdam she never wanted to see again, not if she had to drive through it, and the motorways, although splendid, hardly afforded opportunities to look at the view. But here it was different. Breukelen was small and quaint and as they went along she caught glimpses of charming old houses set amidst green lawns sweeping down to the river's edge, and even, now in winter, with the frost still on the ground, it all looked beautiful. She was wondering where exactly the Professor lived when Mrs Wright said: 'Turn left, dear, and in through the gates.'

The gates, wrought iron and wide open between stone pillars, led on to a sanded drive, curving through shrubs and trees, bare now, but thick enough to hide the house from view. It came into sight round the next bend, a solid, white-painted square mansion, its front door approached by wide steps, its enormous windows twinkling in the pale sun. The drive ended in a wide sweep and then continued round the side of the house, where Emily glimpsed outbuildings. It rather took her breath; the Professor's London flat had seemed the height of luxury to her, but it was entirely over-shadowed by this dignified edifice. 'Well,' said Emily in a surprised voice, 'I didn't expect this. It's—it's like a stately home!'

Doctor Wright grinned at her. He was looking almost his old self now that the journey was over and Mrs Wright gave her a grateful little smile.

'Well, here we are, dear, and how wonderfully you drove. When I think that we might not have been able to come but for you...' She broke off because the front door had opened and the Professor was running down the steps towards them. He greeted them with warmth, kissing Mrs Wright on a cheek, shaking the doctor by the hand and then turning to Emily, whom he neither kissed nor shook hands with; all she received was a placid: 'Well, it wasn't too bad, was it? And you had Mrs Wright to map-read for you.'

He was standing with his hands in his pockets, staring at her, frowning a little, and she felt suddenly dejected and wishful that she hadn't come. Surely he could have smiled?

'It was a very pleasant trip,' she told him coolly. 'Doctor Wright's a little tired, though.'

He nodded carelessly before turning away to walk with his friend back up the steps into the house. Emily, following with Mrs Wright, was still wondering why he seemed vaguely annoyed at the sight of her, when they reached the vestibule and went inside.

She hadn't known what to expect and she found it beautiful; panelled walls and thin silk rugs on the black and white marble floor and a staircase rising at the end of the hall, its branches turning left and right to reach the gallery running round the hall. There was a man waiting by the door, a round, elderly person with a jolly face, the very antithesis of the man in the London flat. The Professor introduced him as Hans to Emily, after the Wrights had greeted him like an old friend, then led the way through the double doors Hans had opened into a lofty room with two great windows at one end and a carved fireplace of great splendour. Here they were welcomed by a brindled bull terrier and a large dog with a shaggy coat and a long feathery tail, witness to a variety of ancestors. It pleased Emily to see a small nondescript cat curled up in one of the handsome velvet-covered armchairs which were arranged around the room; it gave its stateliness a homely look. She felt a little overcome by the unexpectedness of it all and the Professor's politely cool greeting had left her uncertain; perhaps he was regretting the arrangement already. In her mind's eye she reviewed her wardrobe and wondered if it would quite live up to its surroundings. She sat down on an enormous button-backed sofa and watched Hans disappearing with the coats. Presumably they were to drink their coffee and pass the time of day before being shown to their rooms. Coffee, she hoped, would revive her.

It did, but only in part. The Professor did the rest by coming to sit near her presently and enquire after the journey. He seemed so interested that she quite enjoyed telling him about it, and presently the talk became general until their host said: 'I thought we'd have lunch on our own today; there are one or two people coming in for drinks this evening, so we'll dine a little later than usual.' He included them all in his smile. 'I expect you would like to go to your rooms—Bep shall take you up. Maud, you've got your usual room and I've put Emily just across the passage within call.'

Bep, it appeared, was Hans' wife, a very large, stout woman with a red cheerful face who without speaking a word of English nonetheless conveyed her pleasure at their coming as she swept up the staircase with Mrs Wright while Doctor Wright and Emily followed at a more leisurely pace.

The gallery on to which they emerged was, if anything, rather more magnificent than the hall below. The walls were white wood here, and the ceiling was painted; cherubs, scantily draped ladies on what Emily took to be clouds, and a great many wreaths of flowers, the whole gathered up, as it were, into one glorious crowd encircling the domed ceiling above the hall. She was so busy craning her neck to see it all that Doctor Wright had to tap her on the arm to remind her that Bep had sailed away from the gallery and was negotiating a corridor leading to the back of the house. Their rooms were at the end, their doors one each side of a narrow window looking out on to the wintry formal garden laid out below. Emily waited until the Wrights had gone into their room and then, invited by the smiling housekeeper, went into her own. That too had a window, a large one this time, with the same view, and was furnished with great good taste with simple mahogany pieces; a canopied bed, draped in white muslin, a sofa table with a gilded triple mirror in the window, a great tallboy and a small writing desk and chair. There was a small fire burning in the marble grate which to Emily seemed the height of luxury, and drawn up to it, an armchair with a table beside it. She was still gaping at it all when Bep crossed the room to open a door and disclose a small bathroom. Emily stood surveying its pink tiles and mirrors, the piles of pastel towels, the jar of matching soaps, quite bereft of words. If only Louisa were here to see it all! Emily, catching sight of her ordinary person in one of the mirrors, felt that she didn't quite match her surroundings. Bep went away and Emily went to her case on the chest against the wall and opened it. Someone had unpacked for her; she opened the second door and found that it was a clothes closet, her few things hanging forlorn at one end. She remembered that there were people coming in for drinks and wondered what she should wear. She would have to ask Mrs Wright.

That good lady, as though she had heard Emily's unspoken thoughts, knocked and came in, expressed delight at the room, examined the view from the window and suggested that they went downstairs as soon as they were ready.

'What do we wear tonight?' demanded Emily worriedly. 'I'm afraid I haven't enough clothes with me...'

She flung open the closet door and Mrs Wright's kind eye took in the skirt and blouses. 'How sensible to bring a skirt and several tops,' she declared bracingly. 'I've done that too. We'll wear them this evening, dear—Renier always has a house full for drinks, you know.' She went on carefully: 'I believe we're going in to Utrecht tomorrow morning; you and I could slip away and have a look round. And Emily, no one has thought to tell you, but of course, you're getting a salary while you're here...'

Emily turned a shocked face to her companion's. 'Oh, I couldn't! I've not done anything...'

'You drove us here and if Reg wants anything done you'll be doing it, my dear—and I must confess not to have to worry about him at night will be a relief. Not that you'll need to stay awake, or anything like that, but sometimes if he can't sleep, he gets up and roams around, so I'm afraid to go to sleep...'

It was a relief to Emily that she was going to be of some use, after all. 'Look, I'll ask the Professor to have a bell fixed up, then if Doctor Wright wants anything, I can see to it, so you can sleep soundly.'

'That would be lovely, Emily. Now, tomorrow, how about treating yourself to something really glamorous for Christmas night? Renier has the family to dinner and it's quite an occasion. I thought I'd look round for myself, too.'

'Oh, well, if you're going to… I've brought some money with me and I do need another dress, don't I?' Emily looked in the mirror and combed her tidy head even tidier. 'I didn't know about presents…?'

'Ah, yes, we'll see if we can find a few things… Renier's got everything, which makes it very difficult. Just a small something, dear—it's nice to exchange little gifts on Christmas morning, isn't it?'

In bed, hours later, Emily went over her day. It had been delightful, although she had had her misgivings about that to begin with. But lunch had been a very pleasant meal, enlivened by the presence of the Professor's grandmother, a diminutive, rather plump old lady who told Emily in precise careful English that she was eighty-one years old and unlike the young people of today, she enjoyed life to the full. She had eyed Emily sternly and then relaxed with a sharp: 'Not that you look like one of these modern girls, with their ugly trousers and unkempt hair.' She smiled suddenly. 'What do you think of Renier?'

It had been a little hard to answer that because her host was sitting at the head of the table, not quite out of earshot. Emily recalled with shame that she had blushed, although she had replied sedately that he was an excellent surgeon.

Unexpectedly, he had come to her aid with: 'And Emily is an excellent nurse, Grandmother,' to which the old lady had replied:

'Well, I think every girl should be taught to do something useful before she marries.'

Emily wriggled in her comfortable bed at the memory of his bland: 'Are you planning to get married, Emily?'

They had spent the afternoon looking round the house in a leisurely fashion, although half way through Doctor Wright had decided that he would like a rest. So she had accompanied him up to his room, seen him comfortably settled on the chaise-longue before the fire, laid a coverlet over his legs, arranged a table with anything he might require upon it, and then gone downstairs again, but when she reached the big garden room at the back where they had all been, she saw that the Professor and Mrs Wright were so deep in conversation that they didn't even see her, so she had gone to the sitting room and picked up a magazine and while she leafed through it wondered what they were talking about. Doctor Wright, presumably.

She had worn the long skirt and the pale pink crêpe blouse with the ruffles for the evening, and reflected now that it had been most suitable. True, a number of the ladies who had come to visit Renier were very handsomely dressed and most of them had beautiful jewellery, but she had felt satisfied in a modest way that she hadn't looked too bad. At least old Mevrouw

Jurres-Romeijn had complimented her in somewhat outspoken terms, on her suitable appearance. It was a pity that the Professor hadn't had a word to say to her other than the usual polite nothings a host utters to his guests. But tomorrow was another day, she told herself, and went to sleep on the thought.

And a very nice day it was, too. The Professor wasn't at breakfast, and Doctor Wright had elected to have his in his room, so she and Mrs Wright spent an agreeable time discussing their shopping. 'And you know,' said Mrs Wright happily, 'Reg is so much better; knowing you were close by and the bell under his hand, he told me he'd slept all night, and I believe he did.'

They drove into Utrecht in the Jag, with Emily sitting beside the Professor making polite conversation, because to sit in silence was really too much. 'This is a very comfortable car,' she observed, and didn't see the little smile, instantly suppressed.

'Very,' he agreed gravely, and since he didn't seem disposed to say any more she tried again.

'Do you prefer a large car?'

'Er, yes—you see, I'm a large person, Emily. I have a Lagonda V12 though, a 1940 model; it's a two-seater drophead couppé—it's been restored, of course, but I can get ninety miles an hour out of her. I'll take you for a run, only you'll have to wrap up warmly.'

Emily's eyes shone. 'That sounds fun, I'd like that.'

The two men went off on their own in Utrecht. Doctor Wright wanted to renew his acquaintance with the medical staff at the hospital and, Emily guessed, show himself off as a splendid example of the Professor's surgery. She and Mrs Wright, left to themselves, made for the shops and spent an interesting time looking at clothes. Finally Mrs Wright bought herself a velvet dress which, she explained, was suitable to her age and appearance and Emily, carried away by the excitement of the shops with all their Christmas delights, allowed herself—with no difficulty at all—to be persuaded into buying a lovely flyaway chiffon dress in rose pink, its scooped-out neckline bound with a darker satin and with ballooning elbow sleeves. It gave her a glow and Mrs Wright, standing beside her while she studied herself in the looking glass, said softly: 'It's beautiful, dear, it makes you look very pretty, especially if you do your hair in a different style—a little softer, if you see what I mean—such nice hair, too.'

'And have you enjoyed yourselves?' the Professor wanted to know. 'Naturally you went to see the Dom Tower, and climbed its four hundred and sixty-five steps, and probably you had time to pay a visit to the Central Museum and take a quick peep at the Brutenhof Almshouses as well. Probably you didn't get as far as the Devil's Stone.'

'We each bought a dress,' Emily told him, a little breathless, because she was sitting beside him again and he seemed to have that effect upon her.

'And so have I,' observed Mrs Wright from the back seat. 'We've had a lovely time; we thought we'd

compete in the glamour stakes on Christmas night. I
daresay there will be some gorgeous girls there.'

'Of course.' Emily didn't see the lightning glance
he threw at her mediocre profile. 'Franz is bringing a
Vogue model with him, I shall cut him out.' Franz
was his younger brother, Emily had discovered that
from Mrs Wright. There was a sister too, married and
living in Amsterdam, much younger than the Professor. They would be coming for Christmas, together
with a great many aunts and uncles and cousins. 'And
New Year, too, my dear—it will be as much fun as
Christmas.'

Back in the Professor's great house, snug in her
pleasant room, Emily experimented with her hair, re-
did her face, and went downstairs. Presumably there
would be tea, if only she could find the room it would
be in.

She had reached the hall when Hans appeared,
smiling, and led her to a small arched door at its end.
'Tea will be served in here, miss—Mrs Wright is already downstairs.'

The room was small compared with the others,
panelled and richly cosy with moss green curtains and
carpet and pink lampshades to cast a glow over everything. There was a brisk fire burning in the steel
grate, too, and Mrs Wright was sitting by it, looking
at a magazine. She looked up as Emily went in. 'The
men are in Renier's study, deep in blood and bones,
as usual. We'll have tea on our own, shall we?'

It was pleasant sitting there, drinking tea from delicate china cups and eating Bep's little biscuits, and

after a while the men joined them, saying that they
had had their tea, and before long they were deep in
a discussion about Christmas. 'I thought we might
have a crowd in for drinks on Christmas Eve,' observed the Professor, 'friends and acquaintances and
the family, of course—there'll just be family on
Christmas Day. There's a party at my sister's on Box-
ing Day and everyone goes home on the following
day. Then at New Year, it will be the family again—
I thought we might have a dance and ask in a few
neighbours.'

Emily, listening to his quiet, unhurried voice, felt
as though she were in a dream. It didn't seem possible
that only a short while ago she had been making paper
chains to cheer a lonely Christmas.

But loneliness was something she could forget
now; there was so much to do and see; her days were
full. The Wrights had breakfast in their room and on
her second morning she found that she was to share
hers with the Professor. At least, she discovered, she
shared the table with him, but hardly his attention;
that was taken up with his letters and the papers, although his manners were too good to allow her to
feel neglected. But the conversation he tossed at her
from time to time was a little absent-minded and con-
sisted of enquiries as to how she had slept, whether
her breakfast was to her liking and polite remarks
about the weather. After ten minutes or so she told
him kindly: 'Look, do get on with your post and the
papers; I don't a bit mind if you don't talk. My father
never spoke a word at breakfast.' She smiled at him

across the table. 'I'll have breakfast in my room, if you like, it must be vexing to have me here and feel that I must be talked to.'

He had put down the letter he was holding to look at her. 'I do believe you mean that,' he observed in some astonishment. 'It's true I breakfast alone except for the dogs, but if you will forgive me not making small talk, then I should much prefer you to breakfast with me.' He smiled suddenly and she felt warmed by it. 'You are a very restful girl, Emily.'

She stared at him for a long moment and he added with perception: 'You're not going to forget, are you? Will you believe me when I say that from whatever angle I see you, you no longer merge into the background?'

Very nicely put, thought Emily, he'd charm money from a miser's purse. Aloud she said: 'Yes, I'll believe you and even though I—I haven't forgotten I don't hold it against you, you know. Only I don't think I'm prim.'

He gave a bellow of laughter which made her jump. 'No, I don't think so either. What are you going to do today? I suggested to Maud Wright that she took you on a tour of the house—Hans will go with you; his English is quite good. I'd take you myself, but I'm tied up for the next few days. Feel free to do what you like, Emily, and if you want a car, just ask Hans—there's a Mini in the garage eating its head off for lack of exercise.'

She thanked him politely and went on eating her breakfast while he returned to his. They didn't see each other again until the evening and then not alone. She saw that he was tired and although she said nothing he crossed the room to sit with her while they had their drinks before dinner. 'I've had a busy unrewarding day,' he told her. 'I wish I could tell you about it. Sometimes I wonder why I chose to be a surgeon.'

'Because you didn't want to do anything else,' said Emily promptly, 'and for every day that goes wrong, two go right.'

'Do days go wrong for you, Emily? I seem to remember...'

She smiled widely. 'Oh, yes—and mine always seem to come in bunches.'

He twisted his glass idly. 'Do you expect to hear from Louisa while you're here?'

The question surprised her and made her vaguely unhappy. 'No—she doesn't like writing letters. She told me she had a lot of invitations over Christmas.'

'She's the kind of girl who always will. A very pretty girl, your little sister, with a sharp eye to turning things to her advantage, especially men.'

Emily hastened to Louisa's defence. 'She's very young, and—and she was the youngest, you know. They always get a bit spoilt.'

He stood up. 'My youngest isn't going to be spoilt. Shall we go in to dinner?'

The rest of the evening was spent pleasantly enough playing a far from serious game of bridge, although Emily suspected that if the other three had had their way they would have played the game with the concentration it needed. She wasn't good at it herself, but no one seemed to mind her revokings and trumpings, which wouldn't have been quite as bad if she had bent the whole of her mind on to the game, but a bit of it was mulling over the Professor's remarks about Louisa. He couldn't be in love with her after all; just amused. Probably he liked his girls a bit older. She already knew that he liked them beautiful and blonde and unblushing.

Christmas Eve was upon them before they realised it; two men staggered in with a gigantic Christmas tree as Emily was going down to breakfast, and disappeared into the drawing room with it, and there was an undercurrent of subdued bustle throughout the big house. The first of the guests would be arriving after lunch. Emily had peeped into some of the bedrooms upstairs and seen that they were ready with books and tins of biscuits by the beds and flowers on the tables. The two elderly maids whom she hardly ever glimpsed must have been busy.

The Professor greeted her with: 'The tree's here— we'll decorate it after lunch. Do you want anything from Utrecht? It's your last chance.'

She thought. 'No, I don't think so, I've got all my presents.'

He nodded. 'There's some post for you.' He got up and brought her a small pile of letters and two small packages, and she settled happily to opening them. Cards from girls she knew at the hospital, a lovely silk scarf from Mary and George, handkerchiefs from the twins, and in the other packet, something from

Louisa, two pairs of tights—the wrong size, Emily noted wryly.

There was plenty to keep them occupied during the morning. She and Mrs Wright tied the last of their presents while the doctor read his paper and presently Emily put on her outdoor things and walked to the village. They needed more labels and she was nothing loath to trying out the odd word of Dutch she had painstakingly acquired during the week she had been in Holland. She was on her way back when the Professor overtook her in the Jag. He stopped and opened the door for her to get in, observing as he did so: 'Our good Dutch air suits you, Emily, your cheeks are pink.'

'And my nose, I've no doubt. But it's lovely here. Don't you dislike London when you have to go there?'

'There's more social life there—theatres and good restaurants, but this is my home.'

He turned the Jag into the drive and slowed the car. 'Do you like my home, Emily?'

'Very much. It's a bit large—I mean, not for you because you're used to it, but it's…' she paused for a word and couldn't find one. 'It's very beautiful,' she finished. 'You must love it.'

'Well, yes,' he had idled the car to a halt before the door, 'an ancestor of mine built it and we've lived in it ever since. I know every stick and stone about the place and every man, woman and child for miles around, and if that makes me sound deadly dull, I enjoy a night out at a London night club as much as the next man.'

'I've never been to a night club,' said Emily, and then blushed because it sounded as though she was fishing to be taken to one. But it couldn't have entered his head; his face remained blandly polite as he leaned across to open her door.

Decorating the tree turned out to be a hilarious business; it involved climbing up and down a ladder, laden with tinsel or whatever, while those who weren't doing the climbing stood round telling the climber just what to do. Half way through the first of the family arrived—the Professor's sister Evelina and her husband Nikolaas. Evelina was tall and slim and very pretty with the Professor's straight nose and big blue eyes. She hugged her brother, greeted the Wrights like old friends and then hugged Emily. 'Isn't this fun?' she asked everyone in an English almost as good as the Professor's. 'Nik, do go and bring in the presents and I'm dying for tea or a drink.'

'Tea,' her brother corrected her. 'Hans shall bring it in a few minutes.' He spoke from the other side of the tree, standing on the top rung of the ladder while he arranged the star just so.

His younger brother Franz came next, accompanied by a willowy girl with huge eyes and the kind of make-up Emily could never hope to achieve. She shuddered at the sight of the sugary cakes and biscuits which had arrived with the tea tray and drank her tea without sugar or milk, muttering about calories to anyone who would listen to her. Emily wondered if

Franz was serious about her and thought not; he must have been at least ten years younger than the Professor, good-looking, she conceded, but cast in a less giantlike mould than his brother. He was charming to her so that she began to enjoy herself, and when somebody turned on the radio and he caught her round the waist and whirled her into the centre of the big room to dance, she whirled and twirled with the unselfconscious pleasure of a little girl.

More aunts and uncles and cousins arrived presently, so that the old house rang with voices and laughter and finally, when Emily went downstairs before dinner, wearing the velvet skirt and the Liberty top, she had taken Mrs Wright's advice too and taken great pains with her hair; instead of screwing it rather tightly into a big knob on top of her head, she had allow the sides to be looser and rolled her brown hair into carefully pinned coils. She only hoped that they would stay as they were and she still wasn't sure if all her effort had been worthwhile.

But they had. The Professor, waiting in his vast drawing room, his grandmother already sitting by fire, a few of his family already assembled, crossed the silky carpet to meet her. He stopped short in front of her and said, smiling a little: 'You have such pretty hair; I've often wondered why you scraped it back so severely. It's nice. Come and have a drink.'

He was an accomplished host; in no time at all she was the centre of a group of aunts and uncles, who in turn passed her on to more aunts and uncles and cousins and finally she found herself by old Mevrouw Jurres-Romeijn's chair.

The old lady put out a hand and took hers. 'How charming you look, my dear—your hair is different, I think. Renier was quite right when he told me that you grow on one. He hardly noticed you at first, did he? but one of the surgeons told him that and he found out for himself that it was true.'

Emily blushed and wondered if the Professor had told his grandmother to tell her that; he was quite capable of it. She contradicted herself at once. He wouldn't do anything as petty as that; if he wanted to be nasty, he did it in a big way. She saw that the old lady was still waiting for her answer. 'That's very kind of him,' she said in a quiet little voice, and was intensely relieved when one of the uncles joined them and began to talk about the coming festivities.

Christmas Day was something she had never imagined and which she would never forget. The entire party went to the village church in the morning, sitting in the family pews and overflowing into the rest of the little church, and afterwards there was a light lunch before everyone dispersed to do what they liked until tea time. The Wrights already knew many of the Professor's family and Emily, suddenly shy of attaching herself to any of the cheerful, gossiping groups, slipped away and up the stairs to her room. No one would miss her and she could go down at teatime. Perhaps it would be an idea to go for a walk; it was cold but dry and light for another hour or so. She went to the window to look out and when someone tapped on the door she said 'come in' without turning round.

'Now, why did you make off?' asked the Professor, coming into the room. 'No, don't tell me—the family are overpowering—I did warn you. Put on your coat and a scarf, we'll go for a walk—the dogs need exercise.'

'Really?' asked Emily.

'Really. I'll meet you by the front door in one minute.'

They walked right round the park, with the dogs running races round them, barking their heads off, talking about nothing much, sometimes just walking in a companionable silence, and Emily was happy down to her bones; it wouldn't last, she knew that, but just for the moment life was everything she could wish for. No one seemed to have missed them when they got back; they had tea and presently everyone drifted away to dress.

Emily was glad she had bought the pink dress when she got downstairs again; the women's clothes were lovely and so were their jewels. She joined the Wrights for a few minutes and blossomed under their compliments, and when Franz joined them with: 'Hullo, my beauty,' she beamed at him with delight. Elizabeth Arden must be doing some good after all!

It was the Professor who set the seal on her evening with his: 'Emily, I hardly recognised you.' He twirled her round to get a better view. 'Quite superb. And unexpected.'

The dinner party was a large one, and Emily, be-

tween two cousins, enjoyed every minute of it. And
Bep had certainly excelled herself: avocado pears
with a shrimp stuffing, turtle soup, turkey with everything that went with it, and then a giant Christmas
pudding borne aloft by Hans, blue flames licking at
it. Emily clapped with everyone else as it was brought
to table and drank, rather recklessly, a third glass of
champagne.

Coffee was in the drawing room, but first the presents were to be distributed; a lengthy business, with
something for everyone. Emily opening her own presents—gloves from the Wrights, a delicate porcelain
cup and saucer from Mevrouw Jurres-Romeijn, and
old print from Evelina and Franz—paused at the last
unopened gift to watch the Professor. She hadn't
known what to give him; he had everything, so in the
end she had settled for a silver mouse with a long tail,
small enough to go into a pocket or for that matter,
tuck away in a drawer and forget. She studied his face
anxiously as he opened it and was pleased to see that
he slipped it at once into his waistcoat pocket. Only
then did she untie her last present.

It was a small velvet box and inside was her locket
and a little card: 'With best wishes from Renier Jurres-Romeijn.' She fastened it round her neck with fingers that shook and presently when he came to thank
her for the mouse, she asked urgently: 'Did you buy
it—my locket? Was it you who got there before
Louisa?'

He smiled down at her. 'Yes. It goes well with your
dress.'

'Thank you—you've no idea—thank you very much!' She stared up at him, her nice eyes wide. 'It was so kind…'

He laughed down at her. 'I'm not sure if I should feel flattered or not!'

She hardly saw him to speak to on the following day. Several carloads went up to Amsterdam to spend most of the day at Evelina's house on one of the *grachten*; there seemed to be so many people there that Emily decided that she only had the chance to speak to everyone once, and to the Professor not at all. There were several pretty girls there too with their attendant young men, friends of Evelina. They swarmed round Renier like bees round a honeypot and from what she could see, he was enjoying it immensely.

They didn't get back to his house until late in the evening and because Doctor Wright was tired she helped him to bed, saw that he had his supper and his favourite books and then went downstairs to say goodnight herself. Mrs Wright was on the point of going to bed herself. She kissed Emily goodnight with the cheerful remark that Reg hated her to fuss over him and it was a good thing that Emily was there to order him around when he needed it. Emily kissed her back warmly: 'And mind and see that he's got the bell handy, though I think he's going to sleep soundly, he's so tired.'

'Yes, dear. Renier's in his study, telephoning the hospital about something or other. He said you're not to go to bed until he's said goodnight.'

So Emily went and sat down by the fire, and presently the cat got on to her lap and what with the warmth and all the champagne she had drunk, she dozed off. She woke to find the fire dying and the hands of the clock at two o'clock in the morning. She stared at it unbelieving for a moment, then removed the still sleeping cat, turned out the table lamp and started for the door. She was in the hall when the front door opened and the Professor came in. He had his bag with him and he put it down on the nearest chair and took off his coat before he spoke. 'What on earth are you still up for?' he demanded. He sounded so ill-tempered that she chose her words carefully.

'Well, when I came downstairs Mrs Wright gave me a message saying that I wasn't to go to bed until you'd said goodnight. So I went and sat by the fire and went to sleep.'

It seemed prudent to take herself off. She was on the stairs when he caught up with her. 'Emily, I'm sorry—I did say that. But I had to go to the hospital in a hurry and I entirely forgot about you.'

She went on up the stairs. 'It doesn't matter a bit; it was lovely by the fire. But I think I'll go to bed now. Goodnight.' She turned to smile at him before she reached the gallery. He was on the bottom step, incredibly handsome and tired to death. Heaven knew what he had been doing; she'd ask another time. As she got ready for bed she thought sadly that she was the kind of girl a man would forget entirely. She stared at her reflection as she rubbed a nourishing

cream into her pale face. It wasn't a nourishing cream
she needed, it was a new face, the kind of face a man
remembered.

CHAPTER EIGHT

IT SEEMED THAT no sooner was Christmas over than preparations for the New Year were under way. Emily spent a whole morning with Mevrouw Jurres-Romeijn, listening to every detail of what would take place while Emma, the old lady's devoted maid, made coffee for them both. 'Cards,' explained the little lady. 'We all send cards to each other with good wishes, and at midnight we eat *Olie Bollen*.' She paused. 'In English that is oil balls, but that is I think not correct.'

Emily knit her brows. 'Doughnuts?' she essayed, and was pleased to find that she had hit on something near enough to the truth to please her companion. 'And we sing, of course,' went on Mevrouw Jurres-Romeijn, 'and toast the New Year—it is a splendid time.'

Emily left her presently and wandered off to find Mrs Wright to discuss the vexed question of what to wear.

'Oh, the pink, my dear, it's a very dressy occasion, you know. I shall wear the velvet again.'

'Will there be the same people or a lot of new ones?'

'Both—Renier has open house at New Year, he's the head of the family, you see.'

'Lots of pretty girls?' asked Emily.

'Bound to be.' Mrs Wright shot her a thoughtful look. 'Franz will be coming and Evelina and her husband. Franz has a different girl each time I see him. It's time he settled down.'

'Oughtn't R-Renier to settle down first?'

'Oh, he's made up his mind who he's marrying.'

Emily turned away. She said brightly: 'This is such a lovely house for a family, isn't it?'

She dressed carefully for the evening, although there seemed no point in it any more. She admitted to herself that the unlikely chance of the Professor getting even faintly interested in her was now washed out. He'd made up his mind to marry and although he might flirt around with a dozen pretty girls they meant nothing to him. And she wasn't even pretty.

The evening was fun, all the same. Certainly there were pretty girls there, but there were an equal number of young men, all willing to entertain her, and when it was discovered that she danced like a dream, there was no lack of partners. It was almost midnight when Renier swept her away from Franz with the remark that it was his turn to dance with her, 'If,' he added, 'you can bear to dance something as old-fashioned as a waltz.'

Speechless, Emily nodded. Her carefully arranged hair had come a little loose and her cheeks were flushed and she had to crane her neck to see his face.

He danced well, and she—she floated round on air, loving every second, wanting to go on for ever.

Actually it was only a few minutes before the band stopped playing so that everyone could hear the great clock in the hall chime midnight, and at its last stroke there was a sudden burst of good wishes and kissing while Hans and Bep and the maids wove their way around with more champagne.

Emily drank her toast at the last stroke and said in a quiet little voice: 'A Happy New Year, Renier.'

He bent and kissed her cheek: 'And to you, Emily.' He smiled as he said it and the next moment was engulfed in a wave of singing, laughing guests. Emily, caught up between two elderly gentlemen she had never seen before, lost sight of him altogether.

The party went on for hours, but she didn't dance with the Professor again. She saw him partnering one pretty girl after the other and she looked in vain for the one he must surely intend to marry, but he spent no more time with one that the other. It seemed strange, but perhaps she was away or even lived in another country. Emily occupied herself while she danced with imagining what his wife would be like. Beautiful and blonde, of course—an older edition of Louisa.

She was so tired by the time she got to bed that she really didn't care any more.

She was up at the usual time in the morning, she was too young and healthy to notice a late night—besides, Renier would be at breakfast. Only he wasn't; he'd gone out early, Hans told her, an urgent call from the hospital. Emily didn't see him all day.

She had a message from Mevrouw Jurres-Romeijn the next morning, asking her if she would like to go to her rooms after lunch and talk over the party, and since there was still no sign of the Professor although Hans had assured her that he was free that day, and the Wrights had nothing on hand which needed her company, she went along about two o'clock.

There was no sign of the old lady when she reached the wing where she had her rooms. Emily, thinking she had been mistaken, searched through the house for her fruitlessly and retraced her steps. It seemed strange that the old lady wasn't in her rooms. Emily, by means of basic English and the half dozen words she had learned, asked Emma where she was and got a shake of the head in reply, accompanied by spread hands and raised eyebrows. 'Is she out?' Emily tried again.

Emma went away to look in the vast wardrobe in Mevrouw Jurres-Romeijn's bedroom and came back looking shaken. '*Hoed, mantel-weg.*'

So the old lady had got on her outdoor things, but the question was where was she? Emily stood and thought carefully while Emma wrung her hands. Mevrouw Jurres-Romeijn had said something on Christmas Eve; about not going to see one of the retired maids who was ill because Renier had told her not to go on account of the weather. She had sounded very put out, Emily remembered, and moreover she was an old lady who liked her own way. She patted

Emma's stout shoulders, nodding and smiling, and before that lady could burst into speech, hurried away.

It wouldn't be any good telling the Wrights—it wouldn't be any good telling anyone. The household was taking its post-prandial rest and Renier, who would have known what to do at once, wasn't home, nor would he be until the evening. She had watched him drive away with a pretty girl who had called that morning, someone he knew well, she supposed miserably, for she had flung her arms round his neck and kissed him and he had laughed down at her and taken her arm and they had disappeared into his study for half an hour. Emily remembered just how long it was because she had been reading the *Telegraph* to Doctor Wright, and could see both his study door and the great wall clock in the hall from where she was sitting.

She went straight to her room, put on her coat, tied a scarf over her hair, snatched up her gloves, rammed her feet into her boots, and let herself out of a side door. She was just shutting it when Hans came into the passage. He gave her an enquiring look but didn't say anything, and she didn't wait; something told her that she must find Renier's grandmother quickly.

She knew where the retired members of the household lived—a pleasant row of small cottages on the edge of the estate, ten minutes' walk away, but only five if she cut across the park. It was very cold and slippery underfoot and before long her hands and feet were numb, so that she skidded unsteadily on the rutted path. But presently she came out by the cottages,

six of them, all very neat and one or two with lights
shining from the windows already although it was still
barely three o'clock. She hadn't bothered much until
that moment as to what she was going to say and she
hesitated at the first door, but surely just to mention
Mevrouw Jurres-Romeijn by name was sufficient?
She thumped the old-fashioned iron knocker and
stamped her cold feet.

An old woman came to the door, peering round it
in the manner of one who wasn't over-keen to open
it anyway, but her face cleared when Emily asked
politely: 'Mevrouw Jurres-Romeijn is here?' It
sounded the same in both languages and the old
woman shook her head at once and pointed to the
cottage at the other end, so Emily said, '*Dank U, mevrouw*,' in her politest manner and made her way over
the brick path connecting the cottages to one at the
end of the row, where she repeated her performance
all over again, to be met this time with a flood of
information which meant nothing at all to her. It took
a few minutes of hand-waving, nodding and head-
shaking to discover that Mevrouw Jurres-Romeijn had
indeed been there, but instead of going back the way
she had come, had gone on, taking the vague path
which skirted the water meadows. Emily looked at
them now, a bleak stretch of frozen grass fading into
an early dusk. There was a scattering of trees along
one side and what looked like a copse beyond them.
Probably, she thought miserably, the old lady was lying in it, frozen solid to the ground or, worse, had
tumbled into one of the many canals which criss-

crossed the meadows. She nodded at the old woman, waved an arm towards the copse and set off. The afternoon was fast sliding into a cold, grey dusk, and as she picked her way along she felt a few drops of sleet. 'Oh, God,' prayed Emily out loud, 'do for heaven's sake let me find her quickly and don't let it rain until I do.' She meant every word of it, which was perhaps why the rain, or whatever it was, ceased almost at once.

The path she followed was indeed a vague one; several times she missed it altogether and she had no idea where it led. The cottages were on the extreme edge of the Professor's land, so presumably she was on someone else's property, although there was no sign of a house. As she neared the copse and the trees she began calling, standing still and straining her ears for a reply. But there was none, so she plodded on, muttering to herself about the gathering gloom and the weather and why had she ever come to Holland in the first place. But she fell silent as she reached the trees, a clump of firs with a great deal of under-growth; they would be difficult enough to search in broad daylight. She ventured into them, scared now because it was almost dark under their branches and she was convinced that she would never find the way out again and even if she did it would be bound to be the wrong end. 'I wish I had a torch!' She spoke loudly and her voice sounded so strange in the middle of the silence that she caught her breath. At the same time she caught her toe in something and fell sprawling. The something was Mevrouw Jurres-Romeijn, lying very still. Emily scrambled to her knees and bent over her, but when she spoke the old lady didn't answer. 'And I'm not surprised,' said Emily, talking to herself again, 'you probably hit your head on something and now you're half frozen.'

She felt for a wrist and was heartened to find a steady pulse, but the old lady was icy cold. Emily took off her coat and wrapped it round the small body while she thought what was best to do. She could run back to the cottages and tell someone, but on reflection that wasn't such a good idea. She hadn't the faintest idea which way she had come into the trees and it was now so dark she might lose her way even if she gained the water meadows, besides which, it would take a long time to explain what had happened and in the meantime Mevrouw Jurres-Romeijn might recover, take fright, and disappear again, and if she didn't do that, she might freeze to death—after all, she was old.

Emily decided reluctantly to stay where she was and hope that someone would come and find them. After all, Emily knew Hans had seen her go out and if someone called at the cottages they would be able to direct help. She felt her unconscious companion carefully and discovered a badly swollen ankle. There was nothing she could do about that, but she lifted the old lady very gently so that she was cradled in her arms. There was a chance that she would keep tolerably warm cuddled against Emily, although Emily was getting colder with every minute—not only that, she was half sitting, half crouching on the frozen

ground and its icy hardness was boring straight into
her. It was very quiet; no bird was going to open its
beak on an evening like this and no wild creature with
any sense would poke its nose out of its hidey-hole.
Only the branches above her head creaked in the wind
until the silence was broken by the sound of steady
rain. After a few minutes it found its way through the
branches and trickled down her neck and on to her
scarf. She pulled Mevrouw Jurres-Romeijn's fur hat
over part of her face and tightened her hold, suddenly
uncertain if she were doing the right thing. Perhaps
no one would come; Mrs Wright had said that the
Professor wouldn't be back until after tea and if he
were enjoying himself with the pretty girl Emily had
seen, then she for her part couldn't blame him if he
were even later than that. Hans might come, of
course; she cheered up at the thought and began to
shout, astonished that she hadn't thought of doing so
before. She was even more astonished when she was
answered by a distant bellow. 'In the trees!' she
screamed, and then, stupidly: 'Over here!'

She should have shouted in Dutch, of course, only
she didn't know the word for trees. She shouted again
and added: 'Hurry, please hurry!' and caught her
breath as the beam from a powerful torch was shone
over her, and the Professor's voice, sounding quite
harsh, came from somewhere behind it. It was a pity
that he spoke in Dutch, for she couldn't understand a
word of it, and when he switched to English he
sounded as calm as he always did.

'I hurried the moment I heard you scream,' he told

her mildly. He dropped on a knee beside her and
lifted his grandmother out of her stiff, numbed arms,
and Emily, now that they were being rescued, allowed
the tears to stream down her cold cheeks. 'She's been
unconscious all the time,' she said through chattering
teeth. 'I couldn't examine her properly, but I felt her
arms and legs; her left ankle's swollen.' She gulped.
'Her pulse wasn't too bad. She's not—not...?'

'No, she's not.' He lifted his voice in a great bellow
and she saw torchlight through the trees. 'And you?'
His voice was very gentle now, not harsh at all. 'Are
you all right, little Emily?'

'Yes—yes, I'm fine.' People crowded round them
now, half a dozen men with torches, all talking at
once. The Professor spoke to them and the stretcher
someone had been carrying was unfolded and his
grandmother gently laid upon it. Emily's coat was
still wrapped round her, but she had forgotten all
about it. It wasn't until the Professor straightened up
from another quick examination of the old lady and
seen the stretcher bearers on their way that he exclaimed: 'Your coat—where is it? You're frozen, Emily!'

'I put it round your granny.' She was still crying
although she didn't know it any more. She started to
get to her feet and discovered that they were numb
with the cold and wouldn't do anything she wanted
them to do, but now it didn't matter, for the Professor
had taken off his sheepskin jacket and enveloped her
in it with a word to the men standing by, picked her
up, and lighted by his companions, carried her out of

the wood. The rain had turned to sleet and the wind had strengthened its cold breath and she muttered against his jacket: 'You'll catch your death of cold.' But he only laughed, a deep rumble which vibrated against her ear and somehow made her feel quite cheerful again.

From time to time she begged him to put her down, but it was a waste of breath—he took no notice at all, striding steadily over the icy ground until he reached the cottages. There was a Range Rover parked in the narrow lane and the men were putting the stretcher carefully into it. The Professor slid Emily tidily into the front seat and went to take another look at his grandmother, but only for a moment. He got in beside her, Hans clambered into the back while the other men went back to their cottages, and before she had time to realise that her arms and legs were thawing and hurting like blazes, they were before the house. 'Stay where you are,' commanded the Professor, and leapt out, and Emily, tired and shivering with cold and a still remembered fright, was only too happy to do as she was told.

When he came back she asked: 'Your grandmother? Is she all right? Will she have to go to hospital?'

He had got in beside her and flung an arm round her shoulders and she longed to lean against him and have another good howl, but instead she held herself stiffly and she felt his hold slacken. 'No, I don't think so—she's conscious now and her ankle's sprained, not broken. There's no sign of concussion; I think it

was the cold and the shock of the fall. I've telephoned
for a nurse to come out and be with her for the night.
We can take another look at her in the morning, what
she needs now is a sound sleep.' He turned to look
searchingly at her puffy blotchy face. 'And so do you.
Bep is going to see you into bed. A bath first, not too
hot, mind, and I'll come and look you over later.'

'But I'm quite all right, really I am, only cold.'

'And brave and uncomplaining and sensible. You
saved Grandmother's life, Emily. I can never thank
you enough for that.' He sighed. 'The darling, pig-
headed old lady! I should have guessed. I suppose she
saw me go out with Heleen.'

'I saw you go out with her, too.' said Emily, and
could have bitten out her tongue for saying it.

'A pretty girl, isn't she?' observed the Professor
blandly. 'And now—bed, my girl.'

He helped her out of the car because her feet
weren't really quite themselves yet and once in the
hall he picked her up and took her upstairs and
dumped her on the bed with Mrs Wright and Bep
hovering on either side.

'You'll eat your supper,' he told her, 'then I'll
come and have a look at you.'

A warm bath was heaven with Mrs Wright and Bep
fussing round her like two fond mothers, and because
she sneezed twice as she got into bed, Bep fetched a
woollen shawl and insisted on tucking Emily into it
before her supper was brought up to her. 'Eat every
morsel,' warned Mrs Wright, and Emily, quite famished, did just that, and what with the good food and

a kind of delayed relief, she closed her eyes and fell asleep.

When she woke up the Professor was sitting on the side of the bed, holding her hand. As she opened her eyes he observed: 'You look about ten years old with all that hair and that woolly shawl. Bep tells me that you sneezed.'

She was about to tell him that she often sneezed but never caught cold when she sneezed again, whereupon he got up, went to the door, shouted 'Maud!' and came back again, this time to lean over the end of the bed, the stethoscope he had carried in his pocket in his hand.

Mrs Wright joined them so quickly, Emily guessed that she had been waiting just outside the door. 'Now it's me being the nurse,' she declared cheerfully. 'What am I supposed to do?'

'Er—unwrap Emily, if you would be so kind—just the shawl so that I can listen to her chest. I'm not sure how long she was with Grandmother, but it's pretty cold outside.'

So Emily sat up in bed and said 'ninety-nine' each time he told her to and coughed meekly on command. 'Nothing there,' he assured her, and sounded just like the family doctor; a nice mixture of impersonal friendliness and reassurance. 'Stay in bed for breakfast, Emily, and I'll take another look at you in the morning.'

'Very well, and will you please let me know how Mevrouw Jurres-Romeijn is getting on?' She sneezed again and scrabbled round for a hanky and the Professor handed her his. It was enormous, very white, and smelled faintly of the best sort of aftershave. Emily blew hard and felt a silly wish to burst into tears again. She caught the first of them in time, though. 'Oh, dear, now my eyes are watering—perhaps I have caught a cold, after all.'

The Professor was eyeing her closely. 'Perhaps you have. On the other hand...' He didn't finish whatever it was he was going to say but uttered an abrupt 'goodnight,' and walked out of the room.

'He's had a trying day,' said Mrs Wright.

Now he'd gone Emily didn't bother about the tears. She mopped them away carelessly and said: 'How could he have, with that pretty girl—he told me her name—Heleen.'

'Yes, dear. One of any number. They all look alike to me.' She added vaguely: 'It's like putting oil of cloves on an aching tooth, it soothes it for a time, but it doesn't cure it.'

Emily was quite mystified; she had no idea what Mrs Wright meant, suddenly talking about toothache. Probably she was tired too. She sighed, remembering how the Professor had left the room like that, just as though he couldn't bear the sight of her for another minute. And yet he had been very kind when he had found them. 'I think I shall sleep like a top,' she told Mrs Wright.

But before she could curl up for the night Bep appeared once more with a glass of milk heavily laced with brandy. She was to drink every drop, the Professor had said so. She did as she was bid, too sleepy to argue, and then still wrapped in Bep's shawl, drifted off within minutes, greatly helped by the brandy. She didn't wake all night, certainly not when the Professor came into the room on his way to his own bed in the early hours of the morning. He stood for a long while looking down at her. Only her face was visible, the rest was shrouded in wool, her hair spilling out untidily on to the pillows. She was a little flushed and her small nose was pink. There were tearstains on her cheeks too, which she hadn't bothered to wipe away. She looked, if truth must be told, like a very ordinary girl with a cold, but the Professor looked at her as though he had never seen anyone quite as beautiful in all his life.

The cold, routed by Emily's extremely good health, the brandy and a good night's sleep in a warm bed, was nothing more than a vague snuffle in the morning. The Professor, paying her a visit after breakfast, assured her that she had taken no harm from her cold sojourn, agreed that there was no reason why she couldn't get up if she felt like it, and observed that he would be away all day. His manner, though friendly, was distant and he wasted no time on light conversation. Emily had the strong feeling that he couldn't get away fast enough. He did remain long enough for her to enquire after Mevrouw Jurres-Romeijn, though. The old lady had slept all night, he assured her, and had sat up and eaten a splendid breakfast not half an hour since. He intended bringing a colleague back with him that evening to examine her and the ankle would keep her off her feet for a few days. The nurse was to remain and his grand-mother had expressed a wish for Emily to visit her if and when she felt inclined to do so.

'She knew nothing of you finding her, of course,' explained the Professor, already half way to the door, 'but she wants to thank you for saving her life.'

'Oh, pooh,' said Emily, embarrassed to the point of gruffness. 'I didn't do anything—anyone who'd have found her would have done the same.'

He paused once more, his hand on the door. 'Yes, but it was you who found her, Emily.' He didn't return her tentative smile as he went out.

The Wrights were being driven by Hans to see some friends living in Loenen. Emily, up and dressed and assuring Bep that she had never felt better, went along to the floor above. Mevrouw Jurres-Romeijn was sitting up in bed, her hair beautifully arranged as always, a lacy bedjacket trimmed with swansdown that exactly matched the pink quilted bedspread, round her shoulders. She looked remarkably pretty and in the best of health. The nurse who had admitted Emily went away at a word from the old lady and Emily was told to sit by the bed and make herself comfortable. 'Emma's going to fetch the coffee.' The bed's occupant looked Emily over carefully. 'You looked a bit peaked, child. I hope there was no harm done—Renier told me that you were on the ground without your coat for some time. I have to thank you for taking such care of me, Emily, and for saving my life. I am deeply indebted to you.' She put out a delicately thin hand, with its thick wedding ring. 'Come here and kiss me.'

Emily dropped a soft kiss on the old cheek and took the hand in hers.

'I feel fine,' she said gently, 'and I'm so glad that you do too. I'm sorry about the ankle, though, but Professor Jurres-Romeijn said that it wasn't too bad a sprain.'

'Why don't you call him Renier, child?'

Emily coloured faintly. 'Well, you see I've worked for him and seen him on the wards doing his rounds and operating theatre—it seems impertinent.'

The old lady gave a chuckle. 'He wouldn't be pleased to hear that, he's not—how do you say in your English?—cocky.' She gave Emily's hand a little shake. 'Don't you like him, Emily?'

Emily blushed. Whichever reply she made she could see that her companion was going to ask her why, and then she'd have to answer that too. She was saved from answering by Emma coming in with the coffee tray and seized on her respite to start talking feverishly about the weather, the Wrights going out and what charming cottages there were on the estate.

To all of which Mevrouw Jurres-Romeijn gave civil answers, only when they had had their coffee and Emma had gone again, she repeated: 'Don't you like my grandson, Emily?'

'He's an excellent surgeon,' she said at length, aware that her answer was in danger of becoming hackneyed.

'Well, he could be that and quite unacceptable in

every other respect,' her companion pointed out a little tartly, 'but I think that is all the answer I'm going to get.'

'Yes,' said Emily firmly, 'it is.'

The old lady nodded to herself in a satisfied manner. 'It's my birthday in two days' time. I shall be eighty-one, there will be a party which you will attend, of course, for you don't return until two days after that, do you?'

Emily smiled at the old lady. She had known about the party, the Professor had told them about it and she and Mrs Wright had put their heads together over their presents; a frivolous pink chiffon hanky case, to match which Emily had found some fine lawn hand-embroidered hankies. They were to dress for the occasion too and there would be a cake and champagne. Mevrouw Jurres-Romeijn's bright blue eyes sparkled with excitement as she talked about it.

Presently Emily saw that the old lady was growing drowsy. She bade her goodbye, promising to come again in the evening, and went downstairs. It was too early for her solitary lunch, so she wandered into the drawing room and from there to the sitting room and the dining room, looking at all the pictures as she went. Some of them were very beautiful and she supposed valuable too. Presently she was joined by the dogs; Potter the bull terrier and Soapy, so called because, as the Professor said, he was soft in the head. They stayed with her until Bep came to tell her that her lunch was ready in the small sitting room behind the drawing room. They made nice company while she ate it and because she felt a little lonely she talked to them as she did so. She had reached the pudding, an apple tart with thick rich cream accompanying it, when the Professor walked in. She should have guessed who it was, of course, because the dogs had run to the door, but she was deep in thought, wondering about a job and where she should live, but at the sound of his voice telling the animals to behave themselves, she turned round to look at him.

'Oh, they said you would be away all day.'

'So I am officially, but I wanted to check up on Grandmother.' He had sat himself down at the table and Bep arrived silently with a tray of coffee. 'I wanted to check up on you too, Emily.'

'Me?' She didn't quite meet his eye. 'I'm fine. I sat with Mevrouw Jurres-Romeijn this morning. How will you manage about her birthday party?'

'Easily enough. Carry her down to the drawing room and arrange her on one of the sofas. Your cold has come to nothing?'

She bit into the pie and chewed it up before she answered. 'Yes.'

The Professor leaned back in his chair, his coffee cup in his hand. 'If it was a cold. It can resemble so many other things—a gush of tears, for example.'

'I was not crying,' said Emily so quickly that he laughed.

'No? All right, but tell me why you were, all the same.'

'Well, I won't, and it couldn't possibly interest you anyway.'

'What makes you say that?' His voice was very smooth.

'Nothing makes me say it, I just know…'

Bep had brought in another cup and fresh coffee and he poured a cup for her to take to Emily. When she had gone again, he got up and walked round the table and sat down on it, close to Emily, who sat looking into her cup as though it held something much more fascinating than coffee. Presently he stretched out an arm, took the cup from her and set it in the saucer, and when she looked up at him in surprise he bent down and kissed her.

'Emily, you're going back with the Wrights in two days' time—would you stay on here instead?' She was surprised to hear the uncertainty in his voice. 'You could look after Grandmother; she has become very fond of you, and…'

She cut him short, terrified that if she allowed him to continue she would give in without any fight at all. What heaven, she thought, to stay here and see him every day, and at the same time she said sharply: 'I can't—it's very kind of you to suggest it, but I have several interviews lined up…' She plunged into a description of a series of mythical jobs she had been offered, aware that his eyes were fixed on her face and not quite certain if he believed her or not. 'So you see, I couldn't,' she finished presently.

'You are anxious to return to London and work in a hospital there? Carve a future for yourself?' His bland voice had an edge to it.

'Yes, oh, yes, rather! I've always been sold on the idea of being a career girl.'

He got up from the table. 'I'm sorry, I had thought…never mind. The jobs you describe sound splendid, almost too good to be true,' his voice was dry. 'I'm sure you'll make a success of one or other of them.'

He wandered to the door, whistling to the dogs as he went, so that Emily was left quite alone, contemplating a future in which she had no interest at all.

She hardly saw him for the next two days. Mrs Wright was at pains to tell her that he was busy at his practice and had a number of patients at the hospital as well. 'And not only in Utrecht,' she remarked. 'There is a big hospital in Zeist, you know, and he does a lot of surgery there, too.'

All the same, even if he had no time for Emily, he seemed to have it for everyone else. The house seemed full on each successive evening with his friends and Heleen always seemed to be with one or other party of guests. Emily, keeping up her end of a variety of conversations with anyone who chose to speak to her, kept a hawk's eye on the girl, not seeing, in her turn, that the Professor contrived to keep her in view from wherever he happened to be. She was heartily glad when these social occasions were over; she found them hard to bear, for although the Professor was a charming host and was careful to make her feel completely at home, there was never any chance to speak to him alone. Not, she reminded herself very frequently, that she wanted to do that.

She spent a good deal of the morning with Mevrouw Jurres-Romeijn on her birthday. The old lady was in a reminiscing mood, sitting up in her easy chair by the fire, surrounded by presents and cards. They had their coffee together and when they had finished it she asked Emily to open a drawer in the great pillow cupboard facing the bed, and bring her the leather-covered albums there. They were family photos and Emily, kneeling on a cushion by the old lady, looked entranced at the Professor as a small boy, as a youth, a student, a young man. There were other photos too; of his parents and brother and sister, but she didn't do more than glance at them but leafed back the pages to those of Renier, listening all the while to her companion's voice talking about him. When the old lady said suddenly: 'For a girl who has no interest in Renier, you are remarkably thorough in your study of his photographs.' Emily jerked upright to stare into the bright old eyes.

'Well,' she mumbled, 'looking at photos is always fun.'

'I'm sorry you won't stay,' said Mevrouw Jurres-Romeijn.

'Yes, I—I... Oh, I can't, you must know that I can't.' She stopped, appalled at her treacherous tongue, and her companion patted her hand and said in a gentle little voice:

'Yes, my dear, I do know.' She leaned back in her chair and went on in quite a different voice: 'I'm sure you'll make a great success of your new job when you get it, my dear. And now tell me, are you going to wear that charming dress you wore at Christmas? It was so pretty. I have a new one, you know—grey chiffon, and I shall wear my diamonds.'

They talked clothes after that and who would be at the party, and presently Emily went downstairs to take a look at Doctor Wright; he had seemed a little off colour, she had thought, perhaps he had been overdoing things a little. But the holiday had done him good; he was full of plans for the future and the Professor encouraged him in this. The two men sat and discussed it whenever the Professor was free, with Mrs Wright chipping in from time to time. She had enjoyed her holiday too and Emily, thinking about it, supposed that in a strange sort of way, she had as well.

Emily dressed with extreme care that evening. The whole family would be there and just a few friends— close friends, Mevrouw Jurres-Romeijn had said, and although she had met almost all of them at Christmas, she felt shy as she went downstairs just before dinner. She crossed the hall slowly and paused outside the drawing room door and jumped out of her skin at the Professor's soft voice. 'Scared, Emily?'

She whizzed round then and saw him standing in the open doorway of his study, watching her.

She had to do something to give her heart the chance to steady itself. She put a hand up to her neat brown head and gave it a reassuring pat. 'Not in the least,' she assured him frostily.

'Oh, good.' He shut the door behind him and came

to stand beside her. 'Because I am— the whole family, you know—rather a lot to swallow at one go.'

'Oh, what nonsense!' cried Emily, wanting to giggle at the idea of the Professor being afraid of anyone. 'I don't believe you've been scared of anything or anyone in the whole of your life.'

'You're wrong. There's one thing I'm very afraid of: that the girl I want to marry won't have me.'

Emily studied her shoes so that her face would have time to compose itself. 'Of course she will—' she added involuntarily: 'She's so very pretty…'

The Professor looked taken aback. 'Who is?' he asked with deep interest.

'Well, Heleen, of course.' Emily took a step nearer the door. 'Oughtn't we to go in?'

He ignored that. 'You are still determined to carve yourself a career?'

She fixed her eyes on his waistcoat, thinking to herself that she was glad that he wore conventional evening clothes, beautifully cut. 'Yes,' she said at length.

'You have no wish to marry and have a family?'

She didn't answer and after a moment the Professor uttered a satisfied 'Aha!' caught her close in a grip which almost pulverised her rib cage and kissed her with force. 'You remember that, my girl,' he said softly, and opened the door and swept her inside.

CHAPTER NINE

THE ROOM seemed full of people, and Emily, aware that she had met them all at Christmas and the New Year and ought to remember their names, smiled uncertainly. She had a fine flush by reason of the Professor's savage kissing and any of her nursing friends would have declared her to be in a state of shock. She was aware, too, of the Professor's hand holding her firmly by the arm just as though he had guessed that for one moment she had entertained the childish idea of turning tail and making for the door again. It was a relief when after a second of silence everyone started to talk at once, converging on the Professor as he made his way to where his grandmother sat in state, her injured ankle on a footstool, the grey chiffon draperies arranged becomingly about her small person. She put up her delicately made-up face for his kiss, thanked him for his gift, and turned to Emily.

'You look very pretty, Emily, if I were a man I would fall head over heels in love with you,' she chuckled, 'and certainly when you blush so charmingly! Thank you for your gift, my dear. I shall use them and remember you.' She put out a hand and caught Emily's. 'I'm going to miss you very much. You suit this house, you know.'

'It's a very beautiful house,' said Emily carefully. 'I shall miss it too.'

'But not so much that she is prevented from carving herself a career,' remarked the Professor crossly, so that she gave him a startled look. Really, it was impossible to make head or tail of the man! Not that it mattered, she reminded herself silently.

'I'm wearing the diamonds,' observed Mevrouw Jurres-Romeijn, and that surprised Emily too, for the old lady wasn't given to boasting about her possessions; she accepted them as a matter of course. 'They go to Renier's wife when I die.'

'Who's talking of dying on your birthday?' demanded her grandson. 'And here comes the champagne so that we can toast you.'

A tuneful kind of toast it was too, Emily discovered, with everyone raising their glasses and bursting into song. She managed to make out the words too, for the Professor was bellowing them in a rich baritone voice: '*Lang zal ze leven*,' so Emily sang as well, even managing the bit about '*in de gloria*' while the old lady sat in her chair and beamed at everyone wishing that she should live long in glory.

They went into dinner after that and Emily found that she had Doctor Wright on one side of her and Franz on the other. 'And I'm sorry,' she told him kindly, 'that you have to have me instead of that beauty you brought with you.'

Franz laughed at her. 'I'll tell you a secret; I asked Renier if I could sit next to you, you see. You're the only girl I know who enjoys her food and doesn't rabbit on about raw carrots and calories. You've no idea how trying it is when one is made to feel guilty at enjoying a good square meal!'

And Emily, a kind-hearted girl, obliged him by eating each delicious course with just the right amount of enthusiasm, although in truth she had no appetite at all and everything she ate tasted of sawdust.

There were some twenty-four people at table and she knew most of them slightly. The Professor, with his grandmother on his right, sat at the head of the vast table, and his sister Evelina, acting as his hostess, was at the foot; aunts, uncles, cousins and family friends were ranged on either side, and everyone was talking. Emily found time to look around the ladies present, all splendidly dressed if not entirely fashionable, but Franz's girl-friend and some of the younger cousins made up for that in their silver tissue trouser suits, layered chiffons and slinky tunics. Emily felt herself to be not entirely fashionable either, and then was happily reassured by Franz's cheerful: 'You look very nice, Emily. I don't like girls in trousers—not in the evening—nor does Renier.' Heleen, she had already observed, was wearing an orange and silver tissue tunic and trousers; she looked stunning, and her pleasure was dimmed at once by the thought that Renier probably made an exception in Heleen's case. Certainly he looked at her a great deal during the evening, and Emily couldn't blame him—Heleen was devastatingly pretty; Louisa would look like that when she had finished with the modelling school.

'You're not listening,' said Franz in her ear, and

she gave him a guilty look and then smiled because he was smiling too. He was really very like Renier, if only Renier would smile more often.

Dinner lasted a long time, with speeches and toasts and finally the birthday cake to cut and the entire household staff invited in to share it and drink champagne with everyone else, while Mevrouw Jurres-Romeijn sat smiling and nodding like a happy child.

Presently she went to bed, carried upstairs by her grandson. As he sat her down carefully in her chair she said suddenly: 'She won't come for the diamonds, dear boy.'

The Professor didn't look in the least put out. 'No, I know that, Grandmother, but she will come for love, but she has to discover that for herself.' He bent and kissed her. 'Goodnight, my dear.' He smiled down at the elderly face. 'You're a matchmaker, aren't you?'

She nodded. 'I should like you to be happy, Renier, and I have always cherished a wish to be a great-grandmother.'

'I shall do my best, my dear.'

Emily, naturally unaware of this interesting conversation, stayed with Franz, who had taken her under his wing for the evening, shepherding her from one group to another, making it easy for her to talk to everyone, keeping her so occupied that she didn't get near the Professor for the rest of the evening, and he for his part evinced no wish to single her out for conversation. She hadn't really expected it, but she did wish that he would be consistent in his manner towards her. These unexpected and exciting encounters were delightful, but they would have been easier to cope with if he were easy in his manner towards her for the rest of the time. She watched him now, chatting up Heleen. The wretched girl was waving her false eyelashes at him in a most ridiculous manner. Emily, who had very adequate eyelashes of her own, turned her back on the pair of them.

The last day was spent in a visit to the hospital with Doctor Wright where the Professor, looking every inch a man of his calling, treated her with a cool civility which made her wish for a cap and uniform. He had nothing to say to her that wasn't purely professional and bade her goodbye with a careless: 'See you later,' which left her peevish and unhappy. And at dinner that evening the conversation was almost entirely taken up by the route they should take back to England and innumerable messages for mutual friends. Emily, in the velvet skirt and one of the new blouses, had the unpleasant feeling that she was surplus to the occasion; not that she was neglected or ignored in any way, perhaps, she told herself, she was imagining it all. Certainly she felt shy and awkward, in consequence of which her manner was alternately stiff and then, in an effort to appear quite at her ease, much too chatty.

They were to leave during the following afternoon, in time to board the night ferry from the Hoek, and Emily spent a bad night, alternately terrified that the Professor wouldn't do as he had promised and be home to see them on their way, and heartbroken because even if he did, she wasn't going to see him

again afterwards. She went down to breakfast to find
him on the point of leaving the house, but he paused
just long enough to ask her why she looked like something the tide had washed up.

'Worrying about the trip?' he asked with brisk
kindness. 'No need; you're a good driver and Mrs
Wright will be beside you.' He eyed her narrowly.
'Or are you over-excited at the prospect of getting
back to work?'

'How you do harp on that!' she snapped.

'But my dear girl, it's your whole future.'

She longed to yell at him that she had no choice.
Unlike Louisa and Heleen she had no looks to speak
of and no smart chat to intrigue him. She sighed
deeply without knowing it and didn't see him grin.
'I've had a lovely time here,' she told him rather
primly. 'Thank you very much, Professor.'

He said on a sigh: 'Renier. We have enjoyed having you. Grandmother is going to miss you and without you I doubt very much if the Wrights would have
come on their own. You'll be staying with Louisa?'

She remembered that he had asked her already.
'No.'

'Well, I must be going; I've a host of outpatients.
By the way, which branch of nursing do you plan to
specialise in?'

She stared at him, her mind an unfortunate blank.
'I—I haven't decided.'

He nodded carelessly. 'Enjoy your morning.'

Emily was left to her solitary breakfast; the Wrights

having theirs in their room so that Doctor Wright might rest as much as possible.

Renier arrived punctually for lunch which they ate without haste, making plans for the next visit. 'When are you coming to England?' asked Maud Wright.

The Professor shrugged. 'There are two cases I have to see within the next few weeks, but I don't expect to stay any length of time—neither of them are operable, I believe. I go to Brussels tomorrow.'

Emily listened in deepening gloom. She hadn't expected to see Renier again, but she hadn't been able to stifle a tiny hope that she might be wrong. Now it seemed that the remote chance could be scotched.

The actual leave taking took but a few minutes. They had been packed and ready with the baggage already stowed, so that all that there remained to do was to put on coats and hats and get into the car. Hans and Bep were in the hall as they came downstairs, to shake their hands and wish them a good journey, but they melted into the background as Renier came out of his study. He kissed Maud Wright, shook the doctor by the hand and then turned to Emily. For a glorious moment she thought that he would kiss her too, but he didn't, only offered a hand in a quick, impersonal handshake, and went to the door with them. Emily didn't look back as she drove away, nor did she wave, and Mrs Wright, after one look at her pale face, talked cheerful nothings for the next ten minutes or so.

Emily wasn't sure how she got through the next day or two. She had already refused the Wrights' invitation to stay a couple of nights with them while she found herself somewhere to live, but when Dolly rang up while she was still at the Wrights' house having lunch before she went on her way, it was impossible to refuse her offer of a room for the night. 'And Peter will fetch you,' said Dolly. 'He'll be with you in half an hour.'

Emily had been grateful not to have to go to an hotel and they had been kindness itself. All the same the following morning she had cast her eyes down the columns of the paper, made a list of likely addresses, and taken herself off, with the promise that if she didn't find something to her liking she would spend another night at Dolly and Peter's flat.

The first two or three places she went to were hopeless; small, sad little rooms and not quite clean, but by lunch time she found something which would do. It was a top floor room in a row of Victorian houses on the edge of Highgate. It was rather barely furnished, but the view was quite nice and it was clean. There was a gas ring and a wash basin and a small gas fire and it would suit well enough until she had found herself a job. She had some money, enough to last her a month; she paid a week's rent and arranged to go back later that afternoon. 'I'll give you a key,' her landlady told her, 'and I hope you're a quiet girl; I'll have no rowdiness in my house.'

Emily assured her that she didn't much care for rowdiness herself and hoped that Mrs Twigg wasn't going to be too much of a tartar. Her face was stern enough, with a pulled-down mouth and a perpetual frown.

So later on, after lunch, Emily got a taxi, said goodbye to Dolly and went off to Highgate, with the earnest request that neither she nor Peter would tell anyone where she had gone.

'Why ever not?' Dolly had asked, and then: 'Oh, you mean Renier. Look, dear, tell you what—don't tell me the address, then I can say with truth that I don't know where you are—not that we expect him, though he does pop up unexpectedly from time to time.' She had added: 'But you will tell someone, won't you? Your sister Mary? I mean, supposing you're taken ill, I'd never forgive myself.'

Emily promised, just as she promised to meet Dolly one day for coffee. And she would, although she felt sure that very soon they would forget her, especially if they didn't know where she was. It was like starting a new life, she told herself, as she unpacked her few things and sat down to write to Mary. She found the idea so depressing that presently she cried herself to sleep.

She spent the next two days job-hunting; it should have been easy enough; she was a trained nurse with good experience, but her own hospital regretfully told her that they couldn't take on any more staff because there was a shortage of money, and that was the case with the next two hospitals as well. There was a staff nurse vacancy at the fourth hospital she applied to, but it was in the East End with no living-in accommodation and getting to and fro would be too much of a problem. On the third morning she went to an agency, where she was offered several private cases, all outside London, as well as night duty in a nursing home. 'Can you speak Arabic?' asked the woman in the office, and when Emily uttered a surprised: 'Well, no,' was told that she might not suit.

She left the place feeling depressed and a little frightened and to cheer herself up, telephoned Louisa's flat. But her sister, although she sounded pleased to hear her, didn't suggest that they might meet—indeed, Louisa didn't ask what Emily was doing or where she was living. Emily stood with the receiver in her hand after Louisa's hurried goodbye, staring at nothing in particular, until a man with a cross face banged on the door, frowning impatiently. He brushed past her, ignoring her apologies, and she wandered along aimlessly, trying to decide what she should do.

She had several weeks in which to find work, of course, but she didn't want to stay in Highgate for longer than necessary; a room in the nurses' home at one of the big hospitals was infinitely preferable. She paused at a bookstall and bought the *Nursing Times* and the *Nursing Mirror* and got on a bus and walking the last street or two, she bought a bag of apples and a bottle of milk. She wasn't hungry, but she would have to have a meal. Later on, she would go out and get herself some supper, something in a tin which she could warm up on the gas ring. It began to rain as she turned into the road where she had her room; cold, heavy rain so that by the time she reached the door her face was wet and her hair sleeked under her woolly cap. She went slowly upstairs, clutching the apples and the milk bottle, unlocked her door and went in.

There was only one comfortable chair in the room, and Renier was sitting in it. Emily made a funny little sound, half sob, half laugh, dumped the milk on a chair, allowed the apples to fall to the floor and said in a whisper: 'How did you get in?' She took a breath and added: 'Mrs Twigg doesn't like visitors, or—or rowdiness…'

He had got out of the chair and was standing in the middle of the room, making it look much smaller than it was. 'Now when have I ever been rowdy?' he asked mildly.

Emily wasn't going to be sidetracked. 'How did you know?' She took off her wet cap and threw it down beside the milk. 'I asked Dolly not to tell.'

He nodded. 'And Dolly, bless her, told me that she had asked you to give Mary your address—so I rang Mary.'

She was unbuttoning her coat with cold fingers and he crossed the room and pushed her hands gently away and took off her coat. 'Why?' she asked.

The coat followed the cap. Renier's arms encircled her. 'I love you,' he said quietly. 'I've loved you for a long time now—weeks and weeks, and I was beginning to think that you would never love me, always flinging Heleen in my teeth and going on for ever and ever about your career.' He bent his head and kissed her lengthily and would have gone on even longer if she hadn't wriggled a little away from him so that she could see his face.

'Look, it won't work… Oh, Renier, I love you too, but I'm not right for you—I mean, just think of Heleen…'

She wasn't allowed to continue; he kissed her again. 'I have no wish to think of Heleen or anyone else, only you, my darling Emily. I wanted to make you jealous, and surely you wouldn't deny a man the right to choose his own wife.'

'You let me come back to England.'

'What else could I do? Kidnap you? Lock you in the cellars? And if I had asked you to marry me you would have refused out of hand, under the impression, I suppose, that you were doing me and Heleen, or any other girl for that matter, a good turn.'

'Well—yes, perhaps. You see, I didn't know you loved me, Renier.'

'You never gave me the chance to tell you, my darling.' He stretched up and pulled her down on to his knee. 'I'll do it now, before we throw your things into your case and go back to my flat.'

Emily sat up, but he pushed her head gently against his shoulder. 'We must make a few plans, my love; we'll marry just as soon as I can arrange it.'

'But what about Mary and George—and the twins…?'

'If you think that I am prepared to wait until the twins are old enough to be your bridal attendants, then you are grossly mistaken, Emily. Now sit still, dearest, while I tell you what a beautiful girl you are.'

Emily sighed blissfully into his shoulder. It seemed likely that she was going to be rushed down the nearest aisle without so much as a new hat on her head, but somehow it didn't matter at all. She said in a happy voice: 'I'm listening, Renier.'

KATE HOFFMANN

brings readers a brand-new,
spin-off to her *Mighty Quinns* miniseries

REUNITED

Keely McLain Quinn had grown up an only child—so it
was a complete shock to learn that she had six older
brothers and a father who'd never known she existed!
But Keely's turmoil is just beginning, as she discovers
the man she's fallen in love with is determined to
destroy her newfound family.

*Look for REUNITED
in October 2002.*

HARLEQUIN®
Makes any time special®

International bestselling author

SANDRA MARTON

invites you to attend the

WEDDING *of the* YEAR

Glitz and glamour prevail in this volume
containing a trio of stories in which
three couples meet at a
high society wedding—and
soon find themselves
walking down the aisle!

Look for it in November 2002.

HARLEQUIN®
Makes any time special ®